Danny King was born ~~...~~ grew up in a picturesque ~~...~~ Yateley. He excelled at ~~...~~ successfully leave school ~~...~~ cations. He spent the nex~~...~~ freezing his barnacles off in a variety of dead-end j~~...~~ before going to college, gaining some qualifications and landing an altogether different type of job which, while still dead-end, was at least next to a radiator. *Milo's Marauders* is his fifth book published by Serpent's Tail and will be followed by *Milo's Run*. For information on previous and forthcoming books, check out www.dannykingbooks.com.

Praise for Danny King's Diaries

The Burglar Diaries

'One of the few writers to make me laugh out loud. Danny King's brilliant at making you love characters who essentially are quite bad people' David Baddiel

'An absolutely hilarious, laugh-out-loud book by someone who has been there' Bruce Reynolds, mastermind of the Great Train Robbery

'Occasionally hilarious, if morally dubious, *The Burglar Diaries* is well worth buying – and definitely worth half-inching' *GQ*

'This is the sweet-as-a-nut, hilariously un-PC account of the jobs [Bex] has known and loved – the line-ups, the lock-ups and the cock-ups. If ever there was an antidote to *Bridget Jones's Diary* this is it. *The Burglar Diaries* is the first in a series. Long may it run' *Mirror*

The Bank Robber Diaries

'Humorous but horrific, and you know you shouldn't laugh . . . A guaranteed success' *Bookseller*

'It's low on morals but big on laughs, so if you can thieve one, by all means go for it!' *BBM*

'Danny looks set for a long and healthy career going straight . . . to the top of the best-sellers list' *Penthouse*

'*The Bank Robber Diaries* is the best (and funniest) British Crime novel since *The Burglar Diaries*, which was also written by Danny King' *Ice*

'King spends his free time writing for a top-shelf grot mag and hanging out with some "tasty" geezers. He's also written a couple of excellent books about the non-legit lifestyle choice, *The Burglar Diaries* and *The Bankrobber Diaries*' *Loaded*

The Hitman Diaries

'Once again the comic genius and hilarious one-liners have you warming to the anti-social protagonists of Chris, Sid and Vince; more cock-ups than hold ups . . . a thoroughly un-pc but rewarding novel' *BBM*

'It's blokeish humour ahoy in this thoroughly enjoyable tale.. . . . King's writing is sharp, his comedy as black as Donald Rumsfeld's heart and he has a real penchant for dialogue as spoken by criminals . . . the book's hitman protagonist himself [is] a piece of work so nasty he makes Osama bin Laden look like Claire Rayner' *Maxim*

'The action flows as thick as the blood and the jet-black humour will leave you wondering whether to laugh, cry or vomit' *Jack*

'An action-packed tale of murder, mayhem and dating . . . it'll have you hooked' *Mayfair*

The Pornographer Diaries

'It's pretty dirty. And funny too' *Maxim*

'Painfully close to true life for the *Ice* team' *Ice*

'Danny King's filthiest and funniest novel yet' *Buzz*

'A wonderfully funny book for any bloke who's ever perused the top shelf; and for any woman whose boyfriend keeps a porn stash under the stairs' *Desire*

MILO'S MARAUDERS

Danny King

First published in 2005 by Serpent's Tail,
4 Blackstock Mews, London N4 2BT
website: www.serpentstail.com

Printed by Mackays of Chatham, plc

10 9 8 7 6 5 4 3 2 1

This book's for the big feller himself, Clive Andrews. Clive was one of the few people who used to actually read my stuff before I was published, and he's one of the first I'll always send a new manuscript to for an honest opinion. I'll even go as far as to say that some of what you've read will have been influenced by Clive's advice, though I dispute his insistence that he came up with the idea of the paintballing chapter in *The Bank Robber Diaries*. It was 1998 and we were sitting around his flat watching the USA *v.* Iran in the World Cup with more lager and kebabs than doctors would recommend and I was telling him about an idea I'd had for a sequel to *The Burglar Diaries*. We talked about it for a bit, and discussed the notion of two hardened bank robbers having a day out with a load of silly 'paintball warriors', though it was definitely my idea. However, in the interests of fairness here's what Clive has to say:

'I realise it must be difficult for Dan to face up to the fact that one of the most entertaining things he's ever written was the work of someone else, but I really did come up with the paintball idea. In fact, I've been Lennon to his McCartney throughout his literary career. Admit it, Dan, without me you're nothing.'

Did he, bollocks.

Acknowledgements

Here we go, eyes down for a full house. First up I'd like to thank John Williams for continuing to put forward my books for publication and for continuing to prove that you can't disguise three bottles of red with a packet of Smints; to Pete Ayrton, Jenny, Ruthie, Alistair, Lisa and Martin at Serpent's Tail for their sterling work and their sterling currency; to my best mate Brian McCann for asking me if he can be thanked a bit higher up this time as he had to plough through too many names before he found himself in the last book; to his nephews Mark and Pud for proving that not all McCanns think books are just there for fixing wobbly tables; to Rat Sanders, Randy Bummery, Jim Brundlefly, Ollie Scull, Chris Hayward and Robin Percy for all moving to Crystal Palace the very month I move up to North London – unbelievable; to Barrie Smith for helping me update my website and for never going a day without smiling – the simple-minded idiot; to my wonderful girl-friend Jeannie Crockett for her support, warmth, love and unwavering friendship (hmm, I wonder what she's after?); to Jeannie's gene pool, Helen and John, Granny Crockett and Grandma Askew, for making me feel like one of the family, when really I'm just some shifty porno writer who's got his grubby paws all over their precious princess; for

Jeannie's brother, Andrew, for his instant friendship and open invitation to come and stay with him in Frankfurt whenever I want (boy, is he going to regret that come next year's World Cup?); to my mum and dad, aka Dot and Mike, for all the dinners, pocket money and socks; and finally to Gateways supermarket in Yateley (which is no longer there) for allowing me to stack all that pet food for them back in the 1980s and for never checking my pants for choc and fags whenever I waved goodnight at the end of my shifts. The seeds of this book lay in that particular dead-end job. I thank you all.

Good ideas 1

It was Goody's idea.

What am I talking about? It was always Goody's idea. 'Here, let's nick Mr Kelly's motor, have it away outside his house and smash it up. Be a laugh and fucking serve him right for giving us detention again. You in? Come on, don't be a cunt. What's a matter with you? You chicken or something? Cluck cluck cluck cluck cluck cluck cluck . . .' etc.

It's scary to think that a chicken impression at the age of fifteen can end up shaping the rest of your life, but that's how it happens. Peer pressure. How many countless scientists, doctors, mathematicians and bank managers have been lost to us over the years because they were too afraid to lose face in front of their mates? I don't know – quite a few, though, I'd bet – but I reckon for every kid at home doing his homework there's probably a dozen more out roaming the streets looking for their headmaster's house with a big bag of dog shit. At least, there was at my school.

I was stupid and I shouldn't have listened, but then you do at that age, don't you? I always listened.

'Not that way, Goody, this way. Out to the sticks,' I shouted as we headed towards the high street at 60mph.

'Bollocks to that. Let's see if anyone's about.'

'No, Goody, no,' I protested, but I was overruled by

Norris, Patsy (that's Tom Patterson to you) and Jacko (Michael Jackson. Not *the* Michael Jackson, but his mum was a fan, so when she and Mr Jackson got hitched, any lad she had was always going to get lumbered with that name. As it happened, Jacko turned out to be a bit of a fucking fruit-loop too and ended up suiting his name, though as far as I'm aware he can't sing and the only fifteen-year-olds he ever played with was us, when we were all the same age).

'Don't be a prat. We don't want anyone to see us. They could be used as witnesses,' I told him.

'*They could be used as witnesses*,' he repeated, all gay-like, making the wankers in the back crack up.

'Milo's a chicken, look,' Norris yelled and the inside of the motor suddenly sounded like a battery-hen farm.

'I'm not a chicken, but the way you're going we might as well just drive up to the cop shop and turn ourselves in.'

'Good idea,' Goody yelled and turned left through a set of reds and up Park Avenue towards the police station.

'No, Goody, no!' I yelled, but too late: the station approached and Goody slowed, feigning to turn in, but then carried on past it at the last moment. 'Goody, you fucking flid. You're gonna get us all nicked.'

'Fucking flid, am I?' he said, screeching to a halt, then sticking it into reverse and swinging it around. 'Well, if I'm such a flid, perhaps I'd better go back there, then.'

'Hey, Goody, maybe this ain't such a great idea,' someone else other than me finally realised.

'Patsy, don't be a poof. Where's your bottle?' Goody said, sticking his foot down. This time the idiot did actually pull in to the station forecourt and several coppers came out to gawk at us as Goody executed a six-point turn trying to get us out of there again.

'Go, Goody, go, for fuck's sake!' me, Patsy, Norris and Jacko all yelled at him as we drove up half a dozen kerbs and all over the station daffs. 'Go, go, go!'

'I'm trying, but reverse is in a funny place in Kelly's motor. I'm more used to me step-dad's car,' he explained.

We finally extricated ourselves from the cop shop and got back out on to the road, but the Old Bill were already piling into their motors and coming on after us.

'Don't worry, I'm a wicked driver,' Goody reassured us and stuck his foot down.

The two things in our favour at this moment were that we were all sober (well, Jacko had had some Uhu a bit earlier) and that it had gone midnight, so there were fewer people about for us to kill. Other than that, our new day hadn't started out particularly great.

I looked over my shoulder and saw that the Old Bill were right up our arse with blue lights flashing all over their roofs and I had an awful feeling of doom in the pit of my stomach. I looked at the speedo and saw that Goody was doing over 70mph and I couldn't make up my mind whether it would be better for us to slow down and stay in one piece or risk all and try to escape. It didn't look like I had a say in the matter whatever happened: Goody was totally blinkered to whatever me, Norris, Patsy, or Jacko screamed at him as he swung Kelly's car around the streets and played Atari with our lives. It's a terrible feeling to be so completely helpless, and I'm not ashamed to admit this now but I almost began booing my fucking eyes out in the front seat of that Cavalier. In fact, I think I would've, had our little adventure lasted a little longer, but two minutes after it had started it was all over. Goody (the wicked driver) got caught in two minds about whether or not to turn up Richmond Crescent and ended up burying Kelly's motor halfway up the back of a Sherpa van.

'Let's leg it,' he suggested, and we all piled out of the motor and pegged it up the crescent on foot.

I hadn't noticed while we'd been on the road, but there had been two Old Bill motors after us, not just the one, so when the first stopped and spilled its coppers out behind us, the second carried on ahead of us and caught us between them. It occurred to me that we should just run straight at the guys in front. After all, there were five of us and only two of them, so at least our destinies were in our own legs, but Goody had other ideas and shouted, 'Follow me,' then disappeared down the side of a house. Like mugs, we did just that and found ourselves trapped in someone's back garden. When the Old Bill converged on us, their numbers were doubled while our chances were halved. Our only escape route was over the back fence and into the pitch-black woods, so we all started clambering over the creaking wooden panels as four pairs of size tens rapidly closed in behind us. I was almost over – I only had a leg to swing – when suddenly a hand grabbed my ankle. I tried to kick free, but he had some grip on him, and before I knew it there was a second. I kicked and kicked, but I was caught and I knew it. One good yank and I came crashing back down into the garden, hurting my legs and hands in the process, and suddenly they were all on my back, slapping me in the cuffs and threatening me with a good kicking if I gave them any more shit.

'Bloody do it, little bastards! Bloody birch him,' a lady in a nightgown encouraged them from the back door, while the Old Bill thanked her for her contribution and asked her to step back inside.

The coppers pulled me up on to my feet and I looked around to see how many of us they'd got.

There was only me.

Three months I got for that. Three months' youth detention. I'd already been cautioned and had a Community Service Order for trespassing and criminal damage (and a right good hiding from the old man) in the past, so this time I was sent away. I shat myself, I did, that first night inside, but it wasn't too bad in the end – a bit like how I imagine boarding school is, only for total fucking divs. There were a few decent lads there, and if your face fitted in (as mine always does, for some reason) they saw you were all right and showed you the ropes. I even managed to have the occasional laugh, but mostly it was just a case of keeping my head down and eating my greens until it was my turn to go home.

What a fantastic day that was – Christmas, birthday, passing your driving test and losing your virginity all in one. I smiled all morning long until my mum and dad arrived to pick me up and the rest of the day was spoiled with the stuck record of my mum milking as much despair out of the situation as she could muster. It didn't let up for a minute, not even a second, though I couldn't say anything for fear of catching a clout off the old man. So that was it: no celebration, no joy for me that I was out, just misery. Misery and martyrdom and the shame of it all until my head was well and truly done in. I couldn't even escape it as I was pressganged into playing the dutiful son and forbidden from seeing any of my mates again. I wasn't sure how that was meant to work or what sort of a person I was supposed to turn into, but by the fifth day I was ready to take a bath with the toaster.

Fortunately, I was due back at school and the old folks had to let me go, no matter how much they feared letting me out of their sight. Now, obviously, my old school had expelled me after Mr Kelly's car got concertinaed, so I had to go to a new school (a special school) in the next town for problem (or special) children. What a fucking nuthouse that place was. Jesus! I met all sorts of crazy fuckers there, including Bob, who I still know today, and it was with him that I got done next, breaking into the RG News in Parade Way.

We were after fags and sweets. We ended up getting twelve months.

I won't bore you with the details, but I went round the same old merry-go-round again – Youth Detention, release, anguish, grief and the ever-present menace of a wallop, then off into the big wide world again to see what trouble I could get into next.

I didn't go back to school this time around. Well, I'd missed all my exams (though I couldn't actually remember which ones I was supposed to be taking anyway – general and metalwork, I think) so the appropriate powers decided to give up my education as a dead duck and concentrate on getting me a trade. I told them I was interested in working with tools ('crowbars and bolt cutters,' I wrote on my form for a joke), so they found me a YTS place in a local garage, learning and earning a colossal £25 a week. Naturally, this was never going to stretch far enough, so within a few months I started supplementing my income with a little shoplifting on Saturday mornings. I did pretty good at it for a while too and made a stack of money selling my mates albums, tapes, computer games and clothes and so on, and I should've stuck to what I knew, but then Goody came along with a few ideas he wanted to discuss with me.

Three years.

This was just me, by the way, not Goody. That slippery cunt made it away again, leaving me to carry the can again, although plod clocked him good and Goody was forced to run away and join the army, so that was that.

OK, well you know the drill as well as I do by now. The only difference was that this time it was prison, not Youth Detention, and I was now a fully fledged criminal. That's what the judge told me when he sent me down: that I had graduated from being a young offender to being a fully-fledged criminal and therefore I 'must be dealt with as such'. I think he meant it as some sort of put-down, but I was made up by his comments and wrote them down in a diary I started. Mind you, I was about the only one that was. This I could tell from the wail of woe we all heard coming from the public gallery up top when he gave his appraisal. The prison officer in the dock with me gave me the daggers like you wouldn't believe and I couldn't believe they were trying to make me feel guilty for breaking my poor old mother's heart on top of giving me three years. Anyway, it wasn't my fault I was such a disappointment to her; she shouldn't have had such high hopes for me in the first place.

I couldn't go back home after my next release, so I stayed in a halfway house and got my old job at the garage back. I was quite surprised when Glenn agreed to re-hire me, but it turned out he had a few sidelines he'd never mentioned before and he reckoned he could make use of a man of my growing talents. Well, I thought to myself, this is handy.

Five years.

If you lump it all together, add on a couple of lesser sentences for parole violations and my two lots of remand (circa six months and each time acquitted when the case came to court), then take away the early releases and tot it all up, all in all I've done, let me see . . . somewhere in the region of seven and a half years. Seven and a half years? And I'm not even twenty-eight yet.

It's enough to make a man think.

It's even enough to make a fully fledged criminal think.

And this was brought into even clearer focus when Alice stopped coming to visit me. I wrote to her every week for a year and used up half a dozen phone cards leaving messages on her machine. But she never responded.

I couldn't understand why she wouldn't respond. Not Alice. Not my love. The girl who'd stood by me when the rest of the world had turned its back on me. The girl who'd been there for me through thick and thin, who'd told me I was her soul mate and that she was ready to grow old and die with me. Not Alice?

But yes, even her. Alice disappeared off the face of the earth, and I didn't see her for three and a half long years. This had the effect on me that all the courts, probation officers and prison psychologists in the system could only fantasise about, and I did my time staring at her picture, crossing off the days and praying for one last chance.

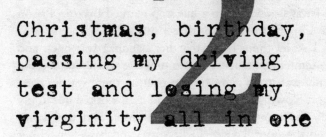

Christmas, birthday, passing my driving test and losing my virginity all in one

The day finally came round again and it was as great as usual. Almost worth doing the time for. Well, perhaps not.

'Mind how you go then, Milo,' says Mr Banyard as he showed me through the gates. I was just about to wish him the same, my good mood at work no doubt, when he added: 'Try to stay out a bit longer this time. We need the cells.'

So that was how it was going to be, huh?

I didn't even dignify his comment with a response. Besides, he'd shut the gate again before I could think of one. I simply touched the door, turned around and started putting some distance between me and my old life.

It was a bit early, I know, but I went and bought four cans of something for the train journey home. I cracked open the first one in the street and almost drained it in one before I was ten yards from the shop. It was the loveliest thing I'd ever tasted. An old woman at the bus stop stared up at me with thinly veiled contempt, so I tried to put her at ease.

'Been on the rigs. North Sea oil. Not allowed to drink on them, you see, so I've been dying for this one.'

I don't think she believed me. Mind you, I can't really blame her. If I had been on an oil rig, why had I waited until I was stood next to a bus stop marked Brixton Prison to have my first beer? Not that it mattered.

As I stood there I saw that her handbag was open and that a tenner had fallen out. No one else was about and the old lady was stood right on top of it, so there was no danger of it blowing away. I already had it all worked out in my mind. The moment the bus came along and the driver opened the door, I'd say, 'Ladies first,' and have her tenner away as I bowed. Pretty sweet. Hadn't been out more than ten minutes and I already had a tenner.

Hang on a minute, I suddenly thought. What's going on here? I'd just spent the last three and a half years talking about nothing else except going straight, and here I was scamming some old lady out of her bingo money before I was even out of sight of the prison gates. I couldn't do this.

Before I had a change of heart, I told the old biddy, 'Excuse me, dear, but I think you've dropped something down there,' and pointed at her shoes.

'Oh. Oh dear, oh dear. Oh thank you, young man. This blooming clasp, it's always doing it,' she said, dancing all over her tenner as she tried to get it out from beneath her feet. 'It's so refreshing to meet someone with a bit of honesty these days,' she said and gave me a little smile. And I'll tell you what: that felt good. Sure, a tenner would've been nice and bought me a few more beers, some choc and some fags, but so what? I had the admiration and respect of a nice old lady. And suddenly that meant so much more to me than all the beer, choc and fags in the world. I'd already been feeling good about myself to start with. Now I felt ten feet tall.

Nothing was going to spoil this day.

A couple of hours later, just as my train was pulling in to

the station, I was absolutely kicking myself. I was so pissed off and kept running the episode over and over in my head to try to remember why having some miserable old cow, who wouldn't even give me the time of day when she first laid eyes on me, think I was honest was better than having a tenner. I couldn't fathom it. Sure, yeah, I'd vowed to go straight and not go nicking any more, but that wouldn't have been nicking; that would've been finding. It wasn't my fault if the silly old fool wanted to go walking around with her handbag open, was it? Why had I opened my big mouth? What an idiot! Bollocks!

I got off the train with that dull ache of a missed opportunity gnawing away at my insides and saw my brother waiting for me at the end of the platform. I walked towards him and we shook hands, said hello and I dismissed the tenner from my mind.

'All right, Mush?' Terry said.

'Not bad, Tel. You alone?'

'Yeah. I think the novelty of seeing you get out has kind of worn off with the boys. Come on, the car's out front.'

'You been waiting long?' I asked.

'A little while,' he replied.

'Yep, me too.'

We found Terry's car where he had left it (not bad for this town) and climbed in. The day was turning out to be a really lovely sunny experience. The car was a bit hot inside, so I wound down the window and smelled the Hampshire air.

It smelled like . . . well, like air, really.

I'd like to say that it smelled like freedom or flowers or kids playing with puppy dogs or something like that but it didn't; it just smelled like air. Mind you, that was a big improvement on disinfectant and piss, so I was more than happy with it.

'This should be a nice little holiday for you, Milo. How long you out for? A month? Two?' Terry started to preach.

'Here we go. Can't I enjoy my first day without the usual lectures for once?'

'Just asking. If I'm putting you up, I wouldn't mind knowing how long for.'

'I ain't going back inside,' I told him. 'Not now, not never.'

'Oh really. What, going straight again, then? That'll be nice.'

'This time I mean it. That's me done. I ain't spending the rest of my life in nick, no way.'

'God, I wish I had a quid for every time you've said that. "I'm going straight. I've changed. Give me a chance,"' he scoffed, doing what I can only assume was his 'me' impression. 'But before you know it, some cunt's talked you into helping him lift a load of tiles or fence his motors or whatever else and you're back inside, wondering how you could've been so stupid and swearing it's the last time. But it won't be, Darren, because you're an idiot. And there's no lesson too blatant you can't ignore.'

'Did you have that little speech all prepared already?'

'Yes.'

'It went well.'

'Thanks.'

'I think you're wrong, though. Yeah, OK, fair enough, I have been a bit of an idiot in the past but those days are well and truly behind me. I've sorted out some very simple rules for me to follow, and if I'm able to follow them then I'll never go back inside again.'

'What rules?'

'If it's dodgy, don't touch it. Don't even think about it.'

'Well, lots of luck with that one, mate, but don't be offended if I don't go sticking the mortgage on you just yet.'

'I won't. I have changed, though, but I can't blame any-one for not believing me,' I conceded. 'It's up to me to prove it. Like, on my way here this morning I saw this old bird drop a tenner and I pointed it out to her and said "Here, look, you've dropped a tenner, you have," and she wouldn't have even noticed if it hadn't been for me.'

'Did you?' Terry asked, looking at me all quizzically. 'Fuck that. I would've had it away,' he said, really pissing me off.

We sat in silence for a moment or two, and I watched the countryside whiz by. So nice to be out in the open again, see a bit of greenery.

'Where are we going?' I asked.

'Thought you'd want to drop your stuff off at mine, then go and get a pint.'

'Nah, come on, let's go round the old lady's.'

'Not a good idea, Darren. She doesn't want to see you.'

'Oh come on, drop me round there. I'll get her some flowers, tell her I'm sorry and all that. Patch things up. Might as well get it over with. I'm going to run into her sooner or later, anyway.'

'It's your decision, but I warn you she really doesn't want to see you.'

'Trust me on this one. I know what I'm talking about. Here, we better stop at the cemetery on the way over and pick up some flowers.'

I rang the bell and Terry stood behind me, jangling his keys. We waited for a few moments before movement behind the frosted glass turned into the door being opened.

'Hello, Mum. I'm out again. Look, I know I've no right to expect any sort of favours from you or anything. All I wanted to do was come by and see you again and tell you how sorry I am for everything that's gone on before. It would be so nice if we could draw a line under all that non-sense and move on. Here, I got you these,' I told her and swung a dozen lilies out from behind my back.

'Piss off out of it, you little scumbag,' she shouted and slammed the door in my face.

'So, do you fancy that pint then?' Terry asked.

'Yes, I could probably go a pint about now.'

Two pounds ninety for a pint. What was all that about?

'Gone up a bit since you went away, has it?' asked Ron as he served us.

'Cor, not many. Who's robbing who now?' I put to him.

Ron unlocked a few padlocks and moved the charity boxes under the counter. 'I'll just put these out of temptation's way in case you feel like evening things up a little,' he said, and I didn't have any grounds for recourse. I mean, the old me probably would've, but I wasn't like that any more. I'd changed.

'Sorry about your jukebox,' I said, and Ron told me it was OK, all forgotten, though it didn't look like it the way that he scowled at me, so me and Terry took our pints and found somewhere comfortable to sit. We had a bit of a chat and Terry gave me all the latest gossip (Goody was back from the army and due along any second; Patsy was still working in RG News and was now divorced; Jacko had won £10,000 on a scratch card and did it all in four months; and someone had new tyres, but I forget who). There was one name he didn't mention, though, and it was noticeable by its absence.

'What about Alice?' I finally asked.

Terry shrugged. 'What about her?'

'How is she? Where is she? What's she up to?'

'You know, this and that,' he said, telling me absolutely nothing. There was some bad news afoot, I could see, so I readied myself for the worst.

'Go on.'

'Oh man, look, I'm sorry, Darren, but she got married.'

'Married?' I took a moment to let this sink in then pressed some more. 'To who?'

'McCann. You know, the youngest one, Brian.'

'Not that fucking idiot? You're joking?' I said, but I knew he wasn't.

McCann? To be honest, I only knew him by sight, so it was a bit of an unjustified overreaction in all fairness, but then I would've probably said the same about anyone. At the end of the day I just couldn't picture Alice – my Alice – as anyone else's Mrs McCann. That was the long and the short of it.

I struggled to find the words, but I didn't quite know what to say. I'd figured she'd have another geezer by now, but married? She was a bit quick off the blocks with that one.

'Is it serious?' I asked, making Terry blink.

'I'd say so, wouldn't you?'

Well, it was probably a daft thing to ask but, like I said, I was struggling for words. I think what I really meant to ask was, was this just a rebound 'marry the first bloke who isn't Darren just to get back at him for going inside again' sort of marriage or was it the real deal? When I finally found the words, it was Terry's turn to not know what to say. He stopped staring at me open-mouthed just long enough to tell me that Alice had a little kid with McCann, so it was probably the real deal.

'Even if it isn't, there's dick all you can do about it now. My advice is to just leave it and get on with your life,' he said, and he got no argument from me. I'd heard this particular sentiment too many times in the past. It's pretty common in nicks. 'Just leave it.' 'Nothing you can do about it.' 'Get on with your life.' 'Put it behind you.' 'Move on.' It's a hard thing to hear, but whenever I saw someone on the receiving end of this advice I always thought it was the right advice. I didn't have to like it; I just had to accept it.

It wasn't like I hadn't been expecting it, anyway; it was just a confirmation of my worst fears. If anything, it was the not knowing that was the hard part. At least now I knew all glimmer of hope had gone, I could 'move on'. Before, when I was just firing letters off into the dark and pleading with the answering machine there was always a chance. Now there wasn't. She was gone (just like that tenner), so I tried to put her out of my mind and forget all about her.

I was just starting on this when a face from the past walked in and called me a cunt.

'Goody,' I smiled back.

'That's my name; don't wear it out. Want a beer?'

'And some peanuts and crisps and pork scratchings.'

Well, that was about all there was to my first day back in the world. Me, Terry and Goody talked long into the night, as they say, but very little of it made any sense after nine o'clock, so I won't bore you with it. There was a kebab involved a bit later on and Goody threw some chips at me for a joke, but that was about it.

Oh, one last thing. Norris came in to see me too, at some stage, but Terry told him to fuck off and tried to start a fight with him. I figured they'd had something of a run-in while I'd been away, so I didn't give it a second thought. But there was more to it than that.

A lot more.

Putting my face about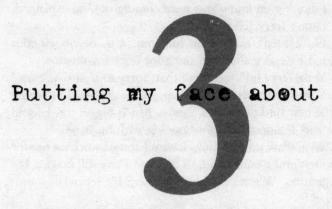

I had a real Stella headache the next morning and a thirst like a bloke who'd just woke up after a night on the Stella. I downed a couple of pints of water, took some aspirins and chucked my guts up down the bog, then downed two more pints of water, took two more aspirins and had a big dump. I think my head was still in prison mode, because Terry walked past and pointed out that in polite society people generally closed the door when they did this sort of thing.

'You not going into work, then?' I asked, when he handed me a cup of tea five minutes later (in the kitchen).

'No, I'm ill. Flu or something, I reckon. I'll phone the office in a second.'

'I'm going to go for a walk. Did you say you'd had some keys cut for me?' I asked.

'Oh no, I forgot. Here, you'd better take mine. Get a set made for yourself while you're out and drop these back off before the evening, will you?' he said, handing me the first key I'd held in three and a half years. 'It's like a crowbar. You use it to get into houses with.'

'Got you.'

First stop was RG News to see Patsy. I thought he would've come down the night before, but he hadn't appeared.

'I didn't even know you were coming out,' he explained.

'Didn't Terry tell you, no?'

'No. Haven't really seen him much, to be honest. But then, I haven't really been out a lot since my divorce.'

'Yeah, Terry told me about that. Sorry to hear that, mate.'

'Yeah, well, these things happen, I suppose. I'm seeing some new bird these days. Sandra. Much bigger tits,' he told me and demonstrated just how big with his hands.

'Well, that's good. Things have a habit of working out for the best in the end,' I said, all the time Patsy still making big tit gestures. 'Where's old Hudson, then? He retired or something?'

'No, better than that. He's dead. Keeled over right here, he did,' Patsy explained, pointing to the floor behind the counter. 'Got it on the security cameras. Want to see it? Everyone else has,' he said, and led me round the back to a little monitor where he showed me a ten-second clip of old Hudson croaking all over the Mars bars. 'I was thinking of putting it on the Internet, but I don't really know how. Do you? Worth a fortune, something like this, I reckon.'

'Sorry, mate, not really my thing, computers.'

'You sold enough of them in your time, you must be able to use them a bit.'

'No, haven't got a clue. Can I have a Dairy Milk bar?'

'Yeah. Do you want to pay for it?' he asked.

'No,' I replied.

'Oh. Oh go on then,' he said, so I grabbed one of those great paving slabs of chocolate that are about three quid, much to his annoyance.

'You know who works next door, of course, don't you?' he said and I did. 'You going in to see her, then?'

'Thought I'd just pop in and say hello. Can't do any harm.'

'You know about . . .'

'McCann, yes.'

'And the . . .'

'Baby. Yes, I do.'

'Oh right. You're not going to smack her one, are you?'

'Of course not. What a thing to say.'

'Then the chocolate's for her, is it?'

'No. But I know she'd like some. Can I take another bar for her?' When he hummed and hawed I called him a cunt and he let me take a second bar, this time a fruit and nut one, so I had one of each in case (and in all likelihood) Alice wouldn't accept a bar of chocolate off me.

'Mind how you go, then, Milo. Give us a call next time you go for a beer and I'll come along.'

'Will do. Cheers for the choc. I'll see you in the week.'

Alice had worked in the chemist's when I was going out with her. Surprisingly, she still did, even though she was married and had a kid these days, but then Alice always did things I could never credit. Go out with me, for one.

'Got anything for a pain in the arse?' I asked when I went in. Alice just frowned.

'Heard you were getting out. Congratulations. I'm glad for you. When did you get out? This morning?'

'No, yesterday. How are you?'

'Married,' she said and held up her third finger for me to inspect.

'Yes, I heard. Congratulations yourself. For everything else too.'

'His name's Mark.'

'Is it? Well, too much to expect you to call him after me, I suppose.'

'What? *Bastard*?'

'Surely I should be the one calling you names but that's not my style. I'm above all that. All I wanted to do was come by and wish you all the happiness in the world.'

'Well, you've done that now, so piss off and don't come in here again.'

'Not even for a packet of plasters?'

'Not even if your head's been cut off.'

'All I wanted was for you to know that I've changed. I'm not like that any more.'

'Good for you, Darren, but you're four years too late. What do you want me to do? Leave my husband and child for you?'

'Well, thanks for waiting.'

By crikey, Alice can move when she wants to. She also had quite a useful left hook on her and I had to put a rack of sunglasses between us before she had me out cold.

'You *bastard*! You utter miserable fucking bastard!'

'OK, let's just take a deep breath and calm down, shall we?'

'Eight bloody years I've been traipsing around one nick or another just to see your worthless arse, and for what? So that you can go and get yourself banged up all over again the minute you get out? You bastard! You bastard, bastard, bastard! Well, no more, Milo. You blew it. You had your chance – no, actually you had more than a chance, you had hundreds of them, and you blew every single one of them.'

'It wasn't my fault . . .'

'Of course it wasn't. "It was Goody's or Patsy's or Glenn's, boo-hoo-hoo,"' she said, wringing the mock tears from her eyes. Everyone was an impressionist.

'I didn't have a choice.'

'You just don't get it, do you? You had a choice; you just made the wrong one. You always made the wrong one. Well, we're both out now, Darren, and I ain't going back, either.'

'Can we at least bury the hatchet over a drink?'

'I'd bury one over your fucking head if I had one.'

'You know, girls shouldn't swear. It's not becoming.'

Sunglasses rack or no sunglasses rack, she came at me again and I had to flee the shop and leg it halfway up the high street before I finally shook her off.

So much for the touching reconciliation scene I'd carried around in my head the last few years. At least it looked like she still cared about me. I mean, you wouldn't get that angry over someone you couldn't give a toss about, now, would you? So that was something, at least. Crumbs of comfort, that's what you have to take from situations like these, crumbs of comfort.

Not everyone was sorry to see me, though. DS Haynes (that's Weasel to you and me) looked positively made up at the sight of me when I opened Terry's front door a couple of days later.

'Didn't take you long, did it, Milo?' he beamed.

'What?'

Weasel and his mate, DC Ross, were good enough to explain things to me on the way over to the station. Apparently, the manager of the local Harvester had got himself lumped over the head while he was dropping off the evening's takings at the night safe in the high street, and Weasel and Ross thought I might be able to help them with their enquiries – or should that be inquiries? I can never remember. Anyway, we found a quiet room and a tape recorder and had a chat about it.

'It wasn't me, I'm telling you.'

'We know it was. Why don't you do yourself a favour and hold up your hands to it? It'll be easier on you in the long run,' Weasel said.

'How many times have I got to say the same thing? I spent the night at home,' I repeated for the tenth time (probably). 'You haven't got a clue, have you? Someone has something nicked and you've got nothing to go on, so what's the easiest thing to do? Drag me down here and try and fit me up. Even if you can't make it stick, you can at least tell the victim you had a suspect in custody but had to let him go because there wasn't enough evidence to hold him with and get out of looking like the incompetent wankers you are.'

Weasel turned to Ross and shook his head.

'Well, I don't know what's up with us. We've gone and done it again. We've arrested an innocent man. Good God, how many's that now?'

'Must be hundreds, Sarge. Don't think we've had a guilty one yet,' Ross replied, deadpan.

It was true what I'd said, though: they didn't have a clue. I mean, I really didn't do it, honest to God. I'd tell you if I had but I hadn't, so this was just a face-saving exercise on their part and I was their prawn. I could see this sort of thing happening a lot over the coming months until eventually they'd get something to stick if I wasn't careful. Suddenly I regretted turning down the chance to have my brief present, but I wasn't about to change my mind now. See, the trouble is, as soon as you demand representation, the Old Bill think they've got the right bloke, or at least that you've got something to hide, and they end up keeping you in for as long as they can possibly hold you in the hope that you'll crack. I really couldn't be arsed with this and figured if I was all friendly and cooperative and answered their questions honestly and openly in a sincere and forthright manner, I'd be on my way within half an hour. Unfortunately, my record kind of counts against me, so that I'm really not a veteran of the benefit of the doubt.

'Listen to me, sunshine, you think you've done time before, but that's nothing compared with what we could send you down for today. Armed robbery? GBH? This is a whole new league you're in, Milo,' Weasel explained.

'If you're so sure I did it, then charge me and prove it in court, but I'm only going to say this one more time: I didn't do it. I spent last night at home watching the telly with my brother. Please go and ask him.'

'Do you know what "Habitual" means, Milo?' Weasel asked.

'I've heard it used from time to time.'

'I'm sure you have. No, habitual refers to a person's nature, their habits, you see? Habitual behaviour is something that is intrinsically ingrained in each of us. It's something constant that we can never escape from, and you know why? Because it's yourself. And you can't escape from yourself. No one can. You, for example, are a habitual thief. And you can no more give up stealing than a lion can give up eating antelopes. It's in your nature. You know, I feel sorry for you, I really do, because you won't ever be able to live a normal life like the rest of us, because what's normal to you is abnormal, indeed offensive, to the rest of us. We can't allow you to act naturally. But you won't quit. You can't quit. You'll just carry on going back and forth to prison, back and forth, until eventually you end up killing someone and they never let you out again. See, you are never, ever, ever going to give it up, unless . . .' he suddenly stopped and paused for dramatic effect.

Oh do please carry on, Weasel, I thought to myself. Tell me how I can break this cycle. Anything, anything, just show me where to sign.

'Unless,' he continued, 'that is, you admit to yourself that you've got a problem. Realise that this is all there is for you, for the rest of your life. This is all that you will know, police stations, cells, prisons and slop-outs – and that's the way it'll be until the day you die, unless you get help. But the only person who can help you is you. And in order to help yourself you have to first admit your mistakes. Start off with a clean slate. Leave your old life behind,' he explained, wiping the table as if it were a blackboard and I was the village idiot.

'Does this work with lions as well?' I asked, making Ross laugh. Weasel shot him a look and he quickly stopped.

'Think you're funny, don't you? Think it's a big joke someone's in hospital with their head all busted up. It's not.' Weasel scowled solemnly.

'I don't think it's a joke. I just don't think I did it. And I don't blame you for giving me a pull – I probably would in your shoes too – but I didn't have anything to do with it, and there's nothing I can do about that. And I'm not about to stick my hands up to something I didn't do just because you want me to stop eating antelopes, so there we are. Where do we go from here? What's the next step?'

'I could keep you in for a couple of days, see how you like that,' Weasel threatened.

'I know you could, but it's not going to change any of my answers and I could do two days standing on my head and you know it, so what would be the point? You know I didn't do this thing last night. You might not have known it before you brought me in but you know it now, and I know you know it, so it's your call.'

I was out on the street less than fifteen minutes later with a stern, 'We'll be watching you' warning, so I went over to Goody's to see if he wanted to come out to play. Goody took me literally (as he always did) and brought his football out, so we went over the park and won the FA Cup a few times each playing penalty shoot-outs before getting bored (and knackered) and going for a sit-down on the swings. It took me back fifteen or twenty years, swaying backwards and forwards on those dirty old tyres, and it surprised the hell out of me just how much my arse had grown since I last played on them. Goody smashed his foot on the ground (just as I'd predicted he would) trying to swing up high, so in the end we just had a bit of a chat.

I think both of us would've rather had a chat over a pint, but who had any money?

'Bound to happen, Milo. She weren't going to stick around waiting for you for ever, you know,' Goody said when I started sounding off again about Alice. 'Birds are like that. They generally want their blokes in their beds at night, not banged up in the pokey miles away. Flesh and blood, she is, just like you and me, flesh and blood,' he explained, then turned all serious, gave me a knowing nod and said one last word on the subject. 'Needs.'

'What fucking books have you been reading lately?'

'I'm a man of the world. I know a few things. It was the same in the army. I had no more luck hanging on to birds than I did my fucking wages, so I knoweth what I'm talkingeth about. Some old slapper you can give a quick poke to when you're on leave's one thing, but love and romance and all the rest of it when you're nowhere in sight for years on end, you can forget about it. Personally, I'm surprised she stuck with you as long as she did.'

'Aren't you supposed to be on my side in all this?'

'Home truths, Milo. No one likes to hear them. Talking of this, though, what are you doing about the old—' then he whistled, which I took to mean sex, '—at the moment?'

'About the same as I did about it inside,' I replied.

'Oh yeah? Terry bumming you in the shower, is he?'

'Yes, that's it. Other than that, not a fucking lot. Should sort myself out with something, though. Might help take my mind off Alice.'

'You know my sister still likes you, Milo,' Goody said, raising his eyebrows. 'You know, Barbara?' he went on, like I didn't know which sister he was talking about. Me and Babs had a 'thing', I think you'd call it, a few years back which I broke off when I got all serious about Alice. Babs didn't go along with this line of thinking, though, and kept on showing up at the pub or my gaff at midnight or anywhere else I might be when I wasn't with Alice and offering it to me on a plate like a desperate groupie, freaking me out no end. She even wrote to me when I went down for my three stretch and told me she'd wait for me until the end of time. Four months later she got married to Colin and started filling the world with kids with learning difficulties. As far as I knew, she was on future Esso employee number four and showing no signs of slowing down.

'Isn't Barbara still married to that Colin matey, though?'

'Yeah, but only in the evenings and weekends. He's not around during the day. You could just pop round and—' then he whistled again '—anytime you like. I'm sure Babs would be up for doing you a favour.'

'Eww! No offence, Goody, but there's something a little unsavoury here that I can't quite put my finger on.'

'Well, the offer's there any time you need it.'

'Thanks, I'll bear it in mind,' I said and gave myself a little swing to help me think it over. It had always been a bit weird shagging Babs in the first place, because she looks just like Goody, only with a wig, glasses and tits, so his endorsement was a real unnecessary turn-off.

'Oh that's what else I was going to talk to you about: work. What are you doing about work?'

'I signed on the other day and they're sorting me out with a few interviews for next week, I guess. Why's that?'

'I could get you a start with this bloke I know, if you like. I do a couple of days here and there for him every once in a while and I'm doing some stuff next week. It's all cash in the hand so you don't have to declare it or nothing.'

'What stuff? It's nothing dodgy, is it? Because honestly, I'm not . . .'

'No, it's nothing like that, just a bit of manual labour: digging ditches or stacking bricks, that sort of thing. Do you fancy it?'

'Not in the fucking slightest, but then I'm not really doing a lot else at the moment, so I suppose I'll have to. What's it like, hard work?' I asked, looking for reassurance.

'You'll know you've earned your money, I can tell you

that. No, it's pretty hard going, but then it's only for a day here and a day there, so it's bearable. I'll give him a bell.'

So that was just what Goody did, and a few days later we found ourselves in a field in the middle of nowhere digging a series of shallow ditches between hedgerows that were designed to keep pikey caravans out of some bloke's field. He came by to see us, he did, him and his Barbour jacket. He bossed us about for a bit, told us not to start any fires with our fags, then disappeared off up to his big house and left us to get on with it.

Goody hadn't lied about the work, either. It was hard labour on an Egyptian scale, I can tell you. The temperature had to be up in the mid-twenties and by the afternoon the ground and my back were well and truly baked to shit. It was the sort of weather where people say, 'Isn't it glorious?' when they get to laze around in beer gardens or by swimming pools or somewhere nice and fun but is an absolute misery to work in. We were out in the sticks too, so the place was fucking alive with legs and wings and little bastards that liked to commit suicide by jumping in my gob every time I opened it.

I hated it.

It was horrible.

And I was fucked.

'No more. I can't do any more,' I almost cried, throwing in the towel with my shovel.

'Here, have some water,' Goody said, handing me a two-litre Coke bottle filled up with tapwater. I drank as much as I could then poured it over my head, washing the sweat from my face and bringing me some merciful relief. When I opened my eyes I saw that the bottle had only about an inch left in the bottom, so I figured Goody better have some of it before it was all gone.

'For me? Thanks. You sure you can spare it?' he said, grabbing the bottle away from me.

'What time is it?' I panted.

'Just gone three. Come on, we've only got another two hours to go then we're done for the day.'

'I'm done for the day already. I can't do any more,' I told him.

'Look, we have to crack on, otherwise Ted'll just knock us for the lot. Come on, chin up and we'll be in the pub before you know it,' he said and went on smashing up more rock-hard ground with his pickaxe. 'Work through the pain barrier,' he told me, so I did and found there was just more pain behind it.

My work rate dropped considerably as the afternoon wore on and I developed a case of the shakes like you wouldn't believe. I even thought I was going to die at one point before Ted finally showed up with our lift back to town and £60 for each of us.

'Is that all you got done? Fuck me, guys, but my old lady could've knocked out twice the holes you've dug today. I can't give you the full amount. I'm sorry but I've got to hold back a tenner each otherwise you'd be taking the piss.'

Goody gave him a little bit of argy-bargy, but I didn't have the energy to barely stand, so in the end we came to an agreement: we got the full amount, but I didn't do no more days for him because I was clearly a big poofter who probably couldn't even shovel peas. This was absolutely fine with me, so we were all friends again and Ted gave us that lift.

'I'm sorry I can't help you more but I've got a business to run,' Ted said on the way to the White Lion.

'That's cool. Honestly, don't worry about it.'

'Goody tells me you've just got out,' he said and waited for me to enlarge on it. When I didn't he struck up again. 'What else you going to do, then?'

'I don't know. Get an office job or something,' I said, making Ted laugh.

'Office job! No offence, pal, but if your record's half as bad as Goody reckons, what office'll ever take you on?'

'I don't know. I'll figure out something,' I told him.

'I hope for your sake you do, because I'll tell you what: you ain't no digger and I can't see you ever being offered anything else.'

The proposition

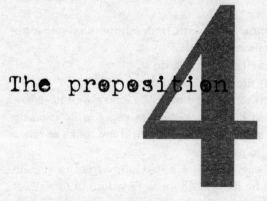

'I didn't think it was that bad, actually,' Goody honestly said, twenty minutes later when we were eyebrows deep in cold lager.

'Not that bad? It was fucking horrendous. And I wasn't even any good at it. Just imagine how much effort I'd have to put into it to be good at it,' I said and shuddered at the thought.

'Honest graft.' Ron, behind the bar, laughed. 'There's nothing like it in the world for getting your thirst up.'

'Ron's right. I really feel like I've earned my money today,' Goody said proudly.

'I don't want to feel like I've earned my money. I want to feel like I've just found it and not have to bother with the earning part,' I replied, and regretted not having had that old lady's tenner away harder than before. I downed the last of my pint as Goody downed his, and we ordered two more and some peanuts and bacon fries to save us drinking on empty stomachs.

'Shall we order some food?' Goody asked.

'Not from this fucking place,' I said, looking at the prices on the menu. How can a BLT – once called a bacon sandwich – cost £4.95?

'We'll get some chips later,' Goody suggested.

'Are you really going to carry on doing days for Ted?' I
asked him.

'Yeah, why not? Bit of cash, fresh outdoors, no one looking over your shoulder all day.'

'I don't know how you can do it.'

'Ah, you get used to it,' he told me.

'I don't want to get used to it. We didn't even have hard
labour inside, so I'll be fucked if I'm going to do it on the
out. My arms ache. So do my legs. And my back's as raw as
a butcher's window.'

'It won't always be this sunny,' Goody tried to reassure
me, though all he did was fill me with visions of snow, sleet,
howling wind and mud.

'I'd rather be back inside,' I muttered to myself.

'Yeah, I think I'd rather be back in the army,' he sympa-
thised.

'Well, why aren't you? Why did you leave?' I asked him,
and it suddenly occurred to me that Goody never talked
about his army days. We talked about football, or the old
days or the jobs I'd pulled all the time, but he hardly ever
put in a word about his time in the army. Admittedly, I'd
never shown any interest before this moment, being that I
was much too preoccupied with my new-found freedom to
be concerned with whatever Goody had been up to, but
suddenly I was intrigued.

'I didn't leave. I was kicked out, wasn't I?' he told me, and
I was intrigued even more. Goody elaborated. 'Discharging
my weapon when unauthorised,' he told me, then gave it to
me in layman's terms. 'I shot someone in the arse.'

'What? You actually shot someone? Who? What? Come
on, Goody, man, fill in the blanks. Who did you shoot?'

'Oh, just some old pikey out in Bosnia. I was there with
the UN for a bit.'

'Why did you shoot him?'

'He was running away and I didn't want him to,' he told

me, as if this was the most obvious thing in the world, and I somehow got the impression that this was the defence he'd used at his court martial.

'You didn't kill him, did you?'

'No. I only clipped him in the trousers. He was fine. Well, not fine, he was screaming like a good 'un and there was blood all over the shop. But you know what I mean. He lived . . . probably.'

'You fucking headcase,' I said, but Goody just shrugged. 'I wonder what it feels like? Getting shot, I mean.'

'Don't know. Didn't speak the lingo, so I couldn't ask him, but it looked like it smarted a bit.'

The conversation carried on in this fashion for a bit, though Goody kept swerving the subject away from his time in the forces in a way that made it clear it was either ground he didn't want to retrace or he was saving it all for his memoirs. I could understand it in a way. I mean, I'd never been in the army, so what would be the point of talking to me about it? I was a civilian and would probably never understand all the shit he went through if he explained it to me a hundred times over, so why waste his breath? I was a bit like that as far as prison went. Sure, if I bumped into another old lag I'd probably take a wander down Felony Lane and compare notes over a couple of beers, but it didn't feel right talking about it with people who hadn't been there. I'm sure all people in specialised occupations feel this way. I bet if you'd never been to dentist school you'd be hard pressed to get a conversation about teeth out of your local gum plumber if you met him down the pub too. In the end, I let the conversation drift to wherever the beer took it and kept my questions for another day.

Though exactly where it drifted to wasn't somewhere I was keen to tread, either.

'You seen Norris lately?' Goody asked. I told him I'd seen

him briefly on the night I'd come out but he'd disappeared after Terry had tried to lump him.

'Why?'

'Oh no, nothing. It's just, I know he was looking for you to have a word with you about something but he couldn't talk to you about it around Terry,' Goody explained, then went all suspiciously whispery. 'It's a job.'

'Oh yes, I see. Milo's not out fifteen minutes, let's see if we can't get him banged up again before teatime, is it?'

'Huh? No, I don't know. That's all he told me,' Goody protested. 'All he said was he had a job, a real big one, and thought you might be interested.'

'Hang on a barley mo'. Is this why Terry clobbered him?' I said, the penny finally dropping. Goody shrugged unconvincingly. 'Well, if you know and Terry knows, how many more fucking people has he been shooting his mouth off to?' Goody again didn't know.

'Might be worth asking Norris for yourself,' he suggested, sipping his pint all nonchalant.

'Yeah, that would be a good idea, wouldn't it? I even chat to him for five minutes about whatever it is he's planning and he goes and does it, then that's me up on conspiracy.'

'Oh come on, don't exaggerate. It's hardly against the law to have a chat with someone about something down the pub, is it?' Goody hammed.

'I'm not interested. I don't want to know. Can't you blokes understand this? I'm not like that any more. I'm completely changed, rehabilitated. Did I tell you about when I first come out and saw this old lady had dropped a tenner out of her bag?'

'Milo, you've told me that story about six times. In fact, on Friday night you said you should've pushed her in the road and cropped the rings off her hands with bolt cutters.'

'I never said that,' I protested and tried to remember if I had or not.

'Oh no, of course you didn't. How out of character that would've been, you fucking thief!'

'Well, if I did, it was only a joke.'

'Conspiracy to prune an old lady. Five years, mate.'

'I think this is slightly getting off the point. All I'm saying is—' I suddenly stopped dead and retraced Goody's recent conversation. I never used to be particularly sharp but years of getting tucked up have given me a bit of a Dodgy-Proposition-Early-Warning System. 'The pub, you said?'

'What?' Goody asked, looking at me with his big "I didn't just do a big shit in your slippers" puppy dog eyes.

'"It's not against the law to chat with someone about whatever down the pub." That's what you said. Norris is coming down here tonight, isn't he?'

'Who knows?' Goody said, looking off towards the clock.

'You bunch of cunts. With friends like you, who needs CID?'

'Look, don't throw your rattle out of the pram. I saw him yesterday and told him we'd probably be coming down here after we knocked off tonight, that's all. There's no conspiracy in it. We're not all meeting up under the grassy knoll or nothing.'

'Fuck this, I'm off,' I said and started necking my pint.

'Too late. I've already got you another one in,' Goody said, frantically signalling to Ron down the other end of the bar with his fingers. 'Look, don't be like that. Just stay and have another one. We don't even have to talk to Norris if he comes in. Just tell him to fuck off or something. Come on, don't go home, stick around, your pint's on its way,' Goody pleaded.

Ron wandered over and asked Goody what he wanted.

'Two Stellas,' he said, shaking his glass about in a hurry, then he pulled out the big guns. 'And two bags of cashews.'

The sheer force of will Goody exerted over me was

impossible to fight. I resigned myself to having another pint but steadied my resolve not to get dragged in to anything I didn't want to touch. I kept saying the word 'no' over in my head again and again as I pictured little oily Norris and his little oily plan as I ate my little oily cashew nuts.

'Don't worry It's probably only scrumping or something like that, anyway,' Goody said when Norris feigned surprise to see us both, but I knew it wouldn't be.

A supermarket.

And not just a supermarket, but that fucking enormous great megastore out where the old gasworks used to be up past the ring road. This was what Norris wanted to hit.

He'd worked there, apparently, stacking pet food and tin foil on the night shift a couple of years ago and reckoned he had all the inside knowledge to clear the place out in under ten minutes. Not of pet food and tin foil, of course, but the £120,000 (at least) in used and untraceable notes that could be found in the manager's safe of a Sunday night. It had to be Sunday, apparently, because this was the only day the takings couldn't be picked up and taken to the bank in the afternoon. In fact, there would be Saturday's and Sunday's money in there, so it was a nick-one/get-one-free special offer kind of day. At least, this was what Norris reckoned.

Mind you, seeing as he also reckoned all we had to do was go marching in there one night, tell everyone to get on the ground, disable the alarm, find the manager, frogmarch him to his office, make him open the safe and then drive off (he reckoned it would take four of us to do this maximum), that just went to show what he knew.

'What about all the shelf stackers? The butchers? The security guards? The ... I don't know, the girls in the office? We just leave them, do we? We just shout, "down on the

ground" and "no calling the Old Bill when we're not looking"?' I asked Norris.

'No, they're wankers, the little cunts I used to work with.
They'd shit themselves in a second and wouldn't dare fuck
with you if you shoved a shotgun in their face,' he replied.

'How are you going to shove a shotgun in their face if
they're scattered all over that colossal shop? You'd have to
round them all up and keep a watch over them before you
could do anything else and that would take blokes. And a
hell of a lot more than just four of us,' I told him, then
noticed I'd used the word 'us', so I started using the word
'no' again and carried on using it until closing time.

'I say we check it out,' Goody said, giving his sausage in bat-
ter a quick breather while we walked along the high street.

'Jesus fucking Christ. Please, Goody, change the record. I
can't even believe I'm talking about this. I've finished, you
dig? Retired. No more. I don't want to even think about it,'
I told him and quickened the pace of my feet and fingers as
they fished about in my cone of chips to demonstrate my
annoyance.

'Milo, man, just think about the money. A hundred and
twenty grand? At least? You've never done anything that
even comes close to something this big before.'

'Yeah, you're right, and I ain't about to start now.'

'Look, we don't have to take the shilling. All I'm saying
is that we should look into it before we blow it out. If it's
as easy as he says it is, then . . .'

But I cut him off with a deluge of hot and soggy pota-
toes spat all over the pavement. 'As easy as he says it is? You
must need your fucking head looking at if you believe anything that bloke says. He's a wanker. The nicks are full of his
sort, who are so greedy for cash they don't even think to
look over their shoulders to see if there's a copper standing

behind them. It's all big ideas and sitting at home watching *Reservoir Dogs* but not an ounce of nous in their heads.'

I wiped my chin and scalded my fingers on a few more chips as Goody tried a different tack.

'Then let's do it without him. Buy what info he does know off him and do the job ourselves.'

This actually made me laugh. 'Yeah, that's what I'd like to do, some big robbery that could get me twenty years, safe in the knowledge that Norris — someone who'd sell out his own granny for a nice fat police reward — was scampering about out there with all the details in his head.'

'He'd be implicating himself if he went to the Old Bill.'

'Look, if you want to go and round up eight or nine idiots and go and do this thing then knock yourself out. I'll even come and visit you from time to time when you're inside. But please, don't ask me to be a part of it. I can't waste any more of my life sitting in a cell.'

'All I'm saying is we look at it. Where's the harm in that?' Goody implored me, really getting on my tits. Man, I hated that. Why couldn't people just take no for an answer? All my life it had been the same — nag, nag, nag. I didn't go round trying to force other people into doing things they didn't want to do, so why did everyone do it to me? No. No. NO!

'You just don't get it, do you? This is my last chance to get my life together. I can't even think about doing a job, not even jokingly. I just love it too much. It's addictive, like a drug.'

'What are you on about?' Goody asked, staring at me.

'Let me put it this way. Have you ever met a reformed alcoholic? I have, and I tell you what, these blokes can never touch a drop again, ever, never. I knew this one bloke, right, and he reckoned he could happily live his life for the next thirty years without so much as a wine gum to keep him going, but if he had one sniff of the barmaid's apron he knew he'd be back sitting in shop doorways knocking back the Special Brew before he knew it. I mean, he knew that, so he didn't put himself in the way of temptation, and it's the same for me. I can never go back to those ways, because I loved it so much.'

Even as I talked, I remembered the shiver of adrenalin I used to experience before a job and the explosion of total head-rushing joy afterwards. Man, that was the best feeling in the world; better than booze, better than sex, better even than getting out of prison, because when you're in prison you always know that one day you're going to get out – you never know (for absolute certain) when you're on a job if you're going to get away with it.

'You know what?' Goody said, threatening me with what was left of his sausage. 'I reckon you've lost your bottle.'

Unbelievable.

How could two people who spoke the same fucking language not be able to make themselves understood? This went back to what I was saying about Goody earlier. Did I press him when he didn't want to talk about his army days? No, I didn't, because I saw that this was obviously a touchy subject for him and moved the conversation on. Why couldn't he do the same for me? I'd explained myself to him over and over again, yet he wouldn't let it go. Yeah, I know we'd both had a few and that both of us had our beer ears on, but, really, how could he be that much of a cunt?

I threw my chips away in disgust, told Goody to fuck off and went home muttering, 'No, no, no,' to myself.

Fat chance 5

'*So, what experience do you have, Mr Miles?*'

'*Well, I can break into and start most cars pre-1994; I know how to clock a milometer; how to pull the wires on the older types of house alarms; I can climb up guttering like a chimp, and I'm almost silent when it comes to windows. I also know how to pick up three CDs in a shop and only put down two, and I could probably do a fair imitation of your signature with less than five minutes' practice.*'

Mr Barnes took a few minutes to look over my patchwork CV, then asked the question I'd been dreading.

'So, what experience do you have, Mr Miles?'

Not much, to be honest, and it showed from the big holes on my CV.

'Well, I have about eighteen months' experience working in the automotive retail and repair trades and I have a HND in mechanical engineering. I've worked in a newsagent's for a couple of months – three or four, actually – a biscuit factory for about three weeks, I used to have my own window-cleaning round, and I have experience of working with old people in the community (eighty hours' experience, to be precise), so I'm very good with people,' I told him, though in truth I'd developed a lifelong hatred for my elders after an enforced summer of Saturday Community

Service around the miserable, smelly, sanctimonious, patronising, nasty, mad and boring, boring, boring old fuckers.

'I see,' he said, setting my CV down on the desk between us and leaning forward, holding hands with himself. 'So how would you say your experience – other than the fact that you're good with people – how would you say this would help you sell shoes?'

What a question!

But, then, what did I expect going for a job in a shoe shop?

'Well . . .' I started, then found myself completely stumped.

I'd had weeks of this shit, and I was getting so bored of it that I could barely manage to disguise my look of utter contempt for these people. I mean, who did they think they were? Fucking shoe shop manager and he thinks he's God.

'How does what you know help you sell shoes?' It didn't. Full fucking stop, by the way.

Unless you've actually worked in a shoe shop before or were a qualified chiropractor, what possible fucking relevant experience was anyone going to have?

I racked my brain desperately trying to think of something to say, but all I could think of was grabbing his tie, dragging him over the desk and giving him the hiding he so richly deserved.

I was so bored of this. So, so, so, so bored.

This was my eighth interview and they'd all been the same. Some crummy little shit in a crummy little suit, getting kicks out of trying to make me beg him into giving me a £5-an-hour job either putting tins in boxes, sweeping up people's hair, waiting on tables, cooking chips, mowing lawns, carrying flat-pack furniture out to cars or delivering pizzas. And now this, selling fucking shoes. I was so sick, tired and bored of it all.

I mean, what sort of a loser was going to tell him, 'Oh

yes, it's always been my dream to work in a shoe shop and
help people find the right footwear for the right occasion.
What brilliant fun that would be. And one day I want to be
the manager, just like you, so that after fifty years I can look
back on my life and say I did that, not too bad, huh?' This
was what this cunt was waiting to hear, but he had about as
much chance of hearing it from me as I did of getting a job
in a shoe shop.

See, the cards were stacked against me from the start. The
JobCentre had referred me for all of these interviews so
everyone I'd been to see had known about my record
before I'd even set foot in their office. And who was ever
going to give a bloke like me a job? Ted had been right
about that one. I didn't even know why they kept agreeing
to see me in the first place. Maybe they were getting some
sort of government grant or tax break or something seeing
no-hopers from the UB40. Personally, I needed the interviews to keep getting my benefits, so this was just an exercise in bureaucracy on both sides of the desk.

Why, then, did they insist on making the interviews such
hard work? And so humiliating too? You know, the benefit
people can cut you off if they hear that you haven't tried at
these interviews. This makes sense in a way, I suppose, otherwise everyone on the dole would simply go along and
kick over the desk the moment they arrived and tell the
man in the suit that he looked like a jerk. But that wasn't it
with old Barnsie here. No, for him it was a power thing. He
was enjoying acting the big man with someone who would
never normally take this sort of shit from a pink-faced,
balding little runt with a girl's hands and glasses. But what
could I do?

In all honesty, of the jobs I'd gone for so far, this one was
far and away the most attractive. No heavy lifting, no driving about in all conditions, no hot kitchens. Just a bit of
rooting around in the back to see if we had any size eights

and holding the female customers' dainty little ankles in a bold, gentlemanly way while I looked up their skirts. Oh yes, it beat digging ditches all right. Not that there was much danger of me actually getting it.

After five seconds of humming and hawing I was still stuck for any sort of answer as to how my experience could help me sell shoes, so in the end I chose to say the first thing that came into my head.

'Well, I'd say my background has helped me keep my feet on the ground.'

Barnsie looked at me in confusion as if he couldn't see what this had to do with anything and said so.

'Well, OK then, nothing. Nothing I've ever done before is going to help me sell shoes, but you know, fuck it, I'm sure I'll be able to pick it up. I mean, how hard can it be?'

Did I just say 'fuck it' in my interview?

'Erm, yes, well, let's move on,' Barnsie suggested, and he didn't get any argument from me. 'Do you have a criminal record?'

This was the first time any of my interviewers had asked me this. I'd joked with Goody that if this question cropped up I'd tell them I certainly did; I held the record for the most car stereos nicked in one night in the whole of Hampshire. Now that I'd finally been asked it, it suddenly didn't seem all that appropriate. I decided to give him the serious answer and just tell Goody I'd said it.

'Yes, I just got out of prison last month.'

'And what were you in prison for?'

I was reluctant to go into the specifics, so I just said, 'Theft,' though Barnsie, the big nosy bastard, wanted to pry further.

'What did you do?'

'I stole some things.'

'Exactly what?'

'No offence, but I don't think that's any of your business,'

I told him in no uncertain terms, and he visibly shrank before me.

'Well, er, no. Quite. I only asked because I have a shop to run and so it's my job to, er, know the people under my employ,' he choked, shuffling papers busily and pushing his glasses up his nose while I stared at him hard.

'I have a record and, yes, it is for theft, but I'm not like that any more. I know for a fact that anyone who takes me on will keep a real close eye on me and I fully understand that. And this is probably why I'm the last person in the world who would ever steal from you. Not because you would be keeping an eye on me, but because I'm desperate to prove to everyone that I've changed. All I'm asking for is a chance. Society as a whole doesn't like criminals. And I don't want to be one any more. So by giving me this job you'll be ridding society of one more criminal, won't you? Not a bad thing to say you've done, you know.'

I didn't get the job. What a surprise! Still, who wanted to work in a fucking shoe shop anyway?

What I really wanted to do was get back in the motor trade. I mean, cars and mechanics were my first love. Unfortunately, there wasn't a garage within fifty miles that would touch me with a fifty-mile-long bargepole. I couldn't even get an interview. Hardly surprising, really, when I thought about it, though. I mean, taking into consideration all the motor vehicle theft and tampering offences I had on my CV, any garage that took me on would have to be absolutely squeaky clean itself, because my presence would bring all sorts of intrusive scrutiny along with it. And how many garages were there like that? No, it looked like I'd shot my mechanical bolt, so what other options were open to me?

In the nick, there were all sorts of vocational courses I could've taken to get myself started, but I'd always been reluctant. I'd mostly concentrated on getting my HND in mechanical engineering and, on the advice of Terry, my English and maths GCSEs. That seemed enough at the time. Why bother learning carpentry or computer programming when I was going to be a mechanic when I got out? Hindsight is a wonderful thing, isn't it? Still, how many of those old crooks who took the computer classes actually managed to get themselves jobs in Dixons when they got out, I wonder? Not many, I can't imagine.

I was quite surprised how much I enjoyed English while I was inside. When I'd done it at school it had simply seemed like work, but in the nick it was almost like a way out. I read a lot of books over my last stretch, thrillers mostly – Raymond Chandler, Dick Francis, P.D. James, Agatha Christie – you know, detective novels. I thought they were great, couldn't get enough of them. I even half fancied having a go at writing a book myself and invented a detective called Dick Danger who went around Hampshire solving murders. The trouble was, though, whenever I sat down to write, I kept getting that wanker Weasel in my head as Dick Danger, so I'd have him slamming his fingers in car doors or falling down stairs or getting his head kicked in all the time so that he hardly had a chance to solve where his teeth had got to before the next boot was up his arse. I wasn't very original with the plots, either. Dick Danger would be called round to investigate a murder on a council estate and figure out it was the butler who'd done it within half a page. After that, I never knew what else to do, so I'd just beat the shit out of Dick Danger again and that would be the end of the book. I wrote about five of them in all. The longest one was only about eight pages long, and my English teacher told me I'd never get them published, so I lost interest. Funnily enough, though, lots of the blokes on my landing loved my books, so there must've been something to them.

Not that any of this was going to help me get a job. And

I did want a job. I couldn't just laze around on Terry's sofa indefinitely until it was time to retire. I had to get out there and do something. Just not digging. Not manual work or lifting or anything hard. I simply couldn't do it. And it wasn't because I didn't want to do it (although there was that to it as well) or that I thought I was too good for it or something. It was just that I wasn't designed for that sort of labour. It would be like trying to win the Grand Prix with a milk float. Even if you suped it up, gave it a high-performance Ferrari engine, racing slicks, took the crates off the back and gave it a head start, it still wouldn't win. Why? Because milk floats weren't meant to race Grand Prix, just like I wasn't meant to dig fucking ditches.

Anything else, though. Anything else at all. Just give me that chance and I'll do it.

On the way home from the shoe shop I bumped into Alice waiting by a bus stop with her little kid in a pushchair, so I stopped to say hello. I was hoping she'd clock the suit (Terry's suit) and see that I'd been for an interview and believe me that I really was serious about turning over a new leaf, but you know what she asked me?

'You in court today or something, Darren?'

'No,' I replied, letting that slide. 'Actually, I've just come back from a job interview and I think it went really well.' I looked down at her sprog and asked, 'Who's this, then? Is this who I think it is?'

'No, this is some other kid I just found outside Tesco.'

I let that one slide too but decided to keep my false compliments about what an attractive saucepan he was to myself. He wasn't, by the way. He was going to grow up to be a right shocker.

'Look, Alice, I think we got off on the wrong foot and I just want to get back on an even footing with you again,' I said, my shoe shop interview no doubt still on my mind.

'Darren, you just don't get it, do you? There is no us, not no more. It's over.'

'Hang on a minute. Can't we even be friends?'

'My friends don't treat me the way you did.'

'I said I'm sorry.'

'And so am I. I'm so so sorry you went away again despite everything I said about not being able to handle being apart from you again. I did warn you not to go down again. You remember me saying that, don't you?'

'Yes,' I told her, but only vaguely. There'd been lots of conversations like that back then, so I couldn't be sure which one she was referring to. At the time I'd taken them as compliments, a sort of 'I love you and never want to be apart from you' touch. I didn't realise they were actually threats. That's women for you, though; they can't just come out and say what they mean, they've got to hide it between the lines all the time and heaven help you if you don't pick up on it.

'Do you want a hand with your shopping?' was all I could think to say.

'No, I don't think I could trust you not to have my eggs away.'

'That's a bit below the belt.'

'Yeah, well I thought I'd get you where you think.'

'Mummy's angry at the nasty man for going away,' I told Mark, who blew a few bubbles out of his nose in response.

'Mummy is not angry. Mummy just wants the nasty man to do what he's best at and go away again.'

'Mummy doesn't like the nasty man, though we used to be friends.'

'Yes, but the nasty man was horrible to Mummy, so they're not friends any more.'

'But the nasty man only wants to apologise and say he's sorry for being horrible.'

'Well, Mummy doesn't want the nasty man's apology. Mummy just wants to get on with her life.'

'I know that, but we live in a small town, so Mummy and the nasty man are going to keep bumping into each other, so the nasty man wants to make peace with Mummy and be friends again.'

'Mummy suggests the nasty man crosses over the road every time he sees Mummy and stops bothering her.'

'You see what she's like,' I said to Mark, though he didn't look like he cared either.

The bus pulled around the corner, so Alice started gathering her bags together. I didn't think she'd even look at me again to say goodbye, but instead she let the hard-bitch façade crumble and talked to me in a tone I just about remembered.

'Look, Darren, this is hard for me but I'll say it anyway, then you can't bother me any more. I did love you once. I loved you so much that it hurt, too much in fact. But when I look back on those days all I remember is pain. And that's not right, all that love and nothing but pain. You hurt me, Darren. You hurt me more than you can ever know and more than I can ever forgive you for. I may even still love you deep down, but I can never forgive you. The fantasy you have in your head about us getting back together – just forget about it. It's never going to happen. You're in my past now, just a memory. I'll try and think fondly of you when I can, but that won't be very often. I'm living for me and Mark now.' (I noticed she didn't say me, Mark and Brian.)

Alice leaned forward and gave me a little kiss on the lips. 'Goodbye,' she said, looking me straight in the eyes, and suddenly I knew it was for real.

The bus door opened and Alice struggled on with her pushchair and shopping and fished about in her purse to pay the driver.

'I have changed, you know,' I called after her, but she

didn't look back, not even through the window as the bus pulled away.

And at that moment I felt sicker than if I'd missed out on all the old ladies' tenners in Britain.

Probably a robbery

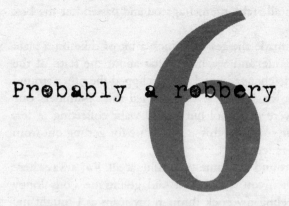

I felt awful for a couple of days and couldn't think about anything else except Alice and how things had gone so wrong between us. It was hard to imagine that we'd once been so in love with each other that we were really quite unbearable to be around. I kept on remembering the jokes we'd shared, the secrets we told each other and the love we made, though this last one was a big mistake because I couldn't help but get the raging horn whenever I looked back and this just made me feel even lower.

Out of sheer necessity I did the only thing I could think of that might help me forget about Alice.

'That was a big load,' Babs congratulated me.

'Urgh,' I groaned to myself and rolled on to my side towards my hastily discarded clothes. 'What time's your old man back?'

'Colin. He won't be home until six, so you've got plenty of time. We can have a chat, catch up a bit. Do you want something to eat?' she asked me, straightening her glasses.

'Er, no. I can't, I'm afraid. I've got to get down the post office and cash my giro,' I told her as I stepped into my trousers.

'Well, do you want a cup of tea before you go? Won't take a mo' to put the kettle on.'

'Um, oh all right, then,' I agreed and passed her the box of Kleenex.

Barbara made the tea and stuck a bit of cake on a plate in front of me, and we had a chat about the state of the world as she changed one kid and clipped the other around the ear'ole for saying he could 'smell shit'. Numbers one and two were at school but would want collecting in less than a hour, so I used this as an excuse for getting out from under Babs's feet.

'Come round any time. Any time at all. I'm always here for you when you want it,' she said, giving me a big sloppy kiss and feeling my cock through my jeans as I fought my way out of the front door.

I got to the end of the path and checked my ego. Nope, I still didn't feel good about myself, so I decided to have a pint and a bag of nuts to cheer myself up once I'd cashed my giro.

The post office was a little sub-branch that looked about a hundred years old. It played home to an old postmaster, who looked about the same age, and a couple of old biddies who sat behind wire meshing and who seemed to know everyone in the short queue by name. I wondered if they'd say hello and ask after my family too after I'd been coming in with my giro for a couple of months or whether they'd just think I was a dole scrounger. No, they looked like a friendly old crew who'd give me the benefit of the doubt and be nice and polite to me as long as I was nice and polite back (be a different matter if I'd landed in this country clinging to the side of the Eurostar, though).

It occurred to me that this was what law-abiding society was all about: mutual respect. Everyone consented to live by a certain set of rules and respect was born out of your adhering to these rules. Basically, these old chaps in the post office were the cornerstone of society, and they'd show me respect and treat me as an equal and peer just so long as I didn't do anything to upset the status quo, i.e. tie them up with piano wire and run off with all their money. So by simply not robbing, raping or murdering any of them, I was automatically earning their respect.

And again, like with the old lady and that tenner, it felt quite good to have that respect. I know it sounds ridiculous, but I could almost see the old ladies and the other customers looking at me and thinking, 'Well done. Well done for not robbing us. Well done for just coming in and using the post office as it should be used. Well done.'

I, in turn, was looking back and standing nice and nonchalantly as if to say, 'I only want to cash a cheque, that's all. You're all safe from me. I don't do that any more. I just want to fit in and have a nice quiet life.'

'Well done. Well done indeed, because, of course, he used to be a bit of a nasty piece of work.'

'Yes, I heard about that. A real thief, completely untrustworthy. Not someone to respect.'

'Well, he doesn't do that any more. He's one of us from now on. He's only using the shop to cash a cheque. He's even going to say please and thank you when he gets his money.'

'Well, you have to respect that, don't you?'

'You certainly do, particularly in light of the fact that this place would be a fucking doddle to rob.'

'Would it?'

'Oh God yes. Look at that security camera up there. The wire's not even connected. It's recording absolutely nothing at all.'

'You mean there'd be no recording of the robbery for the police to study or to use in court? They'd have to rely on a clutch of eyewitnesses to testify?'

'That's exactly what I mean. And look at us, for heaven's sake. Do we look like the sort of people who'd stand up under cross-examination? Half my marbles disappeared years ago, so I'd be no use to anyone.'

'Me too. I can't even remember what day it is most of the time. I just want a cup of tea and a nice sit-down.'

'Now check out the door that leads behind the cash desk. The wood around the catch is all splintered to buggery. One good shoulder charge and it would bust open, no problem. Not that he'd need to bother. Stan's always forgetting to lock it. Look, the door's ajar right now.'

'Oh yeah, look at that. That's dreadful. And they've got all that cash behind there and only a couple of old ladies to protect it.'

'This place would be a piece of piss to do over. A fucking piece of piss.'

'Good job he hasn't come to rob us, then.'

'Yes. Good job he's changed.'

'You have to respect that.'

'Next.'

'You what?'

'Next.'

'What's next?'

'Yes, you with your head in the clouds. Can I help you?'

I snapped back to reality and found myself at the front of the queue and staring at one of the old ladies.

'Are you all right, love?' she asked, as I slipped her my giro.

'Yes. Sorry, miles away,' I told her, and she chuckled good-naturedly and sang the first line of a song I didn't recognise which had the word 'daydreamer' in it. She chuckled some more as she stamped my giro and just started counting out my money when suddenly the door burst open and two guys wearing ski masks crashed in and threatened everyone on to the ground with pickaxe handles.

Everyone dropped down and several of the old ladies

screamed, but I was fixed to the spot in disbelief. Disbelief that this could be happening so soon after I'd just thought about it. Disbelief that I was expected to get down with the rest of the customers. Disbelief that everyone else in here seemed to be surprised that they were being robbed.

'Get down!' the lead bandit shouted, pushing an old fellow to the ground.

'Ged-dan,' his mate told a young mother with a pushchair.

'Get down!'

'Ged-dan.'

'Get . . . fucking hell. All right, Milo?' said matey in the ski mask, stopping in front of me. 'Er, I mean, get down!' he said, suddenly remembering where he was, and pushed me to the ground. I said nothing and did as he said, but the three of us watched each other uneasily as the post office's money found its way into their bags. I was more apprehensive than most and expected a pickaxe handle over the head before the day was out but the lads left me alone and treated me just like everyone else.

They emptied the drawers of cash, stamps and postal orders in about thirty seconds and told everyone to stay where they were for five minutes otherwise they'd come back and beat us all up. One of the old ladies howled with fear at this prospect, and I couldn't help but shake my head at how gullible some people were.

'OK, now stay down and everyone close their fucking eyes. I mean it. Close them, because I'll be checking.'

I didn't understand this part of the robbery but did as they said anyway and closed my eyes. No sooner had I done this than I felt a hand in my pocket and someone tap me on the shoulder. I opened my eyes and saw the guy who'd said hello holding his finger to his lips. I nodded to reassure him I'd stay quiet and he got back to his feet and left with his mate.

The moment they were gone I clambered to my feet and checked the counter for my giro money. It was all gone.

'Didn't you hear what he said? He said we all had to stay down otherwise they'd come back and beat us up,' the postmaster informed me.

'Oh do me a favour!' I informed him back and looked down at all the old sheep on the ground, cowering in fear of their lives at a completely empty and nonsensical threat. Only a few moments earlier I'd been proud to call myself one of them, but suddenly I thought they were pathetic and wanted to distance myself from them as fast as possible. I knew better than to leave the scene of a crime, however, and stuck around outside as the sirens grew louder and louder.

I sat on the steps of the post office and had a cigarette. What I really wanted was a drink, but it didn't look like I'd be getting my giro cashed today. I wondered if I'd still be able to cash it in now that it had been stamped, and suddenly I felt outraged that my money had been stolen along with the post office's.

I was a victim, and it felt bloody awful.

I stuffed my hand in my pocket to see what my mate had been trying to nick and found, to my surprise, nothing missing. In fact, I found quite the opposite. In my pocket, along with my wallet and my johnnies, was one, two, three, four, five . . . five £20 notes. I had £100. Two weeks' dole was only £82, so I was up on the deal.

I rubbed my hands together all cheered up, then smiled and wondered again if I'd still be able to cash my giro.

'They knew your name,' Weasel insisted.

'I'm a popular bloke,' I told him back.

'Wriggle all you want, Milo. We've got you banged to rights for this one.'

Weasel leaned back in his chair and folded his arms all smug and pleased with himself.

'You have to admit, it does look bad,' Ross said, playing the caring, sharing copper to Weasel's wanker.

'I think my client has been extremely cooperative, Sergeant. What more can he tell you?' my brief, Charlie Taylor, asked. Yes, this time I insisted on having a brief present. Innocent or not, I wasn't about to enter an interview room with these two fit-up merchants after being placed at the scene of a robbery by a load of confused old codgers. Besides, it wasn't like I had to foot the bill. No, that was your job.

'Cooperative? We've got him on obstruction at the very least. Either he tells us the names of the men who did over the post office today or we'll charge him. And I do mean that,' Weasel said, stabbing his fat finger on the table repeatedly to underline his point.

'I've told you, I don't know who they were. They were wearing masks. They could've been you two for all I know.'

'They knew your name.'

'What, and you don't?'

'There you have it, Sergeant. He doesn't know. Will you be charging him now or will you be letting him go? Personally, I'd let my client go if I were you, because you and I both know the CPS will throw this whole thing out in the blink of an eye and you'll look even more ridiculous than usual.'

Weasel didn't rise to this. He just hammered the desk some more and told me I was for it, but I could see he was a spent force.

'You know their names,' he insisted for the millionth time, but he was actually wrong. Oh I could've taken an educated guess and named at least one of them, but I wouldn't know for sure if I was right. I'd had only the briefest of exchanges with my masked mate and I haven't seen the vast majority of my friends in over ten years. And we all know what ten years can do to a person. I doubt I'd recognise half the people I shared a class with if they tried to sell me the *Big Issue*. I certainly wouldn't remember their names. And I definitely wouldn't tell Weasel about it if I did.

'I've been in and out of nick since I was fifteen. Think of all those criminals I've done time with over the years. It could be any two out of a hundred blokes. I couldn't say who they were.'

'No? But I bet you could take a bloody good guess, though, couldn't you?' Ross said.

'I'm not guessing nothing. You guess who they were if you want. I don't care.'

'My client will not be making any guesses for you,' Charlie told Weasel, and he was bloody right I wasn't. I mean, what if I guessed it was Harry Madison and it turned out not to be him at all? Knowing Weasel, he'd stitch me up for attempting to pervert the course of justice. Besides, who did he think I was, Mystic fucking Meg?

'You start cooperating or you can go back to the cells and sweat it out in there.'

'Five quid says you can't make nothing stick,' I said and offered my hand to Weasel.

'You've got yourself a bet, my old son,' Weasel replied and took my hand. 'You've got a bet.'

Half an hour later on my way out of the station I asked Weasel if he had that fiver, but the bastard knocked me for it.

'Just get out of my sight,' he said, waving me away, and disappeared back inside before I could annoy him some more.

'Well, thanks, Charlie,' I said, turning and giving my brief's hand a bit of a shake on the steps. 'I think I would've probably been in there for some time if it hadn't been for you.'

'You're welcome, Darren. My pleasure. Now remember, stay in trouble.' He smiled, then drove off in his brand-spanking-new shiny Jag.

I looked at my watch. It was half-past nine on a beautiful summer's evening. And I had a thirst-on like you wouldn't believe.

Terry's tutorial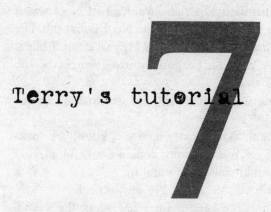

I managed to drag Patsy down the pub, and we had a long talk about his divorce and my job prospects for about an hour or so until we were both on the verge of tears, then Ron called last orders, so I went home via Kentucky's and found Terry sprawled out on the sofa cradling a bottle of lemon vodka.

'You want a drumstick?' I asked and shoved my bargain bucket in his face. I hadn't eaten anything all day and was starving like Marvin, so I'd bought more chicken than I could carry and was now the bloke to be around.

'Gimme,' he said, grabbing a handful, clearly drunk as a skunk on skunk.

'What are you celebrating, then?' I asked, wrestling the bottle out of his hand long enough to pour myself a drink.

'Celebrating? I'm not celebrating, I'm the other one. Commiserating. That's what I'm doing,' he slurred, his eyes all puffy and lopsided.

'Oh. What are you commiserating, then?' I asked and sipped my vodka.

'I got the sack,' he laughed.

'The sack? What for? Had your fingers in the till, did you?'

'Oh yeah, that would be right, wouldn't it? No, I wasn't thieving, I was just . . . shit. Was I shit? No, I wasn't shit. The job was shit, that was what was shit.' He made sure I knew. 'So, then, how can you be good yourself when the job you're doing is shit?'

'I'll go along with that,' I said, but he wouldn't let me have it.

'Go along with that? What would you know, you fuck-ing work dodger? You've hardly done a stroke in all your life, so what would you know about it?'

'Jesus, don't have a go at me. I'm on your side.'

'You get a job and keep it for a few years, then you'll know what I'm talking about,' he said, waving his drumstick at me. 'It's hard, working is. Hard and shit and then they sack you – if you're lucky,' he said, then thought about that. 'Fucking having to get up and go somewhere you hate and do your best, just to keep a roof over your head, and you make a couple of mistakes and that's it, you're out. Go back to GO and start again. Bastards! Fucking bastards! Anderton . . .' he said, attacking his chicken like he meant it. 'What a bastard!' he said but didn't elaborate. All he said was, 'I did my best,' and I believed him.

'So this is the lifestyle you think I should pursue, is it? Work, peanuts, sack?'

'Oh do me a favour, please. Don't make this about you. The world doesn't revolve around you, you know,' he said, patronising me as if he was the older brother.

'Hey, you started it. You're the one who's always telling me to give up the thieving and go straight. Now look at you. What a sorry-arsed piece of shit you are,' I said, then added, 'No offence.'

'The answer to every problem isn't robbing somewhere, Darren,' he said, then chucked his chicken bone through the kitchen door and managed to get it in the sink, which was a good shot. 'More,' he demanded and helped himself to a piece of breast.

'Might solve a few things for both of us right now, though,' I said, trying to get a rise out of him.

'Yeah, we wouldn't have to worry about dinner and rent for a couple of years, I suppose.'

'Believe it or not, you do sometimes get away with it.'

'Don't remember you ever having any great measure of success there, *Milo*,' he said, using my nickname to take the piss.

'That is so untrue. I did loads I never got caught for. Loads and loads, in fact.'

'Bullshit. You were a worse thief than I was an admin assistant. I'll tell you this: if they could sack thieves, you would've got the bullet years ago. Mum was right about you, you know: you really are a lost cause.'

'Oh yeah? I ain't the one lying on the sofa crying his eyes out like a little girl because he's lost a job he didn't even like in the first place,' I said, but instantly regretted how spiteful that had sounded. Luckily, Terry was too far gone to give a shit.

'It isn't the job, it's the money. I haven't got any savings, well, not much, anyway. I've got enough for a couple more mortgage payments – if I live on bread and cheese for the next few months – and then that's me done for,' he explained, and I could tell he was genuinely worried.

'What are you going to do?' I asked.

'Start charging you rent for a start,' he told me, and I suddenly saw the dire pickle we were both in.

'Yeah? Well, what the fuck am I going to do, then?'

'Same as everyone else: get a job and hope you don't fucking lose it.'

'I'm trying, I really am. You've seen all the interviews I've gone for.'

'Darren, you can't pick and choose yourself a cushy

number somewhere warm and fluffy. Now, you already told me they offered you that job in the timber yard, but you didn't fancy it because it sounded like hard work. Well, I've got news for you. My big lazy work-shy brother, from Monday morning, you're going to start fancying it,' he said, sending a cold shiver down my spine and making my hands feel like they were full of a thousand phantom splinters. 'Right, I'm off to bed. My hangover's already kicking in. See you in the morning.'

'Yeah. Sleep tight,' I told him, though there wasn't much chance of him sleeping any other way.

That night I had a dream.

I was in the timber yard and all the pieces of wood looked pricklier than a hedgehog with a headache. I had to shift them from one side of the yard to the other, but I had no strength and my boots felt like they were made of lead. I struggled to shift even the smallest stick and desperately looked around for somewhere to hide and skive. Then I was in the post office and the old lady wouldn't give me any money. I was getting really frustrated with her, because she had a big pile of it behind her and it was just sitting there doing nothing. Beer was £50 a pint and I had 3p. Ron took that then wouldn't even give me a sip. I demanded some beer out of him, but he just told me that my mum had forbidden him to give me any beer and I shouldn't have gone back in prison. I told him I wasn't in prison, I was out now, but then I suddenly remembered I was in prison. But I couldn't understand why I was back in prison and thought I remembered getting released, then I remembered the post office and realised I shouldn't have been in there. I pleaded with Mr Banyard that it was a mistake and that no one had told me I wasn't supposed to be in the post office but he wouldn't wear it and told me to get on and stack those pieces of wood on the other side of the yard otherwise I'd never get out. It was then that I realised the post office was in the corner of the yard and this time I wasn't going to ask for money, I was just going to take it and run and run and run until I'd got away. I was just in the process of doing this when Terry woke me up and asked me if I wanted a chicken Kiev for breakfast.

This seemed like such a ridiculous notion that I assumed I was still dreaming, but I wasn't.

'It's all I've got in. I did all my eggs and bacon yesterday. I've got a bit of milk but only enough for tea. Er, besides, I think I've run out of corn flakes.'

I struggled into an almost upright position and rubbed the sleep from my face. 'What time is it?'

'Almost eleven. You looked like you were out for the count.'

'Fucking weird dreams,' I said and ran over them while they were still in my head. 'All jumbled and all over the place.'

'Yeah, well, that's dreams for you. Did you want a chicken Kiev? I'm ravishing, I am,' he said, not realising what he'd just said and making me laugh.

'No, just tea, please.'

It was about this time that I noticed Terry had a shirt and tie on.

'Where are you going? I thought you got the sack.'

'I've got an interview. Well, more just an informal meet, really, at half-twelve,' he told me, checking his watch, then checking the side of the box of frozen Kievs, then sticking the oven on.

'Already? You didn't waste much time. How have you got an interview already?'

'Informal meet. It's just an informal meet.'

'All right, informal meet. How have you got one already?'

'I've got a few friends, you know,' he said and tapped the side of his nose.

I thought about this as Terry tidied the flat around me and came to the same conclusion.

So did I.

Milo's Marauders

To say I wandered aimlessly that morning wouldn't be true. I was in a daze, for sure, but my feet kept taking me past Alice's house and the chemists like they hadn't yet accepted what my brain had reluctantly acknowledged – that she was gone. Not no more. Not mine at all. Alice's street was just another street to me now, and I had no business in it unless I got a paper round or was turning over one of her neighbours. Gutted. I was overwhelmed with this melancholic feeling of loss that I just couldn't shake. Pining, I believe people in the know call it. I was really down, and not just about Alice, either, but about my whole lot. Alice was just someone I used to turn to to make me feel better whenever I felt down in the dumps, and now she wasn't there my feet didn't know what to do or where to take me.

After a time I spied her coming out of her front door with her little toddler in a pram. Me and my feet followed her to the park and watched her from a discreet distance as she chatted with the other mums and picked Mark up whenever he toppled over on to his nut. I couldn't hear what she was saying, because she was too far away, but I knew it wouldn't be about me. And that just flexed the hurt all the more.

I was miserable.

I'm not saying my life was shit, because you only have to open a newspaper to realise how cushy even the lowliest of us have it in this country, but everything's relevant, isn't it? The geezer in the Saudi jail who gets flogged only once a week while his mates are getting it every day must think he's got it pretty sweet, whereas the Monte Carlo millionaire with the smallest yacht in the harbour could be forgiven for having a case of the glums. You can only judge your life by your peers. And all of my peers seemed to be doing a great deal better than me.

Twenty-seven years old. Most of the blokes I shared a class with all those wasted years ago would've had houses, wives, cars, jobs, kids, holidays and, most important, prospects. I didn't even have the last in that list.

And it wasn't because I wasn't willing or hadn't been trying or nothing, not even Alice could accuse me of that. I just couldn't catch a break. What did I have to do?

I felt like such a loser. And it was the first time in my life I'd ever felt like that. I'd never even felt this way when I'd got sent down all those times, because at least I'd had the respect of other criminals for keeping my trap shut and taking it like a man to offer me some small crumb of comfort. What did I have now? No house. No girlfriend. No car. No job. No kids. No holidays. Nothing. Just a meat-head ex-squaddie with an offer I wasn't allowed to refuse sprinting towards me from across the park.

'All right, Milo? I've been looking all over for you. Well, I went to Terry's, anyway, and you weren't there, so I figured you'd be over here.'

'Well, you've found me now. What's up?'

Goody sat down on the bench next to me.

'Oh nothing, nothing. Just fancied a chat, that's all.'

Goody desperately tried to exercise a little patience before getting on to the subject I knew he wanted to get on to, so I took him all around the houses with the weather, the football scores and how crap music was these days before he finally grabbed the conversation by the scruff of the arse and took it off to the supermarket.

'I had a look at this place Norris was banging on about. Huge place it is, up by the ring road. Have you seen it yet?'

'Do you actually listen to me when I talk?' I asked.

'I'm just sitting here having a conversation. There's no law against that, is there? I ain't saying nothing. All I'm saying is that I had a look out of curiosity and the place was big. I don't think £120,000's an exaggeration, neither. I reckon it's probably more than that. How many blokes did you reckon it would take? Eight or nine, you said?'

How I didn't start crying at that moment was beyond me, but I was just so low at that point that I couldn't resist any more. Before I knew it I was humouring Goody and talking shop once more. I didn't want to (at first), but it just seemed like it would take more effort not to talk about it than to talk about it. And I simply didn't have any energy left.

It was just a hypothetical chat, Goody assured me. Where was the harm in that? So I played his game and told him what he wanted to hear.

'I'd have to see the place first but, yeah, probably eight blokes minimum: one in the van, two to take security, five to round up the staff, then three to sit on them while two cut the alarms and got the money.'

'Eight into £120,000 . . .' Goody started to work out in his head, but I have a mind like a dart scorer when it comes to bread.

'Fifteen grand each. Not too good when you put it like that,' I said.

'I suppose, but not bad either for five minutes' work.'

'But fuck all for five years inside.'

'Yeah, but that's only if we got caught. We wouldn't get caught,' Goody assured me.

'Oh yeah, why didn't I think of that?'

'What else?'

'We'd need somewhere to meet. Couldn't all get together to discuss everything down the pub or round your mum's: look too suspicious, a load of blokes coming and going in eights three weeks before the supermarket's done over by that exact number of blokes.'

'The industrial estate. That place has loads of old drums going empty. We could break into one of those and use it as our hideout.'

'Hideout? Keep it together. This isn't *Batman*, you know. Besides, the industrial estate's still got tons of security cameras up there protecting the occupied units. We'd get rumbled before we held our first meeting.'

'Well, what about the old American base?' Goody then suggested, meaning the little housing estate on the edge of town that used to house the Yank air force and their families when the bomber base was still in use. 'That place is going to wrack and ruin. It's all boarded up now. No one ever goes there except kids, and we can just all meet up after their bedtime.'

'Yeah, not bad. Not bad at all. We could check it out, I suppose. Might do, in the unlikely event we were to actually do this thing.'

'Keep talking.'

We got off our arses and ambled away from Alice and off in the direction of the American base. As we ambled, we drew up a list of blokes who might be interested in doing five years with us. Lots of names were mentioned, and Goody and I discussed their CVs like a couple of shoe shop managers, though the only difference was that, should we decide to go through with this, we couldn't interview anyone unless we were absolutely certain they had the right qualifications and, most important, wanted the job. With a score this big, no one outside the group could know about it. No one. Otherwise the whole thing was off before it had begun.

An old burglar mate of mine, Bex, and his mate Ollie made the top of my list, but Goody told me they were both doing a year up at Erlestoke. This came as a surprise to me, as Bex reckoned he'd never go down. It also occurred to me that I'd won my bet and that Bex now owed me £50. I'd see him in a year's time. Hopefully.

'Well, there's Norris, obviously,' Goody reminded me.

CLIVE MICHAEL NORRIS (29)

Norris started as a shoplifter, then went on to joyriding, burglary and general thievery. Fuck knows how he ever got a job in a supermarket, because he had as much form as I did. Must've been placed there by the JobCentre or something. His speciality was lifting handbags from drunken women in nightclubs, and he showed me how to do it once. What he'd do was sit by the edge of the dance floor and keep his eyes peeled as the place filled up. Then, when he spotted a target and the place was suitably bopping, he'd dance over to her. He'd swing his hips and flash his pearly yellows and she'd naturally turn her back on him or tell him to fuck off or something, so he would. And that would be that, her handbag would be gone. See, while she was distracted by his boat or concentrating on her mates opposite, Norris would do a one-two-three into the straps of her handbag on the floor and dance off with it, trailing it behind his foot. He'd have it under his shirt before he was at the edge of the floor and rifle through it in the bog, then dump it in a darkened corner, minus any money, cards and valuables. He'd do this about five or six times in quick succession, then split before the bouncers had a chance to get their shit together. Not a particularly nice thing to do, but then Norris wasn't a particularly nice bloke. Thieves rarely are.

Quite an eye opener though. According to Norris, the number of birds who went out on a Saturday night with just £5 in their purses bordered on fucking scandalous.

'Who else would you have?' Goody asked.

'Let me have a think. Manny would be another possibility. We used to nick car stereos together.'

'I know. I bought enough off you.'

'But he's married with a little kid these days – fucking everyone is. He could probably do with the money, but I doubt he'd want to risk a real stretch. Especially when he hasn't done anything for so long,' I pondered.

'What about your brother?' bonehead asked.

'What, are you joking? He'd tip off the Old Bill just as soon as look at us.'

'He wouldn't, would he?' Goody said, shaking his head, but I knew better.

'Terry logic: better I get a short stretch for conspiracy than a long stretch for actually doing the job. At the very least he'd tip off Weasel and let us know that he had just so we couldn't go anywhere near the place in a million years. Terry would think he was doing us a favour.'

'I can't believe that,' Goody said, staring at the grass and kicking his heels in confusion.

'I'll tell you who would be up for it, though. My old mate Bob Barker.'

'Barking Bob? That mentalist? Oh come on, you've got to draw the line somewhere,' Goody objected, but Barking Bob was made for a job like this.

ROBERT BARKER (28)

Barking Bob wasn't so called just because we all liked a pun around here. No, he was a premier-league nutcase: built like a shit-brick house with all his brains in his fists, Bob was without a doubt the hardest bloke I'd ever met

– inside or out. I think I mentioned it earlier, but I met him at doughnut school and we got done together doing over RG News, so me and him went way back. Come to think of it, I was probably one of the few blokes in the world who could get away with giving Bob a bit of lip, though I wouldn't want to make a habit of it. Bob had done a bit of everything in his time, though his speciality (other than getting himself barred from every pub in town) was mugging. Bob was a real pro, though, not a little crackhead purse snatcher, and he always made a nice tidy sum in either readies or jewellery from each roll. I guess he'd be what you'd call these days one of your Rolex Robbers. He frequented the flashier parts of London for half the month, targeted dumb Sloanies as they came tumbling out of posh boozers, then had it away with whatever they were sporting. Bob reckoned he'd even done Anthea Turner over once, but I don't know how true that is. A good bloke to have on your side, but a bit unpredictable.

The problem was there wasn't much danger of him doing it without Jimbo.

JAMES JONATHAN JENKINS (24)

Jimbo Jonkers, as he was otherwise known. I didn't really know too much about him to tell the truth, other than he was Bob's Rolex Robbing partner. He wasn't like Bob, though: a little rake, by all accounts, but a rake could still hurt you. Jimbo had the unenviable position of being Bob's best mate. Everyone else in town was scared shitless of knocking around with Bob. Jimbo was more the other way around, too scared shitless not to. I don't know where they met but, once Bob made up his mind this was the buddy for him, Jimbo was in for the duration. To say he was the brains to Bob's brawn wouldn't be right, either; he was more just his little yes-man. Any ridiculously nutty idea Bob had for making a few quid or landing themselves in aggro, Jimbo would be in on it from the ground floor. I wasn't entirely sure about including him on this job, no matter how hypothetical me and Goody were being (as Jimbo might've seen this as a perfect opportunity to get rid of Bob for a few years), but Bob was sure to vouch for him. He always did. And in this game that counts for a lot. More important, though, there was no way Bob would do the job without Jimbo, so one way or another we were all stuck with each other. A quiet sort of bloke with lazy speech. To me, he always sounded like he had a mouthful of marbles.

'Saying all that, though, Jimbo would probably help keep Bob in check on the night, and someone would have to,' I told Goody.

'What's that, five? Who else?' Goody asked, all impatiently, like a little kid on his way to the swings.

I scratched my head and smoked a cigarette, as these things often speed up the thought process, and hit upon another likely recruit.

'Parky.'

LEONARD ROYSTON PARKER (30)

Parky had probably done as much bird as me, though as far as he was concerned every single time was a fit-up. See, Parky was black, which I ain't got nothing against, but Parky seemed to think he was Nelson Mandela or something. He'd scream discrimination at the drop of a pattie and swear his innocence to anyone who'd listen, unless he knew for a fact you knew, then he'd take you aside and laugh and say something like, 'Well, you have to try these things, don't ya?' I'd seen him in action once before, storming into a McDonald's to claim that one of their litter patrol just called him a 'fucking nigger' and

demanding recompense. It almost always worked, as well.
Parky would walk out with dinner for him and his 'wife
and three kids' (his mates) and pass some poor cunt on
the way in who was getting called in to be fired on the
spot. 'They only gave me regular fries, those cunts.' Parky
was primarily a burglar, but he'd been caught more times
than a rash in a whorehouse (once even asleep after getting drunk on the householder's Scotch), though he was
best known for using racism as his defence. In fact, Parky
had done it so many times that the Commission for
Racial Equality once threatened him with legal action if
he ever did it again. He promptly accused them of being
racists. You have to take your hat off to that sort of brass
front.

'Have you thought about Jacko?' Goody asked as we
ambled along together.

'I have, but he's a bit of a stoner, isn't he?' I argued.

Goody looked out across the park and conceded this, but
put in a word for him anyway.

'Well, yeah. A bit, I suppose. He likes a joint, but then
again, don't we all?'

MICHAEL JACKSON (27)

Wacko Jacko started his career with me nicking Kelly's
motor. He broadened out into general thievery and
shoplifting, at first to buy puff and then, later, as a result
of it. He once nicked an ice-cream van and drove all
around the houses with the chimes going at three in the
morning before planting it through Dixons' shutters. I
think the idea was to run away after that, but ideas take a
while to filter through with Jacko, so he filled his pockets
first and was caught a hundred yards down the road with
eighteen Cornettos and a box of flakes under his arm. By
all accounts the copper just looked at him and asked him

sarcastically, 'Do you know anything about the theft of an ice-cream van?' Jacko stared blankly back and replied, 'No.' He did time for that, and when he got out he started dealing instead of stealing. He only catered in grass and black, but he still got three years when he got nicked. This must've shook him up a bit, because he knocked the dealing on the head when he came out and cleaned up for a bit, though he was still a heavy user. Whether or not he'd be reliable was somewhat open to debate, but he was skint, an old friend and suitably experienced.

'Just one more, then.'

'Yeah. You know who I've been thinking about? Patsy.'

'Patsy?'

'Yeah, Patsy. Why not?'

'He works in the newsagent's,' Goody told me, confusing the shit out of me.

'What's that got to do with the price of eggs?'

'Well, he wouldn't want in on something like this these days, would he?'

I laughed.

'No, of course he wouldn't. Not with a life that sweet. Fucking doughnut. Look, Patsy's fucking miserable. His wife gave him the elbow, he's losing the house to her and he has to get up at five o'clock every morning to slap a load of paperboys around. Patsy's desperate to put as much distance between him and this town as possible. He reckons he wants to go and live on a beach in Thailand for a few years. Probably read that shit book.'

'Or saw that shit film?'

'Yeah. Anyway, he reckons he ain't got a snowball's unless he runs off with the week's takings, and he's that close to doing it anyway.'

'Yeah, but wanting in is one thing, having the balls to

actually do it when the time comes is another,' Goody
patronised me.

'Don't worry about Patsy. He's got the bottle. He did
over my uncle's place, didn't he?' I told Goody.

'Did he? What a cunt! Didn't you say nothing to him?'

'No. Well, I couldn't, really. I was helping him at the time.'

THOMAS PATTERSON (27)

Patsy was in Kelly's car with us way back in our teens. He
also nicked a couple of other motors with Jacko that I
was never a part of, and he used to bring his eyes along
with me when I went out shoplifting. Yeah, he was one
of the boys back in his teens but hadn't done much since
then other than scam his employer, RG News. The shop
was part of a chain, you see, so Patsy pulled the same
wage regardless of how much he ripped them off for.
Mostly, it was just selling nicked fags over the counter
and hitting the No Sale button on the till whenever
someone handed him a twenty, but he'd also Mickey-
Dicked with them in other ways too. He once told
me that he hired this dumb schoolkid to lean over the
counter and nick a couple of watches when his back was
turned. Of course, Patsy turned around and caught the
kid red-handed, but the kid ran off and Patsy chased him,
all for the benefit of the security cameras, but, you know,
'Sorry, RG News, the little bastard was just too fast for
me.' Hey presto, the kid found an industrial-sized box of
Snickers that had been accidentally left out the back of
the shop that night, and Mum and Dad Patterson got
Swatches for Christmas. Very nice.

Goody and me wandered around all day long discussing
tactics, equipment and eventualities, and I came away feeling the best I'd done since my first day out. I re-found an
enthusiasm and excitement I wasn't sure I'd ever feel again

and I couldn't wait to go up the megastore and check it out for myself.

Of course, like I'd said before, all this was only hypothetical, but by the time I waved cheerio to Goody I'd been bitten by the bug again.

Suddenly, I no longer felt like an unemployable ex-con with no house, no girlfriend, no car, no job, no kids, no holidays and no prospects.

Suddenly, I felt like a thief again.

Milo to the checkout

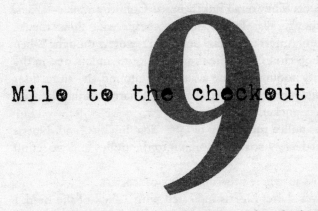

'Yep, I worked here for about two years. I hated it,' Norris told me as we wandered up and down the aisles, pushing a trolley together like couple of the year. We stopped by the dried pasta and tossed in a couple of packs to make it look like we hadn't just come along to case the joint, then carried on. 'Security cameras on every aisle and a big fat cunt called Colin up in the control room watching us when he's not got his face in a bag of crisps.'

Goody and I had discussed the job for about four days before finally roping in Norris. Up to this point it had still all been hypothetical, a bit of fantasy planning to make myself feel good about being fuck-all. Going to Norris upped the ante and made everything that much more serious. I'd wondered about backing out at that moment, but after five days of wearing my old clothes again, I wasn't sure I was able to any more.

And now we were at the megastore, I could almost smell the money.

'Where's the other guard?' I asked, talking as if I meant it.

'There's actually about five or six on during the day. They'll be wandering around the place or standing up by the checkout, acting as a visible presence to dissuade sticky-fingered cunts like us from giving ourselves five-fingered discounts. They're all linked up to Colin by walkie-talkies, and they're all a bunch of meat-heads who think they're Captain America – wankers. Don't worry, though. When the shop closes up, there's only two of them left: one in the security room and one wandering around the shop floor making sure the shelf stackers don't start stacking the stuff in their pockets.'

We pulled up again by the dog biscuits, and Norris dragged a few boxes of Bonio into the trolley and we set off again.

'OK, so where's the manager's office?'

'Over there,' Norris indicated with a flick of the head. I looked past a row of checkouts and saw a door in the wall at the end. Funny, for some reason whenever Norris had mentioned the manager's office I'd always pictured it as being upstairs with big windows overlooking the car park, with a great mahogany desk, a lean-back chair, rubber plants in every corner and a filing cabinet full of Crunchies. I was vaguely disappointed with the nondescript unmarked little door squirreled away in the corner where no one was ever going to notice it.

'What's it like in there?' I asked Norris.

Norris shrugged his shoulders as he struggled to find the words, and I got the feeling it was either really something or really nothing.

'I don't know. It's just an office. Desks, chairs, telephones, rubber bands, that sort of thing. It's an office. Oh, and the safe, of course.'

'But the keys for the safe aren't kept in there with it?'

'No. They're up in another safe in the security office. That one's got an alarm on it, and you have to phone someone with a password somewhere and they turn it off from their end so you can get the keys out, otherwise the place fills up with Old Bill. I seen it happen once, just accidentally like, but they were here like flies on shit in five minutes.'

'What's the password?' I asked, opening a freezer door and sticking a box of economy fish fingers in the trolley.

'Well, I don't know, do I? It's a secret password,' Norris replied.

'Well, how the fuck are we going to phone it through to get them to turn the alarm off, then?'

'Simple. We'll just tell matey up in the control room that we'll blow his fucking head off if he doesn't tell us it. "Oh, and by the way, mate, you're coming with us when we leave just in case you get any ideas about giving us any naughty codewords to tip off the Old Bill." See how he fancies some of that on £5 an hour.'

'The geniusness of your plan is in the subtlety, I see,' I said, but Norris was too busy examining a gâteau to hear me.

'Are we actually buying any of this stuff?' he asked.

'You can if you like. I ain't got no money,' I told him, and he looked all crestfallen like he'd been expecting a good old-fashioned nosh-up when we got out of here.

'The other thing is, the day manager takes the keys home with him for the safe in the security office so we'll have to get them off him first before we can even start threatening anybody. What shall we do? Bring him along with us?'

'No, we'll just have to get the keys and tie him and who-ever's with him up nice and tight. Let's hope he's not throwing a party that night, hey.'

Norris smiled at this, as if the thought of roping to-gether two dozen people in party hats appealed to him. It probably did.

'Mind you, what happens if he manages to get free halfway through the night? We'll all be in the shit then.'

'Yeah, that is a problem. And we can't very well spare a bloke to stay with them just on the off chance,' I pondered.

'We could always take someone else on.'

'Oh leave it out. We're recruiting half of crooks.reunited

for this job already. Let's leave it at eight for now, shall we? No, I've got an idea about how to handle this. Actually, it was an idea I worked on in the nick, though I never thought I'd ever get the chance to use it,' I explained. 'What we'd do is tie him and his missus and his kids up, then tell him we're taking one of his little kiddies with us as insurance. We warn him that if he fucks about or anything like that, we'll do the kid. And we make him believe it by telling him that we read somewhere that you only get about fourteen years for murder these days, whereas we'd get twenty for sure if we were done for just the robbery.'

'You what?' Norris said, staring at me in incomprehension. 'Where d'you read that? That's a right load of bollocks, that is. You kill anyone while you're doing a robbery, let alone a kid, they lock you up for ever.'

'Yeah, I know that,' I told him. 'The point is we make him think we believe it. I mean, if he thinks we're silly enough to believe we'll knock six years off our sentences by rubbing out his saucepan if we're caught, he'll be praying we get away with it even harder than we will,' I told Norris. Personally, I thought it was a good plan when I came up with it: psychology interweaved with mindless violence and all of it a big fat bluff.

'Yeah, but then we get stuck fucking dragging his little kid along on the night and all that *Three Men and a Little Baby* headache.'

'No, don't be silly. We'd just stick a bit of tape on her gob and bung her up in the back bedroom on the way out. Kids and jobs don't usually mix.'

Norris mulled it over and agreed it wasn't a bad idea. Definitely worth a go if we couldn't think of nothing else. I was a bit insulted by this. *If we couldn't think of nothing else?* It beat threatening to blow someone's head off with a shotgun any day of the week. I let this go for now, but Norris had his card half marked for that.

We stopped by the fruit and veg and sexually assaulted a couple of avocados before loading up with oranges and pears and pushing on. As we steered the increasingly heavy trolley together, some middle-aged woman eyed us with curiosity.

'It's all right, we're not bent,' Norris reassured one of them, and we waited until she was out of earshot before we continued.

'OK, so the money's definitely going to be in there. We're not going to open it up and find it full of grumble mags or nothing, no?'

'No, I swear: a big pile of notes all sorted, bagged and bundled. There's coins in there as well, two-pound coins, one-pound coins, fifty pences, twenty pences . . .' I stared at Norris, and he went through the whole lot and listed British currency units for me down to '. . . and one ps too.'

'Really?'

'I mean, there's probably ten grand in coins right there.'

'We'd leave the shrapnel, just take the quids and fifties, otherwise half that dopey lot would get themselves nicked in the post office trying to change them,' I said.

'Yeah, you're probably right,' Norris conceded, and we moved on into cereals.

'Can you draw a couple of plans up for us, upstairs and down, so that I can get a feel for the place? Stick on where the cameras are and, most important, where the exits are. If we do do this, we can't afford to have a single person slip through our fingers when it comes time to round them all up, otherwise that would be our lot.'

I'd been looking about myself as we'd wandered up and down and made a note of all the push-bar emergency exits and mystery side doors here, there and everywhere. Once we'd taken security, we'd have to comb the place from top to bottom looking for stragglers before we could make a move on the money. Or perhaps we didn't? Perhaps the guys who took security could then go on and get the money while the others were still mopping up. I mean, if the guys ran around making enough noise and acting all scary, they might keep any slippery bastards hiding among the stock pinned down long enough for us to do what we had to do and be off. Yeah, that was a better idea. Less time. Less risk. Strike while everyone was confused and bolt before they recognised this as an ideal opportunity to get that George Cross they'd always been after.

'Don't worry. I'll draw some up for you this afternoon. Don't go leaving them nowhere, though,' Norris told me, sticking his hand inside a box of Golden Nuggets and helping himself to a faceful.

'Oi, do you mind? Let's not blow a hundred-grand robbery for the sake of half a box of dried cereal,' I said, snatching it off of him and chucking it in the trolley.

'Don't worry. Everyone does it. As long as you pay for it at the other end, no one gives a fuck. I'll tell you, some of the greedy bastards you get in this place end up pulling up to the checkout with nothing more than a trolley full of wrappers.'

'Yeah, well, we ain't paying for it, are we, so give your greedy guts a rest for five minutes and act like a pro,' I told him. 'And you can sling those peanuts too. Yes, the ones in your pocket. You think I didn't notice, did you? Go on, chuck them in the trolley.'

Norris did as I told him, albeit reluctantly, and I wondered if I'd have to pat him down before we got to the exit.

'You know, you can't tell me what I can and can't steal. It's got nothing to do with you,' Norris grumbled.

'If we're going to do this job, I want everyone – including you – to keep your noses clean. I mean, come on, can't we keep our hands to ourselves just for a few weeks? We are going to be getting fifteen grand, surely that's more than compensation for three or four weeks of honesty.'

'I don't see what one's got to do with the other. All right, no nicking from this place, I'll buy that. But why should I stop doing other stuff that has nothing to do with this?' Norris asked.

'I'll tell you why. Because if you, Bob, Goody or any of the other cunts we rope in gets nicked for something while this is still in the planning, you could easily give the rest of us over as part of a deal. And before you say anything, yes you bloody well would. I know you too well, Norris,' I said, putting my foot down. Surprisingly, Norris didn't argue further. He could see I was more adamant than Prince Charming, so he was never going to win me over. He'd either do as I said for a couple of weeks or ignore my wishes completely and just not tell me about it. If he had half a brain in his head it would be the first. After all, this was Norris's job. Surely he could lay off for a couple of weeks and throw all his efforts into seeing this one through?

'OK, are we about done, then, because I want to get out of here before anyone recognises me,' Norris said.

'Yeah, come on, let's split,' I agreed, stopping the trolley by the long dairy counter and peeling off in different directions.

'Give me one of the fruit gums you just nicked,' I said once we were outside in the car park. Norris dug around in his pocket and offered me the tube. I opened it up and saw that the first one was yellow.

Why did they even bother sticking those ones in?

10

A meeting of minds

'Thunderbirds are go, gentlemen.'

'F.A.B. Milo,' Patsy replied in the gloom.

It had taken a little scouting about on Goody's part, but he'd found us a suitable 'hideout' on the American base, a little boarded-up red-brick end terrace on a ghost town of fifty similar houses. The place was MoD land for now and technically off limits, but there were gaps in the fence all around and nothing to protect other than a couple of derelict streets that would be sold, levelled and built on the moment someone in the MoD found a suitably big enough brown envelope in his corn flakes.

Goody had recruited Parky and Jacko in my name without actually telling me, and before I knew it we were five. I'd had a go at him for this and told him if we were going to do this it was on my terms and my terms alone, but Goody had just asked whether we were going to do this fucking job or not. The new recruits demanded to know the same, and four wills were a lot stronger than one. I had a decision to make: in or out? Before the week was finished with, I was one against seven and there was really only one answer after that. I was in. The job was real. We weren't talking hypothetical any more.

But then, I'd known this from the first moment I'd

allowed it to filter into my brain. It hadn't mattered what bullshit I'd told myself, it simply didn't work like that and I was old and experienced enough to know better. I'd broken my rule – 'If it's dodgy, don't even think about it' – and this was where it had got me. For so long I'd felt like I was swimming against the tide of an overflowing river. The moment I let up, the tide swept me downstream at a hundred miles an hour and deposited me in an abandoned house with seven other villains talking through the job of my life.

And you know what? I was exactly where I wanted to be. Fucking shoe shop salesman . . .

'One condition, though, lads: I'm the guv'nor on this one,' I'd told them all. Norris had roped me and Goody in because he didn't have the blokes. Goody had twisted my arm because he didn't have the know-how. These two factors automatically gave me rank and privilege over both of them. As for the rest of the lads, I left them in no doubt as to who was in charge and why, before we sat down to have our first serious chat. I'd told them all that this job was just too big, too ambitious, to put the infinite-number-of-monkeys theory to the test; someone had to have the final say in all matters, and that person should be me. Anyone who disagreed with me on this was free to drop out, I pointed out, so all seven agreed to let me call the shots (even Bob, unbelievably), but we were never a completely happy ship.

'First things first. We'll need guns, or more immediately, the money to buy guns,' I told my cohorts. 'We're going to have to have a divvy-up and see what we can pile in between us. How much have we all got?'

'Fuck all, Milo. I'm skint,' Parky told us instinctively, a sentiment echoed another six times around the room. 'Nothing.' 'Not a bean.' 'Potless.' Etc.

'Your generosity underwhelms me, lads. Come on, we're going to need some bread, otherwise we can't get the guns.'

'Wha' we need guns for? We cu'd just use bats, carn't we?' Jimbo suggested.

'You can't control a crowd of fifty people with bats, especially when some of them might have a fifty-yard head start on you. No, it has to be guns.' As the room thought this over, I looked across at Bob in the corner and asked if I could have a quick word with him. The room talked among themselves as I took him next door and asked him quietly, 'Seriously, Bob, how much money do you have left?'

'Honestly, Milo, not a sausage. I ain't been working lately,' the lying bastard told me.

'Bob, come on, let's have it. How much did you make from that post office job?' Bob stepped back in amazement as if I'd just pulled the three of clubs out of my top pocket.

'How did you know it was me? Did somebody grass?' he demanded.

'Fuck me, Bob, you said hello to me on the way in. I can recognise your voice, you know? Now I got pulled in by Weasel for that and held in custody for two nights,' I told him, figuring it was my turn to bullshit, 'and I was nearly charged for it, but I never gave you up, didn't even think about it, so you owe me and it's time to collect.'

'Milo, look . . .' he started, but I wasn't prepared to let him get a thought in.

'No, Bob, you look. This is a big job, the biggest any of us has ever done, so we all have to put in on this one.'

'Oh yeah? I don't see any of those—'

'Bob, don't worry about them. They'll do their share in other ways. What I need off you and Jimbo, because, I take it, it was him with you, is the money to buy the shooters. Two grand, that's all. You must've both got away with twice that, anyway.' Bob racked his brains for a reason why he shouldn't have to part with his money but there weren't too many going. An opportunity like this might never come along again, but without the money we couldn't get started, and he knew it. I assured him he'd get every last penny back off the pile before we made the split, and the cheeky bastard even asked about interest. I told him if he was going to act like a bank I'd just stick him up, so he said he'd like to see me fucking try. In the end he agreed to part with a grand for the greater good (for an extra £500 when the time came) and to twist Jimbo's arm into doing the same.

'I'll get it to you tomorrow. Don't go spending it on sweets,' he warned me, wagging his big fat finger in my face.

'Just out of interest, does anyone have a shooter I can borrow this week?' I asked, but nobody did.

'What d'you need a shooter for, Milo?' Patsy asked.

'Picking my nose with, what do you think?'

'Well, I don't know.'

'The bloke I've got to go and see about the guns is a Yardie mate of mine I did time with. He lives up in Salford Quays and I ain't about to go visiting that dangerous cunt holding nothing but two grand and Goody's hand, mate or no mate.'

'Oh I'm coming too, am I?' Goody said, picking up on the breaking news.

Fucking right Goody was coming. Len and me had always got on and had a laugh together, but then I'd never had anything Len had really wanted before (except that bag of liquorice allsorts, and that had gone missing not five minutes after I gave him one of my black twisty ones). Me turning up on his home soil completely unarmed with two grand in used notes that I could never report stolen would be simply too easy for Len not to take. Blimey, put it like that, who wouldn't? No, I needed protection before I even went near that bandit, and if he had a gun I'd need one too.

'What about replicas?' Patsy suggested, but that wouldn't do. If I was buying guns off Len in the first place it meant I needed guns. I wouldn't be able to bluff the liquorice all-sorts-stealing bastard with a replica. No, I needed something that could put a big dirty great hole in him if it came down to it.

'I'll tell you who's got shooters: that farmer matey who lives in that big house past the Dog and Duck,' Parky told me. 'You know who I mean?'

'Yeah, I do.' Goody perked up. 'We dug a ditch for him. You remember that, Milo?'

'Not likely to forget,' I said and thought about my poor melanoma-covered back. 'But you can forget about that place. He's probably got alarms up the yin-yang up there. We'd never get in there in a million years.'

'Hang on a minute,' Jacko said. 'I know who you mean too. That cunt . . .' Then he went quiet again. Just when I thought that was his whole contribution, suddenly there was more. 'What about old Derek?'

Everyone said 'who?'

Jacko continued. 'Derek lives up there with matey. I don't mean at the mansion or nothing, but he's got a little cottage in his grounds, ain't he? He works for him,' he told us, though Jacko didn't specify in what capacity. 'Well, Derek's got guns too. Shotguns. He told us about them down the Duck one night. He's always down there. Him and the missus, both are on Wednesday nights for quiz night. We could turn him over then. It would be a piece of piss.'

Me, Goody, Bob and all looked suitably impressed, so Jacko celebrated by finishing the last of his joint and rolling another.

'Not bad. Parky, you go with Jacko, as you know what you're doing. Don't get greedy and rip the whole place off, because the police will tear this town apart looking for any dodgy tellies and toasters if they've been nicked along with shooters. You clear?' Parky said he was, much too quickly for my liking, so I asked him again. Parky made out he was insulted at the very suggestion he was a two-bit thief who couldn't control himself, so I asked him for a third time.

'Yes, all right, I'm clear. I notice you didn't ask Jacko if he was clear. No, of course not. You can trust that fucking puff-head but make sure the jungle bunny says "yes, masser" before you send him on his way,' he ranted, and we all burst out laughing. Good old Parky, he'll never let us down.

'I'm clear too,' Jacko told me, but I said that was cool, he could take stuff if he wanted because it was OK, he was white and even Parky couldn't help but smile as he called me a racist cunt.

'OK, while you two are off doing that, Norris, you and Patsy check out the day manager as you'll know who he is. Don't let him clock you, but follow him home, check out his place, how many kids he has, alarms, motors, routine, that sort of thing, so that we know where he is when we need him. Might be worth breaking in one night if they all go out too, but do it subtly and don't go nicking anything or balancing ornaments on the edge of ledges or nothing.' Patsy asked what I meant, so I explained that I used to know this guy inside who did this for a joke. Not content with making off with people's stuff, he used to place china or glass in such a way that they couldn't help but knock it over when they got home. He once even spent twenty min-utes arranging for one poor bastard's crockery to fall on the kitchen floor the moment they opened their cupboard door. I have no idea why he used to do this. He said he did it was because he thought it was funny. Still, nice bloke.

'I have got a job, you know, Milo,' Patsy moaned. 'I can't go around playing secret agent all day and night for weeks on end. I've got to be at work.'

'Oh, all right. Goody, you do it instead.'

'Smart,' Goody replied.

'Well, then, I think that probably wraps it up for now,' I said, wondering if there was anything else I could set in motion. 'I guess the only other things to think about are ali-bis and where you're going to stash your cash.' Norris said he was going to stash his in booze, coke and whores, and Patsy asked if it would be all right just to stick it in the post office. Seven expressions of abject horror told him all he needed to know.

'OK, then, let's be off, then. One at a time, though, lads. Let's not be seen as a big group.'

'Actually, there is just one more thing,' Bob said, then turned to Norris. 'You said you used to work in this place but don't any more. Well, I want to know why not. Why d'you jack it in?'

Norris laughed as if this was the most ludicrous thing ever asked.

'What you mean, other than the obvious, that it was stacking shelves for a fucking living?' But Bob persisted and asked him again how and why he'd left. Norris shrugged a few times but when he saw the question wasn't going to go away and his evasion was pricking everyone's interest he finally coughed. 'If you must know, I didn't jack it in. I was sacked.'

'Nicking?' Bob asked.

'Well, obviously,' Norris replied, so I told him to tell us about it in case it fucked us up in some way. I mean, if Norris had already had one crack at the takings, when they disappeared this time around he was bound to get a pull.

'What did you try and nick?' I demanded.

'A tin of shoe polish.'

'A tin of shoe polish?' I think pretty much everyone said in unison.

'You got sacked for trying to nick a tin of shoe polish?'

'Well, I worked in a shop full of the stuff. I'm hardly going to go out and buy a tin, am I?'

A thief's rationale if ever I'd heard it.

Parky and Jacko did over old man Derek's a couple of nights later and landed their hands on two lovely double-barrelled shotguns and a couple of boxes of shells. Parky reckoned they spent half an hour quietly breaking into the steel gun cabinet before Jacko saw both guns sticking out of the umbrella stand. Parky was still miffed about not being able to steal anything else, but I explained again that any video or telly he nicked would've just been too hot to unload. He muttered to himself under his breath for a bit, but left it at that. They brought both guns along to our next get-together and naturally everyone wanted a go on them and called me a miserable bastard when I wouldn't let them.

'Come on, just one go each, so we know how to handle them when the time comes,' Norris insisted, and Parky and Jacko admitted they'd already taken them over the woods and 'whacked' a couple of sparrows.

I was furious and threatened to pull the plug on the whole caper if everyone didn't stop fucking about, but incredibly everyone still moaned. Even Goody, who was meant to be my loyal lieutenant, sided with Norris and said he had a point about everyone getting a feel for firing a gun, so I told them in no uncertain terms that no one would be firing any guns, not down the woods or in the supermarket. And to make sure of this, we wouldn't be carrying any ammo. This got everyone's attention.

'No ammo? Are you fucking joking?' Bob demanded.

'No offence, lads, but I'd rather arm a chimps' tea party than you lot.'

'You can't rob somewhere without ammo, Milo,' Goody ranted, waving his hands in my face as I sawed the barrels off both guns.

'Of course you can. We're only using the threat of violence to get what we want, not the real stuff. I don't want anyone going Rambo nuts the moment we get in there and thinking it's open season on shelf stackers, and this is the only way of guaranteeing everyone's safety,' I explained as the first barrel clattered to the floor.

'There's a world of difference between not using them and not being able to use them,' Goody told me.

'Yeah, you're right. About ten years. If we get done and the guns are empty, they won't throw the book at us like they would if we had bullets – or, worse still, had actually used them.'

The lads weren't having this, though, and nagged, moaned and complained at me to change my mind, but I would've had to have changed it to a bucket of fish to give in to these itchy-fingered cunts.

'You know, you're a bit of a gun's half-empty merchant, aren't you, Milo?' Jacko said, making even less sense than usual.

Only Patsy sided with me and said he thought I was right and that ammo wasn't needed, but he was shouted down as a poof and told to fuck off back to bumming his paper boys.

'Why we even bovverin' a buy proper guns in the first place? Why don't we just get fakes?' Jimbo asked, not unreasonably, but I pointed out that replicas would cost us as much as real guns, most had 'Replica' written on them these days, and if any of us lost one the Old Bill would be able to trace them back to us with ease.

'So we just wouldn't lose them,' someone said.

'What, you mean, like, we just won't get caught?' I asked.

'OK, then, Gandhi, what happens if one of the security guards charges us or won't do as we tell them to or something no matter how much we wave our empty gun in their face? What do we do then? Go home?' Goody asked.

'Well, you don't fucking shoot him, that's for starters,' I said in disbelief, and Goody said he wouldn't be able to without any ammo. 'Look, can't you get it into your thick heads that if so much as one of us pulls a trigger while we're on this job, we all get life – and I get life plus twenty. And that's not going to happen.'

'I'll tell you what, then,' Goody started up again like a

dog with a bone. 'What about if we just have, say, five rounds each, or two in the shotguns. How about that? That way we're not likely to use it because we know we'd have to use it sparingly.'

'No!'

'Four rounds, then?'

'Fuck me!'

'Where's the harm in it, Milo? I'll tell you what, let's have a vote on it. Who thinks we should all have four bullets each? Put your hands up.' Everyone in the room put their hand up except me and Patsy. Goody shouted at Patsy to get his fucking hand up, but Patsy wouldn't budge, so Goody informed me it was a majority win.

'You can vote for gay rights for all I care, mate. You ain't getting any fucking ammo while I'm in charge and that's that. I'm not overseeing a bloodbath.'

There was still much dissension in the ranks until I pointed out that they were all free to drop out any time they wanted, but if they didn't want to they had to do it my way. This was not a democracy. I sawed the last of the barrels off to muted discord and stuffed the guns, barrels and shells into the duffel bag I'd brought.

'You're taking the shells, then?' Jacko pointed out, all perplexed.

'Not on the job,' I told him. 'Only to see my mate up north to make sure he don't rip me off,' and sure enough they all went straight back at it.

'That's not fair.' 'One rule for him.' 'He's a cunt.' And all that etc. Until I could've shot the lot of them.

11

Goody and Baddy

Me and Goody borrowed Patsy's car to drive up to Manchester in (as in borrowed with his permission), though Goody still wouldn't let the old ammo issue go and spent the first fifty miles whining on about it like an obstinate and particularly annoying kid.

'See, I just think . . .' or 'All I'm saying is . . .' or 'I reckon what we should do is . . .', driving me absolutely bananas. He even tried the tack that just me and him should have ammo, then got all offended when I pointed out that as he was the only person I knew who had a track record for shooting people, he was actually the last person I wanted to see with a loaded gun. The conversation was finally dropped in favour of petulance, sulkiness and the repeated re-tuning of Patsy's stereo.

I'd never been to Manchester before but imagined it would look just like it looked on *Coronation Street*. That is to say, shite. As it was, it didn't. It looked, to be fair, just like every other English city I'd ever been to, with more or less the same houses, shops, garages and signposts as everywhere else, only shuffled slightly differently. Naturally, we got hopelessly lost as our atlas featured only the main roads and motorway junctions, so we nipped into the city centre and swiped an A–Z from WHSmith and tried again. Goody even fished out an old army-surplus compass he'd brought with him and showed me which way was north, but seeing as the whole place was fucking north it didn't really make a lot of odds. Another hour and a half of driving around asking the natives which way was Salford Quays and we finally found it. Goody parked the motor in a suitably far-flung spot and we gave Len a bell (Patsy had lent us his mobile too). The car park was weekday busy with a moderate bustle and I was relatively confident our transaction would go unnoticed by the law-abiding citizens of Manchester – if there were any.

'OK, like we agreed, you stay here with the money and the shooter and wait until I give you the all clear to come over,' I told Goody again.

'I know, I've got it. Look, if the shooting does start, though, just hit the deck and keep your head down. I'll take care of those bastards, don't you worry.'

Not the reassurance I was after.

'Goody, mate, this is a friend of mine. There shouldn't be any problems on that score so keep your safety on, OK?'

'Listen, Milo, I'm a professional. I've handled more weapons than you've had prison dinners. I know what I'm doing,' he said, and for a second I thought he was going to salute me and start blubbing at the Stars and Stripes.

'There's not going to be any trouble from Len, so just be cool, OK? The shooter's purely insurance. Len will have his with him too, so there'll be no trouble from either side. Just relax,' I urged him.

We sat in silence for twenty minutes, and I counted the money a couple more times while Goody wiped his hands on his jeans.

'It's the waiting I could never stand,' Goody told me.

'Really? I always hated the getting caught part.'

Len's black BMW circled the car park a few times, and it took a phone call from him before he clocked us. We told him whereabouts we were and he circled around a bit more until he found an empty parking space close by. I gave the money to Goody and told him not to shoot anyone today – particularly me.

Len climbed out of his BMW and gave me a big smile. I returned it with interest as I walked over to him, and we shook hands heartily and told one another how good it was to see each other again. His big mate in the passenger seat stayed in the motor and glared at me through the windscreen while we went through the usual bullshit pleasantries and caught up with each other as much as we dared in under thirty seconds.

'So, who's your pal in the car?' Len asked, looking over at Goody.

'Er, don't know, must be a mate of yours,' I said, doing likewise to his gorilla.

'He got the dough, then, has he?' Len asked, so I told him he did.

'You don't trust me, Milo?'

'Consider where I met you. So, your mate, he's got the old wassnames, has he?'

'They're in the trunk,' Len told me and took me around the back of his motor.

'Don't call it a trunk. It's a boot. You sound like an idiot saying trunk. What do you call your bonnet? You don't call it a hood, do you?'

Len thought about it for a bit before telling me he called it a 'lid'. I wasn't sure about that one. I'd never heard anything on a car being called a lid before, not even on *Starsky and Hutch*, which was where Len seemed to have learned most of his English.

'If this was an American motor you could just about get away with using that sort of language but this is a German motor, so you just sound stupid going around calling things trunks and lids,' I told Len.

'What's German for boot, then? I'll call it that, if you like.'

'I don't know.'

'Well, then, shut up.'

Len 'popped his trunk' and opened a box inside which contained around a dozen assorted pistols and things. I wasn't too knowledgeable about guns and figured I'd have to call over Goody to sort through what was what.

'These are all real, are they?' I asked, looking through them.

'No, some of them are replicas and some are starting pistols,' he replied, keeping a lookout. 'But the others are real.'

'We only want real ones,' I told him, picking out a starting pistol and recognising it for what it was.

'I'll sort you some out. How many do you want?'

'Six.'

'OK. Did you bring a bag?'

'Er, no. Was I meant to?'

Len rolled his eyes. 'Your car's twenty yards away. You want to walk from here to there with an armful of shooters? Muppet! Here, you can have this one,' he said, rooting around his trunk and finding me a small canvas satchel. 'And at no extra cost,' he added.

'You're too generous.'

'Right, there's six in there for you. They're all .22s and they all work. You might have to give them a clean and an oil if you want to be absolutely certain you'll still have five fingers after you fire them, but that's up to you,' he told me, closing the bag and then the box. 'They're £400 each, so you'd better wheel your mate over with the cash.'

'They're not £400. I'm not giving you £2,400 for those pieces of shit. I'll give you £300 each only, but I can't give you any more than that.'

'Look, I told you not to do this to me on the phone,

didn't I? Don't dick me around, Milo,' Len said aggressively.

'We're the ones getting dicked around. You've only just come up from down the road, we've just driven two hundred miles, now you're the one trying to rip us off because you think we're frightened of going home empty-handed. Well, we're not, so don't try and make mugs out of us. You know £1,700 is a good price for those silly things, so let's shake on it and all go home.'

'£1,700?' Len scowled. 'What's wrong with your maths, Milo?'

'Well, Len, I'm buying in bulk, aren't I? You've got to knock off a ton if I'm giving you that much business, it's standard practice. Come on,' I said, holding out my hand. 'Come on.'

Len ticked it over in his mind. To be honest, £1,700 wasn't a good price for what we were getting, but it was a fair price, though just how interested Len was in being fair was not something I was banking on. No, I had a couple of other things going in my favour. Firstly, I knew Len from old. This didn't count for much, admittedly, but then I wasn't asking for much. Secondly, Len had a ready supply of guns brought over from Eastern Europe; cost price to him was not much more than the price of a pair of Levi's, or sometimes just the Levi's themselves. And thirdly, Len could walk away with a lump sum of £1,700 in his hand right now or hang on to them and make a couple of hundred pounds more, and as we all know a bird in your hand's worth two up the bush.

'£1,800 and we'll shake,' Len said, offering me his hand.

'£1,750 and we'll kiss,' I replied, back, holding out for that extra £50 which would buy me a night in the pub tonight. Every penny I saved on the deal was a penny extra out of the collective pot for my pocket. Well, fair was fair;

who the fuck was it who drove all the way to Manchester anyway?

'All right, all right, just give me the fucking money,' he said, as we shook on it. 'You haven't changed, have you, Milo?'

'On the contrary . . .' I started to correct him, then realised he was right, I hadn't. I gave Goody the signal and he clambered out of the motor and made his way over to us as suspiciously as he could, while Len counted bullets out of a little box that was tucked down the side.

'I'll give you six for each shooter. That should be plenty,' Len said, when Goody joined us. 'Now, remember: as long as you don't use them while you're off doing whatever it is you want these for, I can always buy them back off you, half-price, of course. Don't go trying to flog me back no murder weapons, though.'

'Don't worry about that. We ain't going to need no bullets,' I reassured Len, who looked at me in confusion.

'No bullets?' he asked. 'Are you sure?'

'Quite sure.'

'You're the boss,' he accepted and poured the bullets back in the box.

'Er, actually, I'm the boss around here and I say we'll take them,' Goody suddenly jumped in with his size nines.

'Fuck off, Goody!'

'No, you fuck off.' He pushed me, then turned to Len. 'Listen, mate, I'm holding the money so I'm making the buy, and I say we want the ammo.'

At this moment Len's big mate got out of the motor and made his presence felt.

'Goody, just back off. I'm warning you!' I told him, but Len grabbed me by the arm.

'Look, Milo, if you've got some fucking argument with your mate, take it somewhere else, but don't drag me,

Anthony and every spare pair of eyes in this fucking car park into it, otherwise we're off right now.'

He was right, of course. We couldn't make a scene. Four blokes standing around an open BMW 'trunk' was suspicious enough without chucking in an argument to boot. I knew this, and Goody knew this too, the rat-fuck. I quickly weighed my options and wondered whether it would be best all round to start a rumpus and fuck up the deal or bide my time and threaten some sense into Goody when we were far away from here, safe and sound. In the end I decided upon the latter. We still had two hundred miles to drive, and I'd end up fucking myself up as much as Len and Goody if we were collared here with this little lot. And I'm not the martyr type.

'How much dough you got on you?' Len asked Goody and, like a wanker, Goody told him two grand. Len told him he'd give him the guns and the bullets for that two grand, then told me to go fuck myself without waiting for me to say something. Goody handed the money over without a blink, and suddenly my bonus was lost with my authority.

'Good doing business with you,' Goody told Len, shaking his hand, then offering it to Anthony.

'Let's not make it too obvious we're doing business here,' Anthony replied, keeping his hands and his expression out of sight.

'No hard feelings, Milo,' Len said, as he and Anthony climbed back into their motor. 'Business is business, man.'

'Yeah, well, whatever,' I replied, though there was really nothing to say.

'Bollocks,' Goody suddenly remembered and tapped on Len's window as he started the motor. 'Here, I almost forgot. You got any puff?'

'How much you want?' Len asked, probably thinking Goody wanted to shift some back down south.

'Not much, just a couple of joints' worth,' Goody told him, and pulled out a fiver.

'Oh. Oh yeah, here, on the house,' he said, reaching into his pocket and slapping a little bag of green into Goody's hand. 'You take care now, and stay out of trouble.' He smiled, then disappeared off into the wilds of Manchester.

'Stay out of trouble?' I almost laughed, warily eyeing Goody with his canvas bag of guns and drugs.

'Look how much he gave us. There must be a half in here at least.' He grinned excitedly, examining his little present. 'What a nice bloke!'

'You had to do it, didn't you?' I said, totally fucked off.

'Well, look, the way I see it is, it would be stupid not to get the bullets while we're up here. We can always decide whether or not we're going to dish them out once we get back down south. Better to have something and not need it than need something and not have it,' he told me like an old sage.

'Come on, let's get out of here.'

I did all I could to talk Goody out of sharing the ammo out among the lads on the drive back home but my words fell on mutton ears. Goody was convinced we couldn't do an armed robbery without being properly armed, because the bluff would show in our faces and our confidence if we didn't have the means to back up our threats. 'It's all in the psychology,' he told me, and at this moment I realised there was no way I'd be able to control seven separate wills once I'd unleashed them on an unsuspecting target. I mean, if Goody and the others couldn't see reason on such an important issue such as this in the cold light of day, what chance would they have in the heat of the moment when their blood was up and they found themselves face to face with trouble? No, there was nothing left for it. I'd been an idiot to think we might actually pull this off, and now I saw that we couldn't. It had been a nice little fantasy while it had lasted, but if we did it for real someone was bound to get seriously hurt or seriously put away. And I had a feeling I'd get both.

I'd made a big mistake getting mixed up in all this.

I had to pull the plug on it while I still had the chance.

Into action 12

At that particular moment in time I really convinced myself that I wasn't going to go through with the job, yet less than a fortnight later I found myself driving a stolen transit van out of town and into action (as Goody continually put it). I still had a hundred and one doubts buzzing around my mind, but then I always did on every job. It was only natural to fear the worst in these sorts of situations – it made getting away with it all the sweeter.

'What time is it?' I asked Patsy for the hundredth time.

'One o'clock, just gone,' he replied from the passenger seat.

The roads were eerily quiet on the drive to the supermarket. Quiet and dark. All the shopfronts, houses, restaurants and pubs we drove past on the two-mile journey to the target were shut up and sleeping. The only lights we passed were the occasional set of headlights on the road. Everything else was doused in that horrible overhead orange streetlighting that made everything look black and white. Well, black and white and orange. There weren't even any stars about and no sign of the moon. The whole town felt dead, like everyone was holding their breath and waiting to see what we were up to. I was freaking myself out just thinking about it, so I tried to change the subject in my mind and concentrated on being a professional.

'Can we smoke?' Jacko asked in the back.

'What am I, your doctor? Do what you like,' I replied, so Jacko started burning some black into a king-size Rizla.

'Jacko, on second thoughts why not wait until after the job before you do that?'

'I'll need this one just to get me through it,' he insisted.

'Come on, man, we only gonna be twenty fakkin' minutes,' Jimbo, also in the back (together with Parky and Bob), told him.

'I can't do this straight,' Jacko complained, so I told him he could have one small hit on his pipe, just to straighten himself out then, but no joints. Jacko moaned about this, but everyone pitched in on my side.

'If you roll a joint, I'm taking those bullets out of your gun,' Patsy warned him, turning around and threatening him with his finger.

'Fuck's sake,' he muttered at the unreasonableness of it all, as he crumbled himself off a hit into his pipe and made do with that.

'Wha' you even doing with that fakkin' stuff on you?' Jimbo asked, but Jacko didn't answer.

'All right, listen up. We're going to pull up here and wait for Goody and Norris for a bit, so if anyone wants to get out and stretch their legs, do it now but stay out of sight of the road, for the love of fuck,' I told them and pulled in behind a parade of boarded-up shops just a half-mile short of the supermarket. We all clambered out and looked around.

This place was even deader than the rest of the town. Most of the old corner shops and parades this close to the megastore were in a similar condition. All the business had been sucked away by the giant commercial black hole just down the road. Oh they might've sold a paper here or a packet of fags there if they were still open, but it would hardly be enough to keep the family in curry. Bit of a shame, really, when you think about it. I remembered this particular parade from when I was a kid. I used to nick strawberry bonbons from the Spar at the end of the row. Was even caught in there a couple of times. The manager shouted at me and gave me a slap around the ear'ole, as people did in those days. Still, shame he was closed down. I never did get him back for that.

'What do you reckon? They should've done it by now,' Patsy said, indicating towards his watch.

'Don't know. What time is it?' I asked again.

'Ten-past one, just coming up,' he replied, and I agreed, they probably had. Patsy got his mobile out and checked it was on and working OK. It was. They should've phoned by now.

'Still nah word?' Jimbo asked anxiously.

'No. We'll just have to wait,' I told him and took off my gloves to blow on my sweaty hands.

Goody and Norris were the first to go into action tonight. They'd gone to the day manager's house to get the first set of keys we needed. Goody reckoned it reminded him of playing Lara Croft and wondered, if we got away with it, whether they'd make a video game of our robbery. I mean, what can you say to that? Patsy had cased the place with Norris for the last couple of weeks but had a bad case of brown trousers on the night, so Goody had agreed to step in and do the business with Norris. If they got away with it, then we'd all be on our way. If they hadn't, then we'd dump the van a bit sharpish and all race home. That would also be the case if they'd pulled either one of their triggers. I was more anxious about that than them getting caught, I must confess.

'Everyone got their safeties on?' I asked quietly.

'Fuck's sake, Milo. How many more times?' came the reply.

You might be wondering what possessed me to change my mind about dropping out. Well, I'll tell you. I really was going to bale out if the lads insisted on taking live ammunition, but I didn't particularly want the rest of them to go through with it, either, as I'd feel horribly responsible if anything happened. I'd racked my brains as to how I could stop them and finally came up with an idea. Knowing what a load of impulsive halfwits these blokes were, I finally agreed to dish out the ammo and said that we should test the guns first to make sure they all worked. Also, I'd never fired a gun before, none of us had (except for Goody), so it seemed stupid to wait until the day of the robbery to find out what it was like. I rounded everyone up and took them down the fields with a bag of empty Coke cans. I told the lads to fire off three rounds to get a feel for their weapons and banked on the fact that the immature bastards wouldn't be able to resist having one more go after that. And then one more go. Then one more go. Then, shit, I've used up all my ammo! Can you get us some more, Milo? See my thinking? I figured if we used up all the ammo killing Coke cans, I might even reconsider my change of heart and agree to go along and rob the place on my terms. The one thing I never considered was their self-restraint.

All of them took their turns like Olympic marksmen and shot it out with the Coke cans, but not one of them would use up more than their allotted three shots. In Bob's case, he used only two. Most frustrating. I tried to coax them on and called them a load of pussies, but they were having none of it.

'Milo, no. We need these for the job. We're not fucking wasting them.'

'Yeah, Milo, we're not doing this for the fucking fun of it, you know.'

I was unexpectedly impressed with their professionalism and started to wonder if I'd tagged them all wrong. I allowed myself some serious thought over the next couple of days, and the boys continued to impress me with their preparation. They did everything I asked and nothing I didn't. Norris and Patsy excelled themselves by breaking into the day manager's house while the family was out and disconnecting the alarm and unscrewing the latches on a small side window in the utility room, so that they could enter again on the night in near silence. Everyone got their change of clothes, their army greens, their ski masks and gloves. Everyone had an alibi in place, and everyone was focused on their particular roles. Goody taught us how to act in front of any possible resistance, and Norris ran through the plans of the supermarket until we could do our weekly shopping blindfolded.

From a shaky start, we were now finding our feet and behaving like professionals. The fucking about had all but stopped, and there was a growing confidence about them lads that made me believe this might even work. If everything went to plan. If there were no surprises. If everyone stuck to their tasks. If no one lost their heads. If, if, if, if – all that and a few more ifs – then maybe there might be (perhaps) a chance we could actually get away with it. One hundred and twenty thousand pounds, plus all the fags and booze we could load up in the time allotted. We could actually do this. This could actually happen.

This was why I got into nicking in the first place. The rush of risking all and getting away with it. The excitement, the buzz. Who wanted to go to their grave knowing all they did with their lives was work in a newsagent's? Who wanted to dig ditches or sell shoes and spend the rest of their lives living on their brother's sofa? Who wouldn't want to show the world that they were wrong? That I wasn't a loser after all, that I was a player. A big man, if you like.

This was what it was all about. I wasn't no fucking two-bit 'yes, sir, no, sir, three bags full, sir' merchant who'd spend the rest of my life tugging my forelock and breaking my back just so I could earn enough money to pay my income tax, national insurance, council tax, VAT, contents insurance, buildings insurance, life insurance, private pension, HP APR, ground rent, maintenance charges and every other fucking penny you have to pay out in this fucking country before you're even allowed to sit still. No way. Fuck that. I was on that plane with Patsy to Thailand the moment the heat died down and the rest of you could kiss my fucking arse (no offence).

Well, you see, there were a few reasons there, and some of them even made sense. But at the end of the day the real reason I'd opted back in was that I didn't want to miss out. By the end of the week I'd estimated we had a reasonable seventy-five or eighty per cent chance of success and knew I'd never be able to look myself in the mirror again if the lads got away with it and I'd stayed at home bricking my pants. I mean, just think about it: what an amazing thing it would be to be part of something like this. It would be the talk of the town for the next hundred years to come, maybe even the country, and we'd be there sunning ourselves in a faraway prostitute-filled land and laughing our nuts off at how beautiful it was.

Weasel was right. I was a habitual, and it was something I either had to accept or something I had to fight. And which of these promised me a greater shot at happiness?

'Make sure you pick up any butts. Don't leave them for prints,' I said, watching Jimbo step on his fag.

'You fink they'll even know we parked up 'ere?' he asked, picking up the butt and putting it in his pocket.

'Why take the chance?'

'They can get DNA off fag butts now too,' Patsy told us.

'It's true. Anything with your saliva on it – an envelope, a stamp . . .'

'Some big black bloke's cock,' Jimbo laughed, then remembered who else was present. 'Er, sorry, Parky. You nah what ah mean, tho'.'

'Fucking racist.'

'I don't know. Be more racist if he wouldn't suck your cock, wouldn't it?' Jacko observed, and I had to agree with him on this one. We continued in this fashion for a few minutes longer, discussing the merits and drawbacks of sucking Parky's cock when at last Goody rang.

'Hello?' Patsy answered, then looked at me and smiled nervously. 'OK, you know where we are. See you here in ten minutes, then.' Patsy pocketed the phone and we all gathered around. 'They've got it, just like that. Everything went smoothly and they'll be here in about ten minutes.'

A silence descended over us as this sank in. First part of the 'mission' (as again Goody insisted on calling it) was complete. About three miles away, in the nicer part of town, Mr Lincoln, the day manager of the megastore, and his wife and kiddies had been tied up and gagged by a couple of masked men. It had started. Up until now it had been all talk, – well, mostly. Now the real deal was under way. My heart was thumping inside my chest and my mouth was as dry as Lawrence of Arabia's martini. I took a swig of water from the bottle I'd brought, then passed it around. Everyone had a chug and wiped the nozzle, as if subconsciously wiping off their DNA.

'Too late to turn back now,' Patsy said, the tension suddenly audible in his voice.

'Not necessarily. We could still fuck off if we wanted, and we'd probably be all right, but we'd never get another crack at this again,' I told him. 'Want to jack it in? Go and sort your papers out tomorrow? Today, even?'

'I've still got to do that, anyway. Can't disappear straight

away just like that, otherwise everyone would know what
I'd been up to.'

'You know what I mean. You want to go home?'

Patsy thought about it for longer than he should've, but
in the end he told us he didn't.

'OK, then. Right, everyone make sure you've got your
safeties on.'

'Oh give it a rest, Milo.'

Goody pulled up a couple of minutes later, and he and
Norris jumped out of their stolen Saab like a couple of sexually excited baboons and showed us all the keys.

'Everything go OK?'

'Fucking sweet as my nuts,' Goody replied.

'You didn't use the guns or get rough with them, did
you?'

'Oh no. We blew the kids away. Sorry, wasn't that what
you wanted?' Norris and Goody started laughing, and Patsy
asked them if they'd really done that. 'Of course not, you
twat. They were nice as pie. The only shit they gave us was
when we said we were taking the little girl, but they were
all tied up and gagged by that time, anyway, so what could
they do about it?'

'And the girl is . . . ?'

'In the back bedroom under orders to be quiet as a
mouse, otherwise the nasty Mr C will come back and eat
her,' Goody confirmed, giggling and slapping Norris on the
shoulder.

'Poor little girl. She'll probably have nightmares for the
rest of her life about this,' Patsy simpered. I thought about
this and imagined her all grown up and looking like Alice.

'Good,' I said. 'Right, let's get going. We haven't got all
night, you know. Masks down from this point on and only
codenames. Everyone clear?' Everyone said they were. 'OK,
then, make sure your safeties are on and don't go taking
them off for anything.'

'Fucking hell, Milo!' Parky gasped, so I pulled my ski mask down and pointed at him. 'Sorry. I mean fucking hell, Mr A.'

'That's better. Now don't anyone forget and do as little talking as you can. Let's go.'

I climbed back in behind the wheel as Norris, Patsy, Jacko, Parky, Bob and Jimbo climbed in the back and Goody got in next to me. We'd leave the Saab here for now. This was one of our change of motors. We also had the nicked Orion out the front. We'd do the job, drive back here like the clappers, change clothes, change motors, then drive to the edge of town, where Patsy and Bob had left their cars, and change again. Goody thought we should burn out the three nicked motors when we left them to make sure we left no forensic behind, but I thought this was more risk than it was worth. Maybe if we had a bomb or something, then we could do it once we were safely away, but do it the amateur way and we'd all end up stinking of petrol and smoke all night long and that stink stays with you for days. And half of us were bound to get a tug tomorrow. Or today, even.

Patsy, as the most respectable of us, was to be entrusted with the clothes and the masks. While the rest of us were hopefully tucked up in bed, Patsy was to drive down to Pompey or the coast somewhere, somewhere with a pier and a big expanse of water (better that none of us knew exactly where), and sink them all over the side with a few bricks.

And that left just the guns. Personally, I would've preferred them to go the same way as the clobber, but that wasn't a popular point of view. The guns had cost money, and we could get money back on them. Or, in some cases, like Bob and Jimbo, for instance, they just wanted to hang on to them. I told them they'd be fucked if they were caught, but they assured me they had a safe storage place

that had never been turned over in a dozen searches. In the
end I agreed. As long as they didn't implicate any of us if
they got tumbled, then it was their lookout. That's the trouble with this country, guns are so hard to come by for most
of us that as soon as we get our hands on a shooter it
becomes more precious than anything we might ever nick
with it.

We pulled out from behind the parade and started
towards the ring road.

'What the fuck is that?' I heard someone say in the back
and glanced over my shoulder to see what the problem was.

'What's up?' I asked.

'Ah don't know, it's Pats.' Jimbo was laughing. Pretty soon
the others were joining in, so I slowed down and looked
over my shoulder again. Everyone had pulled their ski
masks down and were looking dead scary with it, but Patsy
had some sort of crooked knitwear abortion on his head
that didn't make any sort of sense.

'Well, I'm learning myself how to knit, aren't I? Thought
I'd knit myself some jumpers one day when I was good
enough. Figured I'd make my own mask too to save the
police being able to trace it back to me,' he explained to
much laughter.

'Jesus Christ, I'm doing a job with Nerys fucking
Hughes,' Bob said, shaking his head.

'Oh you lot are cunts!' Patsy moaned, as we all pissed
ourselves at his expense. It was one of the stranger moments
of what was to turn out to be a very strange night, but at
least it lifted the tension for a couple of minutes as we drove
the short half-mile into action.

At least, that was how Goody liked to put it.

Let's do it 13

The supermarket first appeared as a bright glow in the distance which stood out against the black and orange of the surrounding night's sky. A couple of the boys got to their feet and looked over my shoulder at our approaching destination, though no one said a word. All too quickly the laughter over Patsy's mask was forgotten and that knot in the base of my stomach was back. You would've thought after such a career that I wouldn't be troubled by nerves any more, but you'd be wrong. They gripped me like you wouldn't believe. Perhaps it was because this time it was different. This time it was for big stakes. Risking a couple of years was bad enough, but now it was all or nothing. If I was caught on this sort of job with my sort of record, I could expect ten years as an absolute minimum. And if one of these arseholes pulled a trigger, I wouldn't see the light of day again until I was well into middle age. And all for £15,000. It was a sobering thought and one that led me to drive straight past the supermarket turning without even glancing at it.

'You've missed the entrance,' Goody said, punching me on the arm. I made to slow down and turn back, but my arms and legs fought me every step of the way. In fact, my foot started shaking on the clutch so much that it slipped off and I ended up giving the gears some real punishment.

'Fucking hell, Muriel, are you all right?' someone said in the back.

'Just go on and turn around up top,' Goody said, so I stepped on it again and cruised around the roundabout a couple of times until I got my bearings.

'Sorry, lads, miles away,' I said then heard the sound of someone chucking their guts up behind me.

'Oh fucking hell, Patsy. Jesus!'

'I couldn't help it. Sorry.'

'Oh it fucking stinks.' 'Get some air in here.' 'I think I'm going to chuck too,' were the cries from the back as me and Goody frantically wound our windows down.

'Fuck me!' Patsy heaved again, though it didn't sound like anything came out that time.

'Look, it's just nerves,' I reassured him, even though my own guts were doing somersaults. 'Let's just get this done and get out of here.'

'All right, but Patsy . . .' Bob started.

'Mr D,' I reminded him.

'All right, Mr D . . . had better clean this mess up before we get back in the van,' Bob said.

'Here, no, don't leave any of it behind – DNA,' Jacko said.

'I'll DNA you right in the fucking gob if I have to sit in Patsy's puke on the way home,' Bob rebuffed, and voices exploded in the back.

Funnily enough, I found it quite reassuring that I wasn't the only one suffering from pre-job nerves, and this steeled me enough to swing the van into the supermarket entrance and race for the back of the store. Off to the right of the megastore was a twenty-four-hour garage with bulletproof glass, alarms to the local cop shop and security cameras. Norris hadn't taken this into consideration when he'd planned the job, but I had. There was no way we'd be able to knock that place off because places like that are expecting to be knocked off and make provisions for such eventualities. Therefore, we'd have to bypass him. It would require a little more care on our part not to go running around outside with our masks on in front of the pump monkey, but it was do-able. After all, he was the one expecting to get robbed, not the warehouse-sized supermarket next door.

I veered the van away from the garage and motored towards the back of the store.

'Ten seconds!' I shouted, bouncing across the car park lanes and killing the lights. 'Five, four, three, two – good luck, everyone – one, let's do it.'

I pulled to a halt in the long pitch-black shadows at the rear of the store and we all piled out. Fifty yards up ahead was our point of entry, the loading bay. Brilliant white lights illuminated the bay and the lorry park in front of it. The shadows would keep us hidden for all but the last twenty yards if we stuck to the wall. After that, it was a sprint and a jump and we were in.

Bob and Jimbo left us for the front entrance, where they'd wait until we let them in. Parky was sent around to the fire exit on the far side of the megastore and Jacko to the push-bar emergency exit on the rear. We couldn't allow a single person to escape our dragnet. That left just myself, Goody, Norris and Patsy to make the initial assault (as Goody liked to put it).

'OK, keep down and let's go.'

Up on the loading bay someone was moving about. When we got closer we saw it was just some young geezer in store overalls smoking a fag. He had his back to us and was too lost in his own thoughts as to where it had all gone wrong to notice me creep up behind him. I got within a yard, made doubly sure there was no one else around, then, like a flash, clamped my hand around his mouth and dragged him back towards the shadows. The guy went potty and kicked and lashed out with unusually frantic desperation, and it took all four of us to overpower him before I realised why he was fighting so much. He'd just been taking a drag just as I'd pounced and I'd somehow managed to clamp his fag to the side of his face with my gloved hand.

'Ah, you fucking . . .' he started when I let go long enough to pull his ciggy off.

'Sorry about that,' I said, covering his gob again. 'Just an accident. Right, now you be quiet and do exactly as we tell you, otherwise . . .' I threatened him and showed him my gun. The guy nodded, so I took my hand away again and pulled him to his feet. 'The security guard, we want him out here, you understand?'

'Mike? Yeah, sure. You want me to go and get him?' he asked, rubbing his face.

'I don't think so, mate. Just get back on that bay and tell someone else to go and get him for you. Stay where we can see you, otherwise . . .' I showed him my gun again.

'OK, I'm cool. I'm not going to give you no trouble. They ain't my corn flakes.'

'Good lad. Right, now get up there.'

Me and matey stepped up on to the loading bay again while the others stayed out of sight. Matey stood in the open while I hugged the wall. I wasn't sure what we'd do if he decided to martyr himself for the good of his employer; leg it, probably. One thing we certainly weren't going to do was to make a fight of it, that's because this was all a big bluff. In fact, if he did decide to warn everyone that we were out here he would, in effect, single-handedly defeat an eight-strong armed gang and save the day. He would be a hero and be in all the papers and possibly even get a medal from the Queen. He really didn't look the type, though. Like he said, they weren't his corn flakes.

'Jenny! Jenny! Do us a favour. Go and get Mike for us, will you?' he called into the store.

'You fucking get him,' came back the reply.

'I can't. I've got to look after this. Please can you just go and get him for us? It's urgent.'

'Bollocks.'

'Look, you lazy slag . . .'

'What's so urgent that you can't . . .' she started saying and stepped out on to the bay to look straight down the barrel of my gun.

'Don't say another fucking word.' I grabbed her, then pointed down at my three masked accomplices hiding in the shadows. 'Go and join them. They'll look after you.' I pushed her in that direction and told matey to try again.

'Derek! Derek, mate. Look, do me a favour and get Mike for us, will you?'

'What's up?'

'Oh look, nothing. Please just get him, will you?' he said, then had a think about it. 'It's a joke. Go on, go and get him and see what happens.'

'What you gonna do?' Derek sniggered.

'I've got a bucket of shitty water down here. See if you can get him out here, will you?' matey told him, and finally Derek did as he was told and ran off hollering, 'Mike! Mike!' Matey looked at me for approval and he got it.

'Well done,' I told him. 'You've been very cooperative. Just keep it up and you'll have a story to tell the papers tomorrow. They might even give you a couple of quid for your trouble. They do that, you know.'

'Really? How much?'

We didn't have time to speculate, though, as Derek returned with Mike and ushered him towards matey out on the loading bay.

'What's the matter, Graham? I'm busy,' Mike said, and

when he and the sidestepping Derek went past me I
levelled my gun at their backs and told them both to freeze.

'Not a fucking word, either of you,' I growled. Derek
looked at me in total confusion, then looked back and forwards at Graham as if he were still expecting the shitty
water. Goody and Patsy grabbed Graham, Derek and Mike
and bundled them all into the shadows.

'Jacket,' I told Mike, taking the hat off his head and the
keys from his pocket. Mike handed me his jacket and I
slipped my own army-green jacket off and his security uni-
form on (I'd worn dark trousers and a white shirt and tie –
Terry's, which he'd love) and got Patsy to turn them all
around so that I could whip my mask off, and stuff it into
my jacket and put Mike's hat on.

'OK, don't turn around, but show me which of these is
the key to the security room,' I told Mike, handing him the
keys so that he could sort through the bundle to the proper
key. Again, he did as I asked and passed the bunch back to
me by one particular key. 'Wait for my signal, then do it,' I
told the lads.

I took a deep breath, pulled Mike's hat tightly down over
my eyes and headed into the store.

I wasn't expecting to *Where Eagles Dare* my way past
everyone and his wife because everyone obviously knew, if
not respected, their security men. No, all I was aiming to do
was to slip by unnoticed. It was only a couple of short corridors and a staircase to the security room (Norris had done
me a map), so as long as I kept my cap down and my hand
to my face, then there was no reason why anyone should
give me a second look, not even whatshisname in the security room watching on the monitors.

Bollocks.

Whatshisname? I'd meant to ask Mike who was on duty
tonight, so that I could knock on the door and . . . bollocks.
Oh well, it was too late to go back now. I was halfway up

the stairs and almost at the door when the thought dawned on me. Nothing for it but to push on.

A couple of lads in store overalls suddenly appeared at the top of the stairs and passed me on the way down. I almost turned and ran when I saw them but clamped both hands to my face instead and pretended to sneeze. I didn't get so much as a 'bless you' from either of the ignorant bastards, who were far too busy discussing a couple of old boilers they hoped to take to the pictures, and a moment later the danger had past.

I slipped through the doors up top, took a moment to study Norris's map again, then saw the door I was looking for. One last look around to make sure no one was about and I swapped the hat for the mask and stuck the key in the lock. As I did so, I knocked on the door and called out, 'Tea up,' to disguise anything I'd done wrong (us British can always be caught off our guard with the promise of tea – it's how we lost India) and burst in. The guard in the chair still had an expectant look on his face when my gun pressed against his nose.

'Hands now!' I told him, and he stuck them in the air like he was after a beach ball. I quickly yanked his chair away from his station in case there were any foot-level alarms and told him not to fucking try anything.

'Anything you say. Just don't hurt me, please,' he said panicky, and I told him I wouldn't just as long as he was a good boy.

'All the CCs, turn them off,' I told him, then added, 'Nice and slowly.' The guard touched a few buttons and the bank of monitors went blank. 'The tapes for the last hour. Give them to me.' The guard pressed the EJECT button on a couple of machines and the tapes popped out. What next? What next? I thought to myself, hardly believing just how swimmingly things were going. 'Alarms next. Panic alarms, fire alarms and door alarms. Turn them all off now.' I waved the gun about where he could see it to remind him they weren't his corn flakes and he tap-tap-tapped away at his computer for a minute or so before looking to me for a pat on the head. 'Well done,' I told him, then pulled Patsy's mobile from my pocket and gave Goody outside a bell. 'We're in business. Go get them.'

This had been the moment I'd been dreading since the start. Events were suddenly out of mine and God's hands and in the hands of the lads. If anyone was going to get shot, it was going to happen in the next couple of minutes. If the police were going to get called, they'd be here in five. If we'd overlooked anything, anything at all, we'd know about it in ten. This was one of those signpost moments of life. Normally you don't realise a signpost moment is a signpost moment until you look back at it and wonder how you ended up where you did, but I saw this one for what it was and shuddered at the possibilities.

'OK, turn out your pockets. Put your mobile, keys and everything else on the side there,' I told the guard, then demonstrated my charity by letting him keep his fags a moment before wheeling him out of the security room and down the stairs, through a few corridors and into the staff canteen. There were already a few shelf stackers in here having a tea break, so I told them to put their hands on their heads and waited for reinforcements. Goody arrived a moment later with Graham, Jenny, Mike, Derek and a couple of others he'd picked up en route. We got them all sat down and I gave Goody the key to the main entrance.

'Stay here and guard this lot. I'm going to go and let Misters E and H in,' I told Goody and rushed off to open the front door for Bob and Jimbo.

Norris and Patsy were already on their way to the two push-bar exits to let Parky and Jacko in, and the canteen doorway had a line of sight to the loading bay, where we'd entered, so once Bob and Jimbo were inside all possible escape routes were covered (we hoped). It was then just a case of converging on a certain point and herding the staff back into the canteen. That would take care of the lower floor, then we'd go up to the warehouse and do much the same there. If we acted quickly and quietly enough, and kept an eye on the stairs, no one up there would even know what was going on downstairs until it was going on up there. At least, that was the plan.

I sprinted out on to the shop floor and took a second to get my bearings. The giant shop looked unnervingly empty, though I knew for a fact that there were a good twenty-five shelf stackers out there and they all had to be accounted for. I clocked the checkouts and the main entrance behind them and started sprinting for them. Boxes and trolleys were skewed all over the shop, so it was actually more like doing the hurdles than the sprint, and I saw the first few shelf stackers up ahead just staring at me in confusion as I ran.

I almost baulked at the sight of them and fought the urge to turn away. See, at the end of the day I'm really just a thief. I'd always done things when people weren't looking, so having people watch me while I was committing my crimes was bladder-looseningly unnerving. I bullied myself into staying strong and pointed my gun at them.

'Stay exactly where you are!' I told them, though by the way I choked on my words and avoided their eyes as I went past it sounded a very feeble, half-hearted threat from where I was running. I looked back and saw that they'd done exactly as I'd told them to and this boosted my confidence a touch, so that I was able to shout at the next shelf stacker I passed that much louder.

I reached the doors, having ordered at least five people to stay where they were, and flipped through the keys until I found those for the store entrance. Bob and Jimbo were the other side of the plate glass, hopping about on the spot like sprinters waiting around on the blocks. My hands shook and my heart pumped as I fought to stick the key in the lock and get the doors open. I wondered just how long my shelf stackers would stay where I'd told them to stay before they realised this was actually the ideal time to run and hide.

Shouting and screaming broke out over the far side of the store, and suddenly there were people running around everywhere.

'Get back here!'

'Don't move!'

'This is a robbery!'

'Aarrgghhhh!'

I finally got the door unlocked and Bob nearly yanked my arm off wrenching it open to join in the fun. He ran straight into the store and disappeared among the aisles, but Jimbo hesitated and leg-wobbled as I locked the door again.

'You OK?' he asked, and I had to shout at him to get on with it. 'Right!' Jimbo said, taking a deep breath and running into the store. I pocketed the keys and followed ten yards or so behind him.

'This'sis'a'robbery,' he shouted at a group of girls he found huddled together by the pet food. They seemed to understand what he'd said and screamed and looked about in panic as I left him to it and headed up the next aisle. I turned the corner and saw three shelf stackers in overalls sprinting towards me. Close on their heels was one of my mates, though I couldn't tell who at first.

'Don't fucking move!' I screamed and levelled my gun at them. The shelf stackers screeched to a halt when they saw me, one of them skidding straight over on to his arse, and looked to turn again but found they were trapped. 'I fucking mean it. Don't move a muscle.'

Patsy stopped just short of them and waved his gun at them. 'OK, you three, come with me,' he said, though I could hear the lack of conviction in his voice and, presumably, so could the shelf stackers. I wondered if this had been how I'd sounded, and it hit me that a robber's voice was as potent a weapon as his gun. It was all about confidence, as so many things in life are. I kept my gun on the three guys but dragged Patsy to one side and whispered in his ear that he had to be more aggressive with them, otherwise he'd spend half the night chasing them all over town. Then I demonstrated.

'These fucking rabbits run again and you fucking shoot them in the legs!' I shouted, pushing my gun into the nearest's face. 'And I fucking mean it!'

I felt the force in my voice, and when I saw the fight drop from their faces I suddenly realised I was in charge. All my nerves and jitters had transformed into confidence, and I set off in search of more people to shout at as I headed down the next aisle of what I now firmly believed was my supermarket.

The freezer aisle was clear, and Parky and Norris were shepherding people about in pasta and cooking sauces, so I took cereals. The aisle looked empty, though I went down it anyway, just to be methodical. I smiled to myself when I spotted the corn flakes and was just about to look away when I noticed a gap between the boxes. I spun back and kicked and pulled a great load of cereal packets on to the floor, and there, squirreled away among the Coco Pops, was some bloke clutching a mobile phone.

'Get out of there or I'll fucking shoot you!' I screamed at him, and he tumbled out into the aisle, holding up his hands and howling with terror. I snatched the phone out of his hand and studied it urgently.

'Who did you phone?' I demanded.

'No one.'

'Who did you phone?'

'I didn't phone anyone.'

'WHO DID YOU PHONE?'

'Honestly, no one,' he sobbed. 'I couldn't get a signal. It doesn't work in here.'

I checked the signal bars on his phone and saw there was nothing doing.

'If you're lying to me . . .'

'I promise, I'm not, honest,' he bawled, his glasses smeared with tears. I looked around the rest of the cereals and kicked and knocked the whole aisle down around me until I was certain there was no one else hiding. 'You come with me,' I said and pushed him up the aisle. We'd just set off when I heard the one thing I'd been dreading – a gunshot. Me and Glasses looked at each other for a moment, both on exactly the same wavelength, then I kicked him up the arse and double-timed him towards where the shot had come from. I grabbed another shelf stacker en route and stopped another in her tracks as she ran past, and together we all went into the aisle with the smoke and the screaming.

It was Jacko. He was holding one of the shotguns and some bloke was lying on the floor with the whole place splattered red. My heart sank when I saw the two of them like this, and my brain fought to take it all in, but then the bloke started to move and I realised he wasn't dead. When I got closer I found that the red all over the place was actu- ally claret. We were in booze and spirits and Jacko had killed a dozen bottles of Jacob's Creek, showering matey in the process.

'What the fuck you do that for?' I demanded of Jacko.

'He came at me with a bottle and wouldn't take fuck off for an answer. What d'you want me to do, let him smash me over the head and take my gun?'

Much as I was pissed off (though this had more to do with the fright I'd initially got than anything else), I had to concede that Jacko was right. If matey had been determined to come at him, what else could he have done? At least he'd used his nut and showered the bastard with glass and wine rather than white-hot lead pellets. Jacko had done well. He'd kept his head when some Bruce Willis fan had been determined to lose his, and he'd done what he'd had to do to save the situation. It wasn't good that he'd pulled the trigger, as that stuck five years on all of our sentences, but at least he hadn't killed anyone.

I told matey to stay on the ground and my three to stay where they were, then headed up household goods and returned with a length of washing line. Neither me nor Jacko had a knife but one of the shelf stackers came good with a pocket Stanley, so we cut a four-foot length and tied our wine-soaked hero's hands behind his back.

'You've got no one to blame but yourself,' I told him, as we dragged him to his feet and Jacko bundled the four of them off to the canteen.

Just before he left, Jacko turned to me with a big righteous look behind his mask and said: 'Try that with no bullets.'

Point taken.

Safe work

14

I found one more straggler hanging around the fruit and veg. He was just stood there looking bored and put his hands up the moment he saw me, almost as if he'd been patiently holding on for his turn. He was so cooperative that it was almost unnerving. I wondered what his married life was like.

I wheeled him through the store towards where the canteen was and caught hold of Parky as he went past.

'You stay down here and search every nook and cranny – on top of the shelves, underneath them, everywhere. I found one bloke hiding in among the Coco Pops. We're going to go and do upstairs, but we need you to be a constant presence down here until we've got the dough. That all right?'

'Yeah, sure,' he said. 'Here, I heard a bang. Is everything cool?'

'Yeah, Mr F shot a load of bottles of wine up after someone tried to smack him one, but no one's hurt.'

Parky thought about that for a moment. 'Who's Mr F again?'

I turned my charge around to face the wall and mouthed 'Jacko' at Parky a couple of times before he finally got it, then we cracked on with what we both had to do.

I led my last bloke through the back and pushed him into the canteen to join the others. It was a surprisingly poky place for such a big store (the staff must've lunched in shifts or something) with barely half a dozen tables and twenty chairs. People were stood up at the back where they had nowhere to sit, so I ordered them to come forward and sit on the floor where Goody and Patsy could keep an eye on them. Then I saw the small empty table to the side.

'For fuck's sake, B, where are the phones?'

'What? Hey, oh we've been so busy what with everyone piling in I haven't had a chance to collect them yet.'

I couldn't believe this. This was one of the most important tasks of the evening, and I couldn't have spelled it out any clearer to Goody had I tried.

'Right, everyone get their hands, on their heads now!' I screamed at the room, making several girls cry with fear. 'Mr D, go and systematically pat each of them down and get their phones, beepers, pagers and whatever, and stick them on that table there. Look in pockets, handbags and up arses if you have to, but make sure you get them all.'

At this point I turned to address our hostages to keep them in the loop. 'This man's going to come by you and collect all your phones. If you want to make life easy for yourself and us, reach into your pockets now and hold them up in the air where we can see them. If anyone tries to play us for mugs, we'll kill them. We are only after the shop's money; don't lose your lives needlessly.'

There was a brief flurry of activity as everyone except our wine-smelling friend complied. I thought it was because he was up to something but then I remembered he had his hands tied.

'Make sure you pat everyone down anyway,' I told Patsy, then looked at the phone I'd taken off matey in cereals. There was still no signal, and I hoped this would be the case with the lot of them. 'Everyone else upstairs?' I asked

Goody, and he said they were. It was then that I remembered I'd been able to dial out to Goody from Patsy's phone up in the security office, and I wondered if it was only down here that you couldn't get a signal.

I rushed up the stairs towards the renewed shouting and found Norris dashing about from office to office while Bob, Jacko and Jimbo were rounding everyone up in the warehouse. The warehouse was a little smaller than the shop below but more of a maze. There were more aisles, shelves, alcoves and giant stacks of boxes than you could shake a gun at, and I suddenly realised it would be near impossible to find someone in there if they fancied playing hide-and-seek. It was then that it occurred to me that we really hadn't wasted much time thinking this job through properly. Well, desperate times called for desperate measures, as they say, so I stood in the middle of the central walkway, where everyone could see me, and shouted as loud as I could: 'This is a robbery. Everyone out where I can see you with your hands on your heads, NOW!' Then I fired a shot into the ceiling.

Everyone jumped out of their skins, including Jimbo, and a dozen or so shelf stackers tumbled out from between the aisles with their hands in the air. Norris rushed in and asked what all the shooting was about, but I sent him packing back to the offices and told him to check under all the desks.

Jacko gathered all the shelf stackers together and led them down to the canteen, but I wasn't finished yet.

'I mean it. You have this one last chance to surrender or we'll kill you – make no mistake about that – so come out now and you'll be all right. Don't try and be a hero.'

Bob, me and Jimbo stood motionless and listened carefully for any noises. We listened and listened and listened, but it was difficult listening with our ears covered up. As far as I could tell there were no sounds, but then some sneaky cunt lying on his back, holding his breath while he texted the Old Bill, didn't really make many sounds.

'Yes, you,' I shouted. 'I'm talking to you. Don't think we can't see you, you stupid bastard.'

Without warning, someone stood up behind me and almost got his head taken off.

'Sorry, I give up!' he shouted in my ear'ole, and once I'd composed myself again I sent him down to the canteen with Jimbo.

'Right, that's it, then. Mr E, start searching. If they want to play silly fucking games, then that's their lookout. Anyone you find, shoot them in the legs. Start with matey over there,' I told him and waved my hand in no particular direction.

'No, wait. I give up. Don't shoot, please,' some scrawny little wanker begged us, falling over his own arse to show himself. Bob went and got him, then stopped and came back to double-check something with me.

'You still want me to shoot him in the legs?' he asked.

'No, you stupid cunt. I'm just bullshitting them. Don't shoot anyone, for fuck's sake.'

'Got you,' he said and grabbed hold of matey. As he walked him to the stairs, Bob grabbed a Twix out of a box and threw it at the back of matey's head. I'm not sure why he did that; maybe it was to teach him a lesson for fucking about or maybe Bob was just venting his spleen. Then again, maybe he just thought it was funny. Either way, matey got a Twix in the back of the head.

Norris came in and told me he'd found no one in the offices, and when Jacko and Jimbo returned I got them tearing the arse out of the warehouse in case we'd missed anyone. Before heading back downstairs, I checked the signal on my new mobile and saw that there were no bars, but the logo was on the screen. There was a signal — it was a weak one, but that's all it took.

I went down to the canteen and asked the assembled shop workers if the manager could make his presence known. A young guy in his mid-thirties stood up and took a bow, so I invited him to join me and Goody in the security room.

'Are you really the manager?' I asked on our way upstairs. He insisted he was. 'I thought you'd be some old bloke with glasses and a bald head.'

'I probably will be one day.'

'How much do you get paid, then?'

'What's that got to do with anything?'

'Nothing, just curious,' I said, then pointed at the safe in the side of the security room wall once we were up there. 'This,' I said, holding up a little key for him to see, 'is the key to that. The trouble is, if I stick it in, the alarm will go off and the Old Bill will turn up. So what we want you to do is phone through and get them to turn the alarm off. OK?'

'Where did you get that?' the manager asked, looking at my key.

'The day manager sold it to me.'

'Warren sold you it? I don't believe you.'

'Who do you think the bloke standing behind you is?' I said, indicating Goody with a nod of the head.

'That's not Warren,' the manager replied.

'Yeah, good disguise, isn't it?' Goody said, adding: 'Why don't you make the fucking phone call and shut up?'

The manager picked up the phone and started dialling. As he did, I spelled it out for him as clearly as I could.

'Just the password to get them to turn the alarm off, please. If you give the other password, robbery in progress, we'll kill you.'

I gave him the same bluff we'd given the security guard and told him he'd be coming with us at the end of the job, to make sure he'd behaved, and the night manager nodded vigorously to demonstrate he understood.

'Hello? Yes, hello, this is Duncan Bramble at MegaSavers. Could you deactivate the security room alarm, please?' he said into the phone. 'Southampton for the Cup. Yes, that's right, Southampton for the Cup. OK. Thank you. Bye.' He put the phone down and looked at me.

'Are you a Saints fan, then?' Goody asked, tapping him on the arm with his gun.

'Yes, season-ticket holder,' Duncan replied. 'You?'

'Oh I follow their results in the paper but don't really go any more these days. Can't afford it; it's too expensive.'

'Yes, thank you, Baddiel and Skinner. When you're both quite finished, perhaps we can go and get the money and get out of here, otherwise none of us will ever see a match again,' I said, handing Duncan the keys and putting him to work.

Duncan looked at his watch for a few seconds, as if he was waiting for something, then put the key in the lock and opened the door. Sweet wonderful silence, a thief's favourite sound. Mind you, saying that there were probably sirens screaming down at the local nick for all I knew, but there was nothing I could do about that any more.

We grabbed the keys to the main safe and took Duncan downstairs. A few more minutes and we'd have our hands on the cash. Another minute after that and we'd be driving off. Ten more minutes and we'd be swapping cars. It was happening. It was really happening. I could scarcely believe the job of my life was going this smoothly. Nothing could stop us now, other than a shitload of road blocks and police helicopters, obviously, but I tried not to think about that. I was as excited like as a little kid on Christmas morning and just about to unwrap the best present a boy could ever wish for. A hundred and twenty grand in used notes.

'I think there's something you should know,' Duncan said, as we opened the door to his office.

'What?' I asked, not liking the sound of this. I thought he was going to tell me that the police were already on their way or that the safe was covered with laser beams or something like that, but it was neither of those things.

'The safe's on a timelock. It can't be opened until eight o'clock in the morning,' he said apologetically.

'What?' I looked at the safe and saw that it had a big yellow sticker across it declaring this very fact. It took a moment to sink in at first, because my hopes had been raised so much by our cracking progress, but when it did I was truly gutted.

Sorry, son, Father Christmas doesn't exist. It was your dad all along, but he can't be arsed with it this year. Fancy a mince pie?

'I'm really sorry. There's no way around it.'

Me and Goody just stared at the safe in silence, both of us struck dumb with incomprehension and disappointment. I finally found the words to go with my shaking head and decided to share them with Goody and Duncan.

'I don't believe it. I don't fucking believe it.'

'What are we gonna do, Mi ... er, I mean Mr ... er, whatever your fucking name is? What are we gonna do?'

'I just don't fucking believe it.'

'What are we going to do?'

'Unbelievable. Fucking unbelievable. Why can't it ever be easy? Why can't I have one thing go right for me? Just one. I'm not greedy. All I want is one thing, just one time.' Duncan nodded sympathetically and looked like he genuinely felt for me. 'For fuck's sake,' I moaned, absolutely exasperated.

'What are we going to do?'

'Well, for a start we're going to kick Mr C's fucking head

in. Mr C? We really got his name right, didn't we? That little cunt.'

'But what else are we going to do?'

'Stop asking me that, will you? I don't know what we're going to do.'

I checked the time on the mobile just to make sure it wasn't eight o'clock now and found that it wasn't, not by a long way, in fact.

'Can't we break into it somehow?' Goody asked.

'Do you have any idea how to break into a safe?'

'No, not really. Don't we have to tap the handle with a hammer or something?'

'No, you haven't. Great.'

'Well, why don't you? I thought you were supposed to be the fucking master criminal around here. How comes you don't know how to open the fucking thing?' Goody complained.

'I thought I did. That's why I went and got the fucking key,' I shouted back.

'Oh man, this sucks. Let's go and get him now.'

'What are you going to do?' Duncan asked when we'd calmed down a little.

'I don't know, mate. I'll have to have a think about it,' I told him and spent the next five minutes doing just that.

It was obvious we weren't getting into the safe tonight, no matter how much we sulked. I toyed with the idea of taking it with us, but there was no way on earth we'd be able to lift it, let alone get the van up any hills with eight tons in the back, so that was the end of that idea. Dynamite was out of the question too, because we didn't have any and wouldn't know what to do with it if we did. Acid and drills the same. Going home empty-handed looked to be about our best option, but there was one other alternative.

I checked outside and saw that everything was sleepy and quiet, then I came back and asked Duncan a few things.

'What time do you open in the morning?'

'Eight o'clock. Why?'

'But we can't come back er . . . Mr . . . er . . .'

'And what time does your night shift knock off?'

'Seven.'

'And the day workers start rolling up then, do they? At seven?'

'Yes. What are you thinking?'

'I'm thinking, Duncan, that we might not be going any-where for a while. No one knows we're here, so we could just wait around until eight, then get the money,' I explained. Goody looked about as convinced as Duncan and asked me if I was feeling all right.

'What about all those idiots who are going to be rolling up at seven? What are we going to do about them?'

'We'll just stick them in the canteen, same as we did with the others. It'll be easy – easier, in fact, because we can just nab them as they come in.'

'And the first lot? We can't just let them all go at seven, otherwise they'll go running to the Old Bill.'

Thank fuck Goody was here to point this out to me, as this was exactly what I was going to do.

'Of course not, you fucking spanner. They can just be a bit late, can't they? An extra hour's not going to kill anyone. If anyone needs to make a phone call, we'll let them use the shop phone and tell whoever they want that they're doing an hour's double-bubble. That'll do.'

'You can't keep us all prisoner for—' Duncan checked his watch '—six-odd hours.'

'Oi you, nose,' Goody warned him. 'What about the cus-tomers? If this place is meant to be open at eight, it's going to look a bit weird when they find the doors are still locked and no one's around.'

'Oh we'll just stick a sign in the door: "BACK IN TEN MINUTES" or something like that. They can wait. Anyone

who goes shopping at eight in the morning deserves everything they get, so fuck 'em.'

'You can't do this!' Duncan insisted, like I hadn't heard
him the first time.

'I can't do a lot of things, but that's never stopped me in
the past,' I replied. 'Right, come on, let's go and fill the
others in.'

15
The longest night

I broke the good news to everyone in the canteen and weathered the complaints for a full minute or so to let them get them off their chests. I don't think I've ever pissed off that many people in one go before and can't really recommend it as a laugh. Bob and Patsy, who were standing guard over our prisoners, complained as loud and as sulkily as the sulkiest of shop workers, and I had to yell at everyone to shut their cakeholes before I could be heard again.

'You tell me, then. You tell me what you want to do,' I asked Bob once I had quiet.

'Well, I don't know, do I? You're the brains. You figure something out.'

'I have, and this is it. Now we're just stuck with it and that's the end of it.'

'Can't you break into the safe, Mr A?' Patsy asked.

'No, I can't. Can you?'

Patsy said he couldn't, so I asked the same of Bob and he said he couldn't either.

'Can anyone here break into a safe?' I asked the assembled shop workers. None of them could either, or if they could they weren't owning up to it. 'Right, then, that's it. Now, Mr E and Mr B, you stay here and carry on guarding this lot. Mr D, you come with me.'

Bob started off with me before I had to remind him that he was Mr E and that it was actually Patsy who I wanted, so the two traded places and Patsy headed for the door. 'Actually, before we go, whose phones are these?' I asked, picking up two mobiles off the big pile of confiscated phones. A couple of our guests said they were theirs, so I took a note of their numbers and gave one to Patsy. 'Save using your own phone any more, just in case.'

'Just in case of what?'

'Look, find yourself a bush up by the main road and keep an eye out for trouble, will you?'

'Trouble?' he asked, looking at his new phone.

'Yeah, you know, Old Bill, SAS, the A-team, I don't know, just give us a call on this number if anything comes our way.'

'Oh fucking hell, Milo . . .' he started to moan until I pointed out that if the worst came to the worst, and the Old Bill did turn up, he'd be the best placed to have it away on his toes. 'Er, yeah, sure. I'll keep a lookout, then,' he said and disappeared off into the night. Just before he left, I wagged a finger at him and told him not to fall asleep on us. 'Are you joking?' he replied. 'I'm doing everything I can to stop myself from shitting my pants as it is.'

I checked the signal on the phone I'd taken and compared it with my other phone. Nothing. I'd have to make sure I stayed upstairs most of the night if I wanted to hear from Patsy.

I went and found Parky out on the shop floor and got exactly the same reaction from him as I had done from Bob and Patsy, then went through *déjà vu* all over again with Jimbo, Jacko and Norris upstairs, making sure that Norris and everyone else knew that this was all Norris's fault. Once I'd convinced them all I really couldn't crack safes, I put Jimbo and Jacko to work loading the van up with fags and booze.

'Drop them off and come back for more when you're done. If we've got to be here all night, we might as well make good use of our time and nick a load of shit while we're at it.'

'Where are we taking it?'

'Er . . . good question. Hang on a minute, I think Parky told me once he's got a lockup somewhere. Go and touch him up for the address and the key and don't get yourselves nicked. All right?'

'Yeah, all right.'

'Come and see me before you leave and I'll time you. If you're gone more than an hour we'll figure out you've been nicked and clear out. If you do get nicked, you have to stay schtum for an hour to give us a chance to get away. Are you clear?'

'Nicked? I'm not getting fucking nicked,' Jacko said, as if that were the most preposterous thing he'd ever heard.

The two Js went off in search of fags and booze while I went and had another look at the safe. I took a tin of soup with me when I went and gave the handle several good whacks just in case there was something in what Goody said, but all I succeeded in doing was splashing chicken and veg all over the place. I don't know what I was thinking about, but you do silly things when you're desperate, don't you? Seriously, though, I mean, who'd buy a safe you could crack open with a tin of Cross & Blackwell's anyway? I started cleaning it up with a bit of kitchen roll then thought bollocks to it and left it as it was. If nothing else, it would confuse the shit out of the Old Bill when they finally rolled up.

I checked on all the drawers, then had a look under all the tills, just in case there were a few quid tucked away here or there. Then I had a look behind the fag counter and then around the perfumes; I checked out the customer services desk and then had a root around behind the deli but I didn't find a sausage. Actually, I found plenty of sausages behind the deli but you know what I mean. Parky came over and asked me what I was doing and, to be honest, I didn't really know. I think I was just trying to keep busy to pass the time, but I didn't have any real direction at that precise moment.

'You want me to just keep walking round this place all night?' he asked, and I suddenly realised he didn't have his mask on any more. Or at least, it wasn't pulled down over his face; it was just sitting up on his head like a woolly hat.

'What are you doing? Get your fucking mask down,' I told him.

'Oh man, my face was getting all sweaty.'

'I don't give a shit if you were coming out in boils, we're wearing these things for a reason, you know.'

'There's no one about. We've got them all banged up in the canteen. They can't see me from there.'

I thought about what he said and decided he had a point. I looked around just to make sure no one was about, then pulled my mask off to great relief. My face was wet and my hair matted with sweat, and I gave both a much-needed rubbing. I took my gloves off too and dried my paws as best I could against my trousers before slipping them back inside my cold, clammy gloves. I hadn't expected to wear these things for so long, and it was pretty hard work on the old boat race, so I figured I'd go and relieve the lads in the canteen, let them step outside and unmask for five minutes too.

'Look, Parky, you're probably right and everything but keep your mask down when you're walking up and down the aisles just in case there *is* someone hidden among the shelves. If you want to give yourself a break, just step into the office for five minutes or something.'

'Oh fuck that. There's no one here. We've got them all,' he complained.

'Parky, do you want to take that risk for the sake of a sweaty face?'

'Yes, I do.'

I realised I could stand here and have this conversation all night with the stubborn bastard and he'd still do whatever he wanted, so in the end I decided to let him risk it.

'Oh bollocks to you, then. Do whatever you like. You'll be the one who gets picked out of a police line-up, though, not me.'

'Do me a favour – ain't you heard? – we all look the fucking same to you lot anyway,' he told me, then cracked open the can of Tango he'd been holding and wandered off scratching his arse.

I made good on my promise and gave first Bob, then Goody, a five-minute breather outside the canteen door, then went upstairs and did the same for Norris. While I was upstairs, I phoned the phone I'd given to Patsy to see how he was getting along and had a brief chat with him. He told me he'd picked a spot by the main road where he could look along both ways of the bypass and still keep an eye on matey in the twenty-four-hour garage.

'He's not stirred or nothing?'

'No, just sitting there serving the odd late-night shopper. What a shit job he's got. Imagine that.'

This was a bit rich coming from someone who worked in a newsagent's. The only difference I could see between Patsy and matey was that matey sold his wank mags during the night.

'OK. Well, keep your eyes peeled and let us know if you see anything you think we'd want to know about. All right, see ya.'

'Yeah, bye.'

'You want a Snickers?' Norris asked, his hand in a box of them.

'Er, yeah, go on, then.'

'Look, honestly, I know you won't believe me, but it isn't my fault the safe's got a timelock on it.'

'This had better not turn out, in any way, shape or form, to be my fault,' I warned him.

'It's no one's fault. It's just one of those things that happens in the course of life.'

'What are you talking about? It's not just one of those things, it's your fucking fault. You should've known about the timelock from the start.'

'How am I going to know a thing like that?'

'Well, I don't know. Perhaps you could've read that big fucking sticker plastered all across the front of the safe.'

Norris stuck out his lip and shrugged that one off.

'What's done is done. We could all go on about who should've done what to what until the cows come home to roost, but it ain't going to make any difference so what's the point? Personally, I never saw the sticker. When I saw the safe it had the door open and the old was's name was hidden. That's my excuse, if you think I need one.'

'You really are a wanker, you know that?'

'Sticks and stones . . .'

'Believe me, if I had any right now I'd be using them,' I told him, grabbed another Snickers and put some distance between us.

I went down to the canteen and asked our guests if anyone needed to use the khazi. A couple of the blokes and obviously all the old ladies did, so I got gave Mr C (Norris) a shout to come down and help us with the babysitting while Bob and Goody chaperoned everyone with their hand up to the bog.

'Don't let them shut the doors on you, all right?' I told Bob on his way past.

'I can't be expected to go with a complete stranger standing there watching me,' one of the old battleaxes moaned.

'Why not? We have to,' Bob told her. 'How d'you think we feel?'

'Look, he ain't going to be watching you. He'll have his back turned.'

'Will I?' Bob asked, like this was news to him. 'Oh yeah, right. Yeah, whatever.' Then very quietly he whispered to me, 'I bet she loves it really, the dirty bitch,' and led her away, asking her if she didn't mind doing it in front of people she knew, then.

Jimbo poked his head around the door and told me him and Mr J were off. Mr J, I took to mean Jacko, even though he was meant to be Mr F, but I let this go because I didn't want to seem petty. I checked the time on the mobile. It was coming up to quarter to three, and I made sure Jimbo knew to be back within the hour.

'Okee-dokee,' he replied and scooted.

'Here, mate, look, I'm fucking starving. Any danger of a bit of nosh?' Graham (the shop worker we'd first grabbed at the loading bay) asked. This didn't seem like an unreasonable request or even one that would put us out much, considering where we were, so I said I'd have some sandwiches brought in for everyone. It was at this moment that Duncan, the manager, showed his true colours.

'If you want sandwiches, you'll have to pay for them. We're not thieves, even if they are,' he told his gobsmacked staff.

'I don't fucking believe you,' was the general consensus, with a few 'you cunt's throw in for good measure.

'Hey, hey, hey, you're not in charge here any more. I am,' I told him. 'And everyone gets a sandwich on the house. I don't know if you realise this but they're not your sandwiches any more. They're mine. I'm stealing them, and I'm free to give them to anyone who's hungry.'

I couldn't believe the pettiness of the man. What was it with blokes like this? I'd met hundreds of his type in my life, and I'd no doubt meet hundreds more, but this was probably the one and only time I was in a superior position to one of them, so I was going to make the most of it.

'Right, everyone, you name it, you've got it. Mr C, start taking orders.'

'All I can say is that the supermarket will take a very dim view of anyone foolish enough to take advantage of this situation,' Duncan warned everyone.

'And I'm telling you this: anyone who doesn't eat a sandwich will be summarily executed on the spot, so none of you has a choice,' I told everyone, no longer feeling like the biggest villain in the room.

'Smart. You could force me to have a bag of Wotsits and a can of Lilt too if you like,' Graham told us, so I told him he had it. 'Or better still, a can of Stella. How about a beer?'

I weighed this up in my mind and decided that if this would keep everyone happy and calm, then why not? Just a couple, though. I didn't want everyone getting steaming and starting a punch-up.

'I'll have some brought in for you.'

'Can you put them in the freezer first, just for twenty minutes or so, so they'll be nice and cold?' Graham then asked.

'Fucking hell, mate, is there anything else you want?'

'Something to read? Some mags and stuff would be nice. It's a bit boring in here, to be honest. And my arse aches. Can I stand up and stretch my legs?' Several other people chipped in and said they'd like that too.

'Oh for fuck's sake,' I muttered to myself and figured out how I could do all this. 'All right. Wait a second.'

Bob, and then Goody, came back with their charges, so I told Goody to go and give Parky a shout and round up a couple of trolley-loads of sarnies, crisps, chocolate, soft drinks, mags and beer for everyone, then told Bob and Norris to stay with me while we watched over everyone as they stretched their legs. We let them all stand, four at a time, just for a minute or so, then got them sat back down on the floor until finally everyone was done. Then some more people needed a piss and others wanted tissues or a drink of water or a pillow or a blanket or this, that or the other, and this basically went on all night.

After everyone had eaten (and boy could they pack it away?), Graham sparked up a fag and Duncan got straight on his back again.

'Put that out at once. This is a non-smoking building. You know that perfectly well.'

'I'll go outside, then, shall I?'

'Listen, Duncan, your rules don't count tonight. If anyone else wants to smoke, go ahead.' At which just about everyone in the canteen breathed a huge sigh of relief, put their hands in their pockets and pulled out their fags.

'You can't do this. This shows no consideration for the non-smokers in this room who don't wish to get cancer,' Duncan whined.

'Oh give me a break, will you?' I told him but he wouldn't listen.

'No, I demand you provide us with a second non-smoking room for all those who don't wish to breathe in second-hand smoke.'

I couldn't believe the balls on this cunt. How could he talk to me like this? If I was Alan Rickman in *Die Hard*, he wouldn't dare talk to me like this because he'd just get a bullet in the head.

'I'm not dividing up my men to guard two rooms. Now we've only got a few more hours to get through and no one's going to catch cancer from second-hand smoke in that time. But if I hear any more complaints from you, Duncan, you will catch a hole in the head from a first-hand bullet. You got that?'

Duncan pulled a defiant face, though I could see my message had finally sunk in: we were in charge, not him.

Time drifted by, and I swapped everyone around so that Parky and Norris were guarding the shop workers while Goody and Bob patrolled the upper and lower floors. I stayed upstairs as much as possible so that I was in contact with Patsy, and at twenty to four he phoned through to say that the van was coming back. I met Jimbo and Jacko down at the loading bay and asked if there had been any problems.

'Nah, none. Just workin' flat out an' only just made it back in time,' Jimbo said, looking at his watch. 'You wan' us a make another run? There's still plenty a room in 'is lockup.'

'Yep, go for it, but better make it the last one. You don't want to risk being seen unloading fags and booze into his lockup after sunup. OK, go on, get your skates on. Get Bo . . . er, Mr . . . er . . . B or, you know, whoever, to give you a hand loading up.'

Jimbo and Jacko got to it, so I gave Patsy another call to check everything was OK. Patsy naturally threw in a few additional complications to do with the fact that he wasn't going to be at the newsagent's in time to do the papers if he had to sit around behind a bush all night, so I told him that that was just hard tits on everybody, wasn't it? His customers would just have to go without papers for one morning.

At half-past four Jimbo and Jacko set out with another great load of fags and spirits, and Norris and Parky gave me a call and told me they needed my help in the canteen again. All the Stellas, Guinness, Pepsis and Bacardi Breezers and everything else we'd so generously provided had come back to haunt us. The entire room was busting for a piss, and at that moment even the most bashful of birds was ready to squat over a bucket in the corner of the room. I rounded up

Bob and Goody, and the five of us spent most of the rest of the night shepherding as many people as we could safely watch over backwards and forwards between the bog and the canteen.

This was rapidly turning into the longest night of my life, and for the first time since I'd dug that ditch with Goody I was really feeling like I was earning my money. Who could've guessed stealing could be such hard work?

And there was still a long way to go yet.

Sunup

'No, I can't. I'm sorry, I'm not allowed. What . . . ? It's not my fault . . . Ben, please. Just for once you'll have to make breakfast for yourself . . . What?'

Bob looked at me and rolled his eyes behind his mask. At half-six we'd let everyone who needed to make phone calls use the landline in the canteen to explain why they wouldn't be home at the normal time. Only a handful had felt the need to inform their other halves and most had simply been a case of 'Sorry, honey. We're stocktaking this morning, going to be a bit late, bye,' but Georgia's old man was less than understanding.

'No, I'm not being selfish, it's you who's being selfish . . . No, I told you I can't . . . What's that . . . ? Well, go and have your breakfast in the café, then, see if I care . . . No, don't, you can't.' Georgia looked up at Bob and told him her old man wanted to talk to the manager. 'I guess he'd better talk to you,' she said. Bob took the phone and asked him what the problem was.

'Listen, mate, she has to work until nine today, otherwise we're going to give her the bullet.' Georgia looked at Bob in alarm, but he dismissed her concerns with a nonchalant wave of the hand. 'Why can't you make your own fucking breakfast? What are you, a fucking spastic or something?

What . . . ? The fucking manager, that's who. Who the fuck are you . . . ? Oh you reckon, do you? Well, you come on down here, then, if you think you're fucking man enough. Cunt.' Bob slammed down the phone and told me we were expecting another guest. He then turned to Georgia and advised her: 'Jesus, love, you want to give him the fucking boot.' I wondered if she got that a lot.

Jacko and Jimbo were back again and they, together with Goody and Parky, had squirreled themselves into little hiding places in the loading bay. There was no longer any point patrolling upstairs or the shop floor, because it seemed pretty logical that if anyone had managed to avoid us and call the Old Bill, the Old Bill would've been here by now. Besides, the loading bay was where we needed every available hand from now on in. The seven o'clock shift would be arriving soon, and all the other doors were locked bar this one. Either they'd simply turn around and go home (which I'd do in their boots) or they'd come around this way, in which case we'd have them. After we'd taken care of them, we'd have just one more hour to wait, then we'd be out of here.

A familiar-smelling smoke came drifting towards me from Jacko's hiding place, and I told him to put the fucking thing out as I inspected the troops. I suddenly realised he'd probably been skinning up every time he was out of my sight, so what sort of state he was in now was anyone's guess.

'Just a normal rollie with a little bit in it to straighten me out,' he reassured me. Fucking junkie.

When I checked on the canteen, Norris came up and told me he was concerned.

'Duncan's been looking at me again. I think he recognises me, even with my mask on.'

'Oh for the love of fuck, go and swap places with Mr F' – at which point I naturally had to mouth 'Jacko' at Norris's furrowed brow – 'He can keep an eye on everyone in the canteen. You help out in the loading bay.'

Norris leaned in and asked me very quietly: 'Do you think we should kill him?'

I stared back at Norris and asked him if I could see his gun. He handed it to me and I emptied his bullets into my pocket and told him I didn't want to see him anywhere near Duncan again.

'Oi, give me back my bullets.'

'Not a chance.'

'Give them to me now.'

'Shoot me,' I told him and pushed him out to the loading bay. 'Trouble with the staff,' I explained to half a dozen quizzical stares.

The first newcomer we nabbed wasn't part of the seven o'clock shift but Georgia's angry old man. Patsy phoned through just in time to tell me that some crazy-arse stuntman was on his way up to see us, and Goody laid him out with the butt of his gun after he'd screeched to a halt and charged in screaming he was going to tear someone's head off. We couldn't trust this unpredictable nutter in the canteen with the others, so we tied his hands and feet, stuck a gag on him and bunged him in the meat locker to cool off, in every sense.

At ten to seven the first people started to roll up (who turns up for work ten minutes early, especially at that time of the morning?). We grabbed them, bagged them and frogmarched them into the canteen with relative ease. We worked so efficiently, in fact, that we were like some criminal production line, with Goody and Parky at the front passing them back to Jimbo and Norris, then on to me in the corridor, then finally to Jacko and Bob, who got them all squared away.

'How many are we expecting, Mr A?' Goody asked, but I didn't know.

'I'll go and check with Duncan.'

Just as I said those words, some bloke came around the corner from outside, clocked Goody in full battledress and took off like a rabbit.

'After him!' Goody screamed, and him and Parky belted out of the loading bay and into the early-morning sunshine. Norris and Jimbo looked at me in panic, so I yelled at them to get out there too. Not only could we not let matey get away, but if anyone else turned up and saw us chasing him across the car park with masks and guns it would be game over.

I rushed to the edge of the loading bay and peered outside. Goody and Parky were right on top of matey, literally, while Jimbo and Norris were hiding among the parked cars. While they were out there, a little Fiesta pulled up and a young girl got out. Jimbo sneaked around between the cars and pounced on her from behind. The girl turned kicking and screaming, and gave Jimbo a right good hiding, and it was only when he pulled out his gun to protect himself that he finally gained the upper hand over her.

Just as he did this, a little MG pulled in and some bloke got out. Norris jumped up and stuck his gun in matey's face and screamed at him not to move.

'Fuck that. Get them inside quick,' I shouted across the car park, and the lads picked up their new hostages and ran with them towards the loading bay. Another motor pulled in before they were home and the guys dropped on to their faces.

Some bloke in a suit got out and started over towards the loading bay, but stopped and back-pedalled a few steps. He looked down at where Jimbo and Jimbo's hostage's legs were sticking out from between two parked cars and asked if everything was OK. I leaped from the bay like a horny salmon and charged towards him, screaming at the top of my voice for him to get his hands in the air. Matey jumped out of his skin and wobbled his legs about as he watched me charge. He looked like a sprinter on the blocks waiting for the gun, but when it came it pointed straight in his face and warned him not to move. I grabbed him by the scruff of the neck and ran him back into the loading bay, as Goody, Parky, Jimbo and Norris all did the same.

Once we were all safely inside, I gave the car park a quick scan and breathed a sigh of relief when I saw that we'd got away with it. I looked at my mobile: it was a quarter-past seven. We'd grabbed around fifty people already; there couldn't be that many more turning up now. We'd done it.

But only God knew how.

Me, Parky and Goody led the latest lot into the canteen while Jimbo and Norris waited for stragglers. When we went through the doors I was staggered at just how many people we'd managed to cram into this small space. It was like looking in the back of a lorry in Folkestone. There was next to no floor space any more, and what little there was was strewn with crisp packets, sandwich wrappers and beer cans, so that you had to really watch your footing.

Something Parky clearly didn't.

He tumbled over either someone's leg or something on the floor and went crashing on to his back, firing a shot into the wall as he fell. This must've startled Bob, because he squeezed his trigger too and blew a big lump out of the pillar in the middle of the room. Goody immediately turned, dropped to one knee and fired two shots at the open doorway. Me and my hostage were right in his line of fire and both of us had to dive to avoid being shot in the face. Finally, for reasons he could never explain, Jacko turned and used his second shotgun cartridge to blow the stack of mobile phones to bits. Stoned, probably.

Parky's and Bob's shots ricocheted around off the concrete-block walls and bounced all around inside the canteen, like two peas in a whistle, while almost a hundred people screamed and dived behind each other for cover. All this took place in probably just under half a second, but it was the noisiest and most panic-stricken half a second of my life.

I cautiously sat up once I was sure the carnage was over and looked about the place. Dust and gun smoke hung in the air as a blanket of people slowly started to stir.

'Wha' the fuck wazzat? Ay heard shootin'?' Jimbo said, poking his head around the door as we wriggled our fingers in our ears to try to stop the ringing.

'Is everyone OK? Is anyone hurt?' I asked. 'Everyone check yourselves and those next to you and make sure you're all OK.'

I got to my feet and started wading through the mass of bodies, shaking anyone who wasn't moving to make sure they were OK, as Parky, Bob and Goody all did the same. Jacko just stood near the door, clutching his heart and shaking with shock.

'Wha' 'appened?' Jimbo asked him, but Jacko couldn't say.

Miraculously, and with much relief, everyone seemed to be fine. All we'd killed in our little shoot-out were three walls, all the mobile phones and a BLT. Several girls were crying (and one of the blokes) and this time I said it like I meant it: 'Right, will everyone please put their fucking safeties on?' I turned to Goody and looked at him accusingly. 'And what the fuck did you think you were shooting at, Rambo?'

'Sorry, Mr A. Army training – just sort of kicked in. When under attack, always defend the point of entry.'

'You fucking doughnut! You could've blown my fucking head off.'

'*Could've*? "Could've" never hurt anyone.'

'What?' I said angrily, but Goody simply checked his gun. 'Everyone, we're going to be having words about this later.'

'Excuse me,' some young girl said at the back. Jimbo told

me that he hoped he wouldn't be included in these words, as he hadn't joined in the Battle of the Canteen. In fact, he was the only one of us who still had all his original allocation of bullets left – except he didn't say it in so many words. 'Excuse me,' the girl asked again, putting her hand up in an effort to get my attention.

'I want everyone to clear out of this room. No, not the shelf stackers. You stay where you are. I'm just talking to my men. Everyone, we're guarding them from outside from now on. Come on, let's move,' I shouted.

'Excuse me,' the girl said again, this time a little louder.

'What?' I snapped back at her, as if I didn't have enough on my plate already. If she wanted a piss she'd just have to tie a knot in it. We had only another forty-five minutes left, and I was fed up dealing with these moaning Minnies. Unfortunately, it wasn't a piss she wanted.

'Sorry about this,' she said all tearfully, 'but I think I've been shot.'

My heart stopped dead at that moment. These were the words I'd been dreading (or at least a variation of them). I think I would've rather heard anything else at that moment. 'This is the police.' 'You're under arrest.' 'You're going down.' Even, 'You're hit, Milo' – anything but this. I dashed across the canteen towards where she was huddled and pushed my way through the crowd. Her left arm had a big red stain on it and blood was dribbling down her fingers.

'Look away, darling. Look over there,' I told her, then used a shelf stacker's Stanley knife to carefully open up her sleeve.

Halfway up her forearm I found a small hole no bigger than the size of a pea, which was steadily seeping blood. I twisted her arm ever so slightly to get a better look, and she let out a blood-curdling scream right in my ear'ole that shit the living daylights out of me.

'Mr B, get your arse over here,' I shouted.

'Let me through, let's have a look,' Goody said, pushing everyone aside. 'Can we give her some room, please? Back the fuck off.'

Goody squatted down beside me and checked the wound. He ran his thumb over the swelling, bent it at the arm and told her to keep it like that until he could make her a tourniquet.

'It's nothing,' he said, though it didn't look like nothing to me. 'The bullet's just under the skin. No broken bones or severed arteries. It's just a ricochet. If you'd been shot directly, it would be a lot worse than that. You'll be fine, love, no problem.'

'Are you absolutely sure?' I had to ask. Knowing how keen Goody was to get his hands on the money, I did briefly half wonder whether or not he'd lie about this so as not to jeopardise his score.

'Of course I'm sure. I'm trained, aren't I? Basic field dressings and first aid. I could even probably take the bullet out for her if she wanted, but as I don't have the proper kit or any anaesthetic I think it's probably best we leave it for the hospital.' Goody turned to Duncan and told him to fetch a first-aid kit.

'Mr G, go with him,' I said, but Parky just stood there motionless. 'Mr G – yes you – go with the manager.'

'Me?' Parky finally said.

'Yes, you, for fuck's sake.'

'I thought I was Mr H.'

'Nah, ah'm Mr H,' Jimbo told him, and I had to yell at Parky to just fucking go with him.

'I'm not going to die, am I?' The girl sobbed miserably, tears running down her paper-white face as she shook like a leaf.

'Don't be silly,' Goody told her. 'It's barely a scratch. The doctors'll sort you out in five minutes. You won't even have to stay over. Have a tiny scar on your arm, that's all.'

'It really hurts,' she moaned.

'Look, she's going into shock. Gather up all the coats and cover her up, keep her nice and warm,' Goody said, setting the security guards to work. 'Look, what's your name?'

'Hazel,' she croaked, her lip wobbling all over the place.

'OK, who here is a friend of Hazel's?'

A tear-streaked girl next to Hazel put her hand up. Goody rolled his eyes and asked, 'Anyone else?'

Graham came forward with a load of coats and said he knew her, so Goody told him to talk to her and keep it nice and positive. Reassure her that she was going to be fine and not to let her drift off.

'Shouldn't we give her a little nip of brandy or something? Isn't that what they do in the movies?' Graham suggested, so Goody agreed and sent Jimbo off to find some brandy (if he hadn't already stashed it all away in Parky's lockup).

'She needs a hospital,' Mike, the security man, insisted.

'Yes, and you can take her to one in exactly forty minutes,' I told him.

'No, she needs to go now.'

I looked at Goody, who just shook his head.

'No way. If she was in serious danger then, yeah, we'd let you take her. But you heard the man, it's only a scratch. I've been here far too long to chuck in the towel now, so you'll all sit down and shut up!' I stood up and made for the door. 'OK, everyone not needed in here, let's get the other side of the doorway, please.'

I tossed all the remaining mobiles into one of the trolleys and wheeled it outside just as Parky returned with the medical kit.

'Where's your man, Duncan?' I asked, incredulous.

'It's cool, chill out. Mr N is with him,' Parky replied.

'Who?'

'You know, Mr N.'

'We haven't got a Mr N,' I said, then suddenly realised who he meant.

Norris.

I dashed off up the corridor, then out on to the shop floor and towards the manager's office, and when I got there I found Duncan up against the wall with Norris's gun pressed against the back of his head.

'Imagine that, hey? Brains all over the place, bullet ripping open your nut. Oh God, no. Oh God, this can't be happening, – this can't be happening, but it is, because I fucking mean it. I'll do it to you in the blink of a fucking eye, you piece of shit. You and your fucking family,' Norris was telling him.

I grabbed Norris by the shoulders and threw him across the office, firing into a stack of folders just inches from his head to remind him I still had bullets even if he didn't.

'What did I tell you?' I screamed at him.

'He knows who I am,' Norris protested.

'Frankly, I'd be amazed if he didn't by now.'

At this moment my phone rang and I saw that it was Patsy, so I told Duncan and Norris to give me a moment.

'What's up?'

'I've been trying to get hold of you for ages. What was all that shooting I heard in there?' Patsy asked, the concern audible in his voice.

'You could hear it out there?'

'Yeah, like pretty muffled, but I heard it. What the fuck are you doing in there?'

'Just some guns went off by accident,' I told him. 'Nothing to worry about.'

'Bullshit. Tell me the truth. What's happening? Have you shot anyone?'

I weighed up whether or not to tell him the truth. Knowing Patsy as I did, I figured he'd be on the first plane to Thailand if he knew we'd left some young girl with a bullet in her arm, and we simply couldn't afford to be left that exposed. Besides, what good would it do him to know someone in here was shot? He didn't need to know, and I didn't need to tell him. It was as simple as that.

'No, no one's been shot.' Duncan looked at me, but I put my finger to my lips. 'You have my word on that.' And he could if he wanted, it made no odds to me; my word's never been that good for anything anyway.

'You promise?'

'On my mum's life. Just walls and the ceiling. Everything's fine. Just keep your bottle for another half-hour and we'll have the money. You OK?'

'Yeah, OK, Milo.'

'OK, see ya.'

I returned to the problem of Norris, or rather the problem Norris had made for us, and realised there was only one way out of this, and killing Duncan wasn't it.

'Now, you listen to me, Mr C. Duncan doesn't want any trouble, isn't that right, Duncan?' He said it was. 'And Duncan knows that that's exactly what he's going to get if he goes blabbing to the police about anything, don't you, Duncan?' Again, Duncan said he did. 'Because Duncan is a very shrewd man. All he wants is for us to leave and for his staff to walk free, because Duncan knows that if he manages that, the papers will praise him, his employers will reward him and we will never, ever, ever come calling again. He also knows he will find an envelope with ten grand in used notes dropped through his letterbox in the next week if he keeps his mouth shut.' This got his attention. 'Now, that would be nice, wouldn't it, Duncan?'

'That would be very nice, Mr A,' he confirmed.

'So there you have it, Clive Norris of Rockmount Road, we have Duncan and Duncan has us. An arrangement me and Duncan and everyone else has no problem with. In fact, the only one who has a problem with it is you, so if anyone's going to end up with a bullet in the head, guess who it'll be?'

I could've added, 'Oh, and guess whose cut the ten grand's coming out of?' if I'd wanted to, but there was no point mentioning that until we had the safe open, in case Norris decided to fuck us up somehow.

I took Norris's gun away from him and sent him off to the loading bay and checked the time. It was half-past seven. Thirty more minutes and we'd be done. Jesus, I was exhausted, running on nothing but adrenalin, but, like I said, thirty more minutes and we'd be done.

'Were you serious about the ten grand?' Duncan asked surreptitiously as we walked back to the canteen. 'Because I'll take it if no one finds out about it. I've got no problem with that at all.'

I smiled to myself. The corrupt old cunt (or young cunt, in this instance). Only a few hours earlier he'd been spouting the rule book at anyone who fancied a sandwich, now suddenly when no one was around he was happy to negotiate himself a big fat backhander as a payoff for keeping vital information from the police – information that could help recover his employer's money, if not their sandwiches. Some people are pure class.

'You know what, Duncan? I like you. You're my sort of bloke.'

Tick tock, tick tock.

'It's your own fault if you're cold. If you'd learned how to make your own Rice Crispies you wouldn't be here, would you?' Bob was taunting the angry boyfriend inside the meat locker.

I checked the time and saw it was quarter to eight. Fifteen more agonising minutes to chalk off.

'You might as well let him out of there now. He's tied up,

anyway, and probably too frozen to start anything, so just bung him in a corner and keep an eye on him,' I said.

Tick tock, tick tock.

Jacko came up and fretted over the state of the girl with the arm. I asked him what he wanted me to do about it. He didn't know; he was just saying. 'Well, then, shut the fuck up and get back to where you were. Jesus, can't everyone just leave me alone for fifteen minutes, please?' I looked at my phone again. Still fifteen minutes. Bollocks.

Tick tock, tick tock.

I pulled one of my gloves off and started chewing my nails. I didn't want to leave any possible DNA, so I chewed up the pieces into little tiny bits and swallowed them. Come on, come on, fifteen . . . no, fourteen minutes to go. This mobile had better not be fast. I was more nervous now than I had been for the entire night and had butterflies flapping around in my stomach by the swarm.

Tick tock, tick tock.

Jimbo, Parky, Norris, Goody and Jacko were all in their ambush positions around the loading bay. We'd bagged another three people in the last quarter of an hour (one a delivery driver) and more were likely to show. Me and Bob stayed back and kept an eye on the canteen door while Duncan, the newest member of our gang, told everyone not to try anything silly this late in the day. 'Just keep calm, as we've been doing all night, and it'll all be over very soon. Don't take any risks, because it's not only your life you'll be risking but those of your friends and colleagues next to you.' And my ten grand too, I could see him thinking. He looked at his watch and started biting his nails as well.

Tick tock, tick tock.

My phone beeped slightly, then went silent. I looked at the screen and it said, 1 MISSED CALL. I figured that could only be Patsy so I moved towards the front of the loading bay, where I could get a better signal and called him back.

'What's up?'

Patsy hissed something into the phone, but I couldn't make it out.

'What? Say it again. I can't hear you.'

At that moment two police cars tore around the back of the supermarket and screeched to a halt in front of the loading bay, just feet from where I was standing. I stared at them in abject horror as machine-gun-wielding uniforms jumped out and took aim at my face.

Tick tock . . .

17

Up shit creek without a boat

'Armed police. Get your fucking hands in the air, NOW!'

'Never mind,' I squawked down the phone and dived headlong into a tray of out-of-date rolls. 'Police! Police! Police!' I shouted, scrambling back towards the safety of the canteen on my right hand while using my left to shield my arse from bullets. The lads in the loading bay all did likewise and scurried away like crabs into the bowels of the supermarket.

'Don't fucking move!' the Old Bill were shouting but we were equally vocal.

'Don't fucking come in. We've got hostages. We've got hostages!'

Someone – and I still don't know who it was to this day – fired a warning shot back at the Old Bill, and they responded with a few rounds of their own. I was still blindly crawling along on my belly when things around me started exploding. I've never been so scared in all my life.

'Don't shoot, don't shoot. Hold your fire, for fuck's sake,' I screamed, and it must've got through to all parties concerned because the shooting stopped and the Battle of the Loading Bay was over. (Incidentally, as you can probably tell, the names the Battle of the Canteen and the Battle of

the Loading Bay were terms Goody coined for these little
incidents. I just thought I'd throw them in to add a little
colour.)

We scrambled to the relative safety of the canteen corridor and took shelter behind what we could find. Jimbo
looked down at what he'd chosen to hide behind and found
it was a trolley loaded with Calor gas bottles. He looked
about to see if there was anywhere less explosive to hide
and found that everywhere else was taken.

'What are we going to do, Milo?'

My phone vibrated in my pocket and I saw that I'd
received a text message. I keyed it open and found it was
from Patsy. POLCE R CUMIN. Thank you very much, Radar
O'Reilly.

I realised if we were to make a break for it, it would have
to be now, before they turned up in force. OK, they had the
loading bay covered, but perhaps they hadn't quite got
around to the front yet.

'Let's go!' I shouted at Goody and the rest of them and
shot off up the corridor towards the shop floor. We burst
through the swing doors and were pelting for the main
entrance when we saw SAS-wannabe cops swarming
through the open doors.

'How the fuck they geddin 'ere?' Jimbo asked as the
seven of us skidded over on to our arses and legged it back
the way we'd just come.

'We've got hostages! We've got hostages,' yelled Goody at
the advancing Old Bill, while Bob went for the more familiar: 'Fuck off, why don't ya!'

We made it through the swing doors again, and I told
Goody to hold them back to give us a chance to think. I
hoped they'd only just arrived and were simply taking up
positions, rather than storming the place for real, but I seriously doubted that. We probably should've got one of those

radio scanners that monitor police frequencies. Annoying how you always think of these things afterwards, isn't it?

'Don't shoot at them, for fuck's sake. Just yell at them not to try anything,' I told him.

'Oh that should do it,' Goody cracked, and I had to remind him this was Civvy Street, not the Western Front – the Old Bill would talk before risking anyone's life. Even ours.

We made it back to the canteen and I found Duncan and Mike, the security guard, poking their heads out of the door asking us what was going on.

I shoved them both back and told everyone to get down on the floor, then sent Jimbo and Bob forward to keep the Old Bill at bay.

'What are we going to do, Milo?' Parky asked me.

'I don't know – about twenty years, I should imagine,' I replied. Jacko looked at me, then started putting an enormous joint together. I knocked it out of his hand and told him to give it a rest for five minutes.

I had to think. Had to think.

What had gone wrong? Where had they come from? What had we missed? Everything, probably. The day manager, for a start; we'd never intended him to be tied up for so long. An hour at the most was all we thought we'd need to keep him quiet for. But eight hours? No matter how scared he was, sooner or later he was going to wriggle out of his ropes and find his daughter upstairs, and that would be that, the bluff would be over. Or maybe it wasn't him, maybe we missed someone when we took the place. Maybe there was someone upstairs right now, hunkering down among a thousand tins of baked beans, texting his mates to phone 999. Or then again, what if someone in the canteen had had a phone? We needed to miss only one to cause problems for ourselves. They hadn't used it before, because they thought things would turn out OK, but they may have changed their minds when they saw us blowing lumps out of Hazel's arm. I didn't know, and I couldn't guess. I was sure I'd find out soon enough, so I put that matter out of my head and tried to concentrate on what our options were.

It had been five minutes since the Old Bill had shown up, and I was still standing here a relatively free man. OK, that told me they weren't storming the place, just cutting off our escape routes. Pretty bad, but could be worse. Well, perhaps not. But we were still in charge of the situation for the time being. As long as they were out there and we were in here, our destinies were in our own hands.

At least, that's what I tried telling myself. Unfortunately, I knew all too well where this one was going to end up, and it made me feel sick to the pit of my stomach thinking about it.

I'd done it again, hadn't I?

After everything I'd said over the last three years, I'd done it again. Oh my fucking God. Only this time, I'd done a real proper job on myself. Twenty years easily. Life, more than likely. We'd shot someone, for fuck's sake. So what if they weren't dead? So it had just been an accident. So what? We'd still shot someone during the course of a robbery and that was all the judge needed to throw the book at us. Well, he'd throw the book at *them*, and I'd get the whole fucking library. Oh my God. Oh my fucking God.

Life in prison, not out before I was at least forty-seven. Maybe even fifty. But you know what was the most annoying aspect of it, the whole situation? The fact that all those smug bastards would be slapping themselves on the back and congratulating themselves about how right they were about me once again. Weasel, Terry, Alice, Mum and Dad, all of them will be saying, 'See, we told you. Once a crook, always a crook,' even though this was such bollocks. I wasn't like that any more, I told myself as I stood there in a ski

mask and battle fatigues, holding a hundred people at gun-
point hostage while police helicopters circled overhead.

'Bollocks.'

Sometimes that's all there is left to say.

'Is that the police?' Duncan asked.

'Yes, you can kiss goodbye to your ten grand now,' I
replied, loud enough for the whole canteen to hear. Well, I'd
lied. I didn't really like him.

'I don't know what you're talking about,' Duncan said,
but suddenly everyone else did.

'That ten grand you said you'd take for keeping your
mouth shut,' I explained, pulling Norris's mask off of his
head.

Two birds with one stone, I believe they call that.

Norris made a grab for the mask, but it was too late –
everyone had seen his face and, judging by their expressions, lots of them recognised him.

'You!' Mike said, getting to his feet.

'But why?' the others were saying.

'What a wanker!' Graham shouted.

'What did you do that for?' Norris demanded.

'Because you don't need it any more.'

'Why not?'

'Because you're going to prison for a very long time,' I
told him.

'Then you don't need yours either, then,' he said and
reached for my mask, but I pushed him away.

'I do. See, they don't know who I am yet.'

'They soon will . . .' Norris started, so I shoved my gun
in his face and told him that was inadvisable.

'Get out of here and go and keep Mr B company.'

I shoved Norris out of the canteen and Parky asked me
what I was doing. I told him Norris's goose was cooked as
soon as he fucked about with Duncan; it was his own fault.
But Parky looked uncertain.

'Whatever you say, man.'

'Milo, get out here. They're on the foghorn,' Bob shouted down to me.

'I see we've given up our codenames now, have we?'

'What? Well, you know what I mean. Anyway, get out here.'

I was just leaving the canteen when Duncan came rushing up to me and asked me why I'd fucked him up like that. 'Why did you try and stop those people eating sandwiches?' I asked by way of response.

'They were the store's sandwiches. I had to say something, it's company policy. More than my job's worth if I hadn't,' he insisted.

'Is it company policy to take ten-grand kickbacks?' I asked. 'Or is it only company policy when it's everyone else?'

I pushed him back into the canteen and told Parky to watch over everyone for a mo', then made my way forward to where Bob and Jimbo were squirreled. We couldn't see any coppers from where we were, just a mass of flashing lights, and I wasted a few more seconds pointlessly wondering if leaving them on like that drained the batteries.

'This is the police. Come out with your hands up. We have the place completely surrounded. You can't get away. Give yourselves up now before someone gets hurt.'

'Bit late for that, boys,' Bob quipped.

'Glad you find it funny, Bob, because that little nick's probably doubled everyone's sentence,' I told him, wiping the smile off his mask.

'What are you talking about? Goody said it weren't even a scratch,' he complained angrily, but he was growling at the wrong guy.

'It doesn't matter. They won't care. We're all looking at life for that.'

'Life!' they both choked.

'You arseholes all wanted to be the big men and bring ammo along. Well, then, now you've got to pay the price. I told you this would happen, but no one wanted to listen to old scaredy-cat Milo, did they? Well, you've fucked it for us all.'

'But that's not fair,' Bob protested. 'It was an accident. We didn't mean it, and Goody saw to her good.'

'Wha' about me? Ah never done nothink. I weren't even there,' Jimbo protested, but I just shook my head. 'Ow, fuck me!'

'Well, if I'm gonna do life, I'm gonna take a few pigs with me before they get me,' Bob muttered rather worryingly.

'I wouldn't do that if I was you, Bob.'

'Why the fuck not?'

'Because your gun doesn't work; it's one of the faulty ones,' I told him.

'Hey, what's wrong with it?' he said, looking it over.

'Here, give us it and I'll show you.'

Bob handed me his gun and, as with Norris, I emptied out the bullets and stuffed them into my pocket.

'It's out of ammo,' I informed him, then handed it back.

I moved away as quickly as I could but Bob was straight on after me, rugby-tackling me to the ground and punching me in the small of the back as Jimbo fought to pull him off.

'Give me those fucking bullets. Give 'em back!'

I shoved my gun in Bob's face and promised to blow his brains out if he didn't get off me, but he was so incensed that he completely ignored the threat and carried on pummelling me. It wouldn't be long before he had the best of me, so out of sheer desperation I fired a shot just past his ear and he rolled off me, screaming and clutching the side of his head. This brought a fresh burst of several shots from our friends outside, and the three of us squeezed behind boxes and shelves and shouted at them not to fire.

'That was just a tin can falling off a shelf, that's all,' I told them, hoping they'd believe it. The shooting stopped and they yelled at us to throw out our weapons. 'It was just a tin can, honest. You want us to throw all them out too?'

'Come out where we can see you. Keep your hands on your head at all times,' the foghorn told us.

'You'll shoot us.'

I then heard Goody up the corridor shouting something at someone. I couldn't make out the words, but it sounded like roughly the same thing as I was shouting back here. In between us was a shitload of crying from the canteen, so I yelled at Parky to close the door to make sure no more stray bullets found any of our guests.

You know, it was funny. I was almost on the verge of starting to feel a bit bad about shitting the good people of MegaSavers up so much when I thought, 'Fuck 'em,' it was a story they could dine out on for years. How many of them would feel bad for me when the judge banged his hammer shortly after saying the words 'twenty years'?

'I'm fucking deaf. You've made me deaf, you cunt,' Bob screamed. He ripped off his ski mask and looked at the blood that was trickling out of his ear.

Bob was a mate and all, but I didn't feel bad about it. He was going to try to take out some coppers. That would've meant life plus life for the lot of us. None of us would've ever seen the light of day again.

I wondered whether or not I should take ammo off everyone. We could only do ourselves harm with it now.

I opened my gun and was about to empty my last round out when I had a change of heart and reloaded with Bob's and Norris's confiscated cartridges so that I had a live round in every chamber. Well, I figured, I could trust myself. Besides, I had the most to lose out of everyone. If anyone deserved ammo, it was me. Jimbo watched me doing what I was doing but didn't say anything. I'd have trouble getting his bullets off him, I realised. But then, as he still had his original allocation of three, he was clearly the least trigger-happy of the lot of us, so perhaps I wouldn't need to worry about him after all.

After a while Bob stopped growling and the three of us sat in silence while the police shouted demands through loudspeakers. A moment later telephones started ringing all around the supermarket. I think they were hoping I'd be near one, but I wasn't.

Half an hour later news of the situation must've made the outside world, because all the mobiles that were left stand-ing in the canteen suddenly burst into life and Parky asked me what we should do about them.

'Shall we answer them, Milo?'

'We're not running a phone-in, Mr G; just turn them off. And will everyone please stop using my name?'

The police weren't going anywhere out back, so I decided to go and check up on Goody and see if he had any ideas about how we were going to get out of here. He didn't, but he did apologise for dragging me into this whole mess in the first place, which I thought was pretty big of him under the circumstances. Norris just glared at me with his red sweaty face and muttered about how I'd get mine when the time came.

'I've got news for you, Norris. The time has already come. I've got mine already. I've got mine for the rest of my life, so don't you go worrying about that.'

'What are we going to do, Milo?' Goody asked me, a popular question, it seemed, this morning.

'I don't know,' I told him. 'I just don't know.' I examined my prospects as I examined my loaded revolver and an old phrase from the telly kept spinning around my head again and again.

You'll never take me alive, copper.

Cornered rats 18

Twenty years.

Jesus Christ!

The reality of our predicament finally sank in. I'd panicked at first, but now I suddenly saw what I'd done to myself. Twenty years. That's what we were facing, and it wasn't just a number, it was a sentence, something we'd actually have to do. Playtime was over. We'd rolled the dice and lost. And look at what we'd risked this for. Seven hundred and fifty pounds a year. It ran my blood cold just thinking about it. How could we have been so dumb? Or more to the point, how could I?

OK, the robbery might've worked, but it would've worked just as well without ammo or with only blanks or something, and we would've got only half of what was coming to us, though that would've still been a number that would've seen me blubbing and screaming as they dragged me out of the dock by the ankles and off to prison.

What had I done with my life? And I mean 'my life'. The first sixteen years were basically me sleeping in a little room, lights out by nine, no girls, no alcohol and no freedom. Then I went to a Youth Detention Centre and none of that changed, then I went home again, then to prison, then to prison again, then . . . oh well, I've been over this ground already. Now I was looking at twenty straight years behind bars. I'd be a middle-aged man by the time I got out. And how long would I have left after that? Maybe another twenty years, if I was lucky (and if I managed to stay clear of the nick that long, which I seriously doubted) before finally being confined to the littlest room of all for the rest of eternity. Fuck me, I really *Carpe Diem*ed, as Mork said, didn't I?

Was it really worth going on? Wouldn't it be better just to pulled the GAME OVER trigger and hope to get another go somewhere down the line when robots were ruling the earth?

No, I couldn't do that. But then I couldn't go back to prison, either. And topping myself in prison would be a lot more painful and drawn out than sticking the shooter in my gob and saying goodbye to my brains now. Or would it? We'd always assumed that blowing your brains out didn't hurt because it was instantaneous, but then that's only because no one who's ever done it has come back and told us it did. It might actually be the most painful way in the world to kill yourself. We just keep on doing it because we don't know any better. Like lemmings all jumping off a cliff thinking they're going to land in jelly and blancmange at the bottom. Of course they're not, but they keep on doing it all the same, because there's no cunt up top warning them about all the sharp rocks and broken lemmings down below.

What am I talking about?

Whatever, the point was that I really didn't fancy killing myself, but at least it was a fallback option: the James Bond cyanide capsule to be taken only in the event of everything else going tits up. And we did have other options. Didn't we? This was a massive supermarket. We had enough food and clothing in here to keep us and our hostages fed, washed and warm for a year if need be, and I wasn't going anywhere until I'd figured out a way of actually getting us there.

'Milo.'

I snapped out of it and looked around at Goody, who'd peeled his mask back.

'Look, if we're not going anywhere for the time being, maybe we should get that little girl to the hospital. Give her over to 'em,' he suggested.

'Fuck that,' Norris suddenly protested. 'They'll see that she's been shot and we'll all be for it. You said yourself if we hurt anyone we'd all get twenty years.'

'Yeah. Well, we have, and we will,' I told him.

'But they don't know that yet. We could just keep her quiet. Get her not to say anything,' he said. I looked at Goody, who told us both she'd lose her arm if she didn't have that bullet taken out. 'Well, then, you do it, Good'. You said you could.'

'Fuck's sake, Norris, give it up. Why would she want to do us any favours? At the moment I imagine she wants to see us all strung up from lampposts with Rik Waller swinging on our ankles. No, come on, let's get her out of here. Good', you come and give us a hand, as you know what the score is. Norris, you stay here and don't let any Old Bill through.'

'No, wait.' Norris was imploring us, but we weren't in the mood for listening. We went back to the canteen and sent Parky out to keep Norris company, then had a look at Hazel before deciding whether or not we could move her. She was as white as a sheet and shivering in a way I didn't like, despite being buried under so many coats she could've been mistaken for the front bedroom at a party.

'She ain't going to be able to walk, Mr A,' Goody told us.

All eyes were on us, and I felt vulnerable in the middle of such a mass of people. They could've easily jumped and disarmed us both if they'd thought about it, but no one did.

Perhaps the threat of the others outside kept them at bay or perhaps they recognised that we were trying to help their friend. Whatever it was, they kept their distance, which was pretty decent of them.

'You, mate, what's your name?'

'Graham.'

'Look, the Old Bill's outside, so we're going to give her up and get her to hospital. Give us a hand getting her out of here and you can go with her. Deal?'

'Yeah, cool. What do you want?'

I sent him and Jacko off to find something to stretcher her out on, and they came back with the canteen door. Hardly an extensive search. We carefully loaded her on to the door, then made a white flag out of a broom handle and as white a tea towel as we could find, then the four of us – me, Goody, Graham and Hazel – picked our way through the debris of the loading bay towards the sunshine. Goody (mask down again) and Graham carried the door; I waved the flag.

'Goody, what is a white flag, anyway? Is it just a truce? We're not telling them we're surrendering or nothing, are we?'

'Bit of both, really. Perhaps we'd better tell them what's on our minds before we go any further,' he suggested.

I looked out at the sea of guns and told them not to shoot.

'Don't shoot. Hold your fire. We're bringing someone out. Hold your fire.'

We waited until we got a few reassurances in that direction, then stepped off the loading bay and out into the car park, still waving our whitish tea towel. There were a staggering number of Top of the Pops about, stretching back as far as the eye could see. Armed response units, uniformed Old Bill, CID: you name them, they were here to nick us. I didn't even know we had this many cops in town. And they were everywhere: behind cars, crouching down on either side of the loading bay, on the roof. There was even a police helicopter circling overhead. I couldn't believe it.

Blimey, we're going to be made to pay for this lot, I thought to myself. It would've been the perfect day to pull a job in town if it wasn't for one thing: all the town's villains were inside MegaSavers with me.

'You got an ambulance here?' I called out, and the lead cop got on the blower and summoned one from around the front.

The sight of all the cops left me in something of a daze, and I ended up wandering a little too far from the safety of the megastore. So much so, in fact, that a couple of the bastards were able to edge forward and quickly grab me, Goody and Graham and pin us to the ground, while another lot whisked Hazel out of it. They searched us all over for weapons, but me and Goody had left our shooters inside with Jacko for safekeeping, if you can call giving that fucking flake a couple of loaded guns 'safekeeping', so they had to make do with confiscating Graham's Stanley knife.

Naturally, the wankers tried to slap the cuffs on me but I was having none of it.

'Get the fuck off me. Get off me. We're not surrendering. This is just a truce. We've still got men and hostages in there, you know. Now, get the fuck off!'

I didn't think they were going to listen for one horrible moment, and I suddenly had one more regret to go along with all the rest, but then a voice commanded them to unhand us and a moment later we were free again.

One of the bastards had really sunk his knee into my back, and I winced as I got to my feet and called them all cunts. I looked over at who had given the order to unhand us and saw that it had been some uniformed chief inspector done up like Bus Conductor of the Year marching up from the back. Walking side by side and in step with him was a face that made my heart sink even further (if that was possible). It was Weasel.

'Oh great! Super-cop's here. That's all we fucking need,' I whispered to Goody after the Old Bill backed away.

One of the Old Bill reassured the inspector we were unarmed, so he and Weasel approached to within talking distance.

'You men, wait up. I want to talk to you, wait up,' the inspector called to us. 'Is anybody else hurt in there? Is everyone OK?'

'Yeah, they're fine, but fuck knows how, what with you lot shooting up the place like it was the OK Corral,' I told him, looking accusingly at all the armed coppers around me.

'My men only fire when fired upon. You shoot at us and we will return fire, and I can guarantee you we are better marksmen than you.'

Goody leaned over and whispered in my ear, 'Oh yeah? How comes we're the only ones off the mark so far, then?'

I could see Weasel looking at me very suspiciously as we spoke. He wasn't a hundred per cent certain of who I was, but I could see it in his eyes: he was almost there.

'Who are you?' the inspector then asked Graham.

'Graham,' Graham told him.

'He's not with us. He's just one of the shelf stackers in there. He's a mate of the wounded.'

'Can I go with her?' Graham asked, but the inspector told him he'd have to talk to him first and sent him away with some Robocop.

'All the best, then, lads,' Graham wished us as he was led away.

'Yep, cheers, mate. Mind how you go. And remember, be back with the helicopter by half-ten, all right?' I called after him, to which Graham gave me the thumbs-up.

'Nice bloke,' Goody observed.

'When you're ready?' the inspector said impatiently.

'Look, we're not nutters or anything like that, but we've got almost a hundred people in there under our ... er ... protection—' the inspector let that one go '—and we don't want anyone else getting hurt: not us, not them, not even you lot, believe it or not. Well, maybe him, I suppose,' I conceded, looking at Weasel.

'Milo!' Weasel suddenly clicked. 'I bloody knew it.'

'Well, aren't you the clever bastard. Give yourself some shit on a stick.' One of the armed coppers next to us laughed but quickly shut up again when Weasel threw him a look.

'You know this man?' the inspector asked him.

'Yes, sir, I do. Darren Miles. An old acquaintance of mine.'

'How about this one?' he said, pointing to Goody. Weasel stared at him hard, but he was all out of guesses.

'Never mind all that. We want assurances from you lot that you won't shoot at us again or try and storm us when we're not looking. You give us those and we can guarantee the safety of our guests,' I said.

The inspector said he could guarantee that, but then he would've probably said anything and guaranteed us a Fun Bus Trip to the Moon if he thought it would stop us decorating the canteen with checkout girls. Didn't mean it would happen, though.

'Now, why don't you all come out?' the inspector asked.

'To what: twenty years?'

'You won't get twenty years, not even half that. Not even a third.'

'Not even a quarter?' Goody pressed him hopefully, but the inspector didn't have much to say about that.

'You've played it pretty sensibly so far, so you come on out before all this goes any further and I'll make sure the judge hears all about it. After all, at the end of the day what have you actually done? False imprisonment? Reckless endangerment? Possession of firearms? Serious offences but hardly A-list crimes. With cooperation and good behaviour you'll all probably be out again in three or four years,' he lied.

'Bollocks! You'll bang us up for life,' I said angrily. 'They're just words, empty promises. I wouldn't trust those any more than you'd trust me with your wallet.'

Weasel took a big step forward into our faces and spelled it out how he saw it.

'Well, how about these words, then? If any of you little fucks lets off one more shot I'll personally guarantee that every last one of you does go down for twenty years: no deals, no parole, no nothing. And if you take another pot shot at us, we'll shoot the fucking lot of you in the fucking heads. How do you like those words?'

'He can't say that,' Goody told Inspector Blakey, then turned to Weasel and said the same thing. 'You can't say that.'

'I can say it and I can do it. Now, you get your friends out here right now and tell them to keep their hands up where we can see them otherwise we might not realise they're surrendering,' Weasel said. The inspector remained silent throughout Weasel's stirring speech and that told me all I needed to know about our chances of seeing daylight again if we believed him. 'And take those fucking masks off, both of you.'

Goody was about to when I stopped him.

'In our own good time. Now, we'll go back inside and explain the situation to the lads. It may take a little time to convince them all to come out peacefully. Do we have your word on it that you won't try anything while we're talking in there?' I asked, and the inspector said I did.

'Now, how about letting the people in there go?' the inspector suggested, casting a real slur on my intelligence.

'What? One thing at a time, Henry Kissinger. Those

people in there are the only things stopping you from grabbing me and him right now and giving us a fucking good
kicking.'

'We wouldn't do that,' the inspector denied.

'You might not, but that fat fuck would,' I told him,
chucking a thumb in Weasel's direction.

'You want to watch that mouth of yours, Milo. It might
end up getting you into trouble,' Weasel said rather sinis-
terly.

'Well, how about letting some of them go, then? How
about the women? That's usually what people do in these
situations,' the inspector urged me.

'I've seen the same films as you, mate, and I've seen what
always happens at the end of them too. If you don't mind,
I'll do things my way, the safe way. The more people I've got
in there the less likely you are to come in like *Who Dares
Wins*. Now, all good things come to those who wait.'

'Well, just you make sure you see to it that we're not
waiting too long, Darren. The longer you stay in there, the
harder it will be on yourself when you finally do come out.'

We agreed on a temporary truce to give us time to dis-
arm and straighten things out with the guys inside and
arranged a phone connection to the line in the canteen for
when I wanted to communicate with them next. I turned
to go back inside when the inspector grabbed Goody and
told us he'd hang on to him for a while.

'Surely there's no need for you both to go back in there?
He can stay out here with us, it simplifies things.'

'You're breaking our trust already. Look, I can't just go
back in there alone, otherwise the guys will never listen to
me. It'll look like I've handed him up and are planning
to do the same with the rest of them next. Both of us need
to go back if we're going to talk them round. Jesus, can't
you see that?'

The inspector and Weasel stared at me suspiciously.

'Besides, Mr B here has to give himself up if we're going to get ourselves a fair deal. At the moment he's in your custody after you caught him and that's shit you can use against him. Come on. Fuck's sake, where are we going to go? You've got the place surrounded.'

The inspector finally let Goody go, and we moved away from them and back into the shop.

'You notice he didn't say not even a quarter?' Goody said.

'What d'you expect, the Nobel Peace Prize?'

'What are we going to tell the others. How are we going to get them to come out?'

'We're not,' I told him.

'We're not? But you just said . . .'

'Do me a favour. You didn't believe any of that old bullshit that was flying backwards and forwards back there, did you? No, fuck that. I much prefer it in here,' I told him, stepping back into the sanctuary of MegaSavers.

Our fifteen minutes

19

Isn't it amazing? Goody spends months and months bending my ear into doing this job, then at the first sign of trouble he turns around and starts bending my ear to give up. I mean, what was it with the bloke?

'But you told him we'd give ourselves up!' he was saying along with a dozen other things.

Fucking Goody, he'd been in the army so long that he couldn't even comprehend not doing something some bloke with pips on his shoulders suggested. Oh it was all *Mission: Impossible* and cowboys and Indians while we were getting away with it, but the moment some authority figure marched into view and told us to pack it in, Goody was *yes sir*-ing him all the way to Parkhurst.

Still, even though I'd lied to the inspector, I reasoned he was probably good for his word about not trying to storm us (at least, not for the next hour or so). After all, if the whole thing went tits up and turned into a massive bloodbath, we'd only have our lives to lose; he, on the other hand, had his career and pension to kiss goodbye to. I gave it ten minutes for word to filter through to all his subordinates, then took the opportunity to gather all the lads together on the stairs just across from the canteen to see if anyone had any ideas about getting us out of here.

Norris was still making little deals in his head about trying to convince the girl we'd shot not to press charges, and perhaps talking to the supermarket and seeing what they'd say, and this, that and the other, and not making a lot of sense in between. Jacko was very much resigned to his fate and was trying to smoke as much of his gear as he possibly could before it was taken away from him (he was even looking around for condoms to swallow what he could of it).

Bob was still seething with anger with me for not letting him 'off some pigs', and every now and then I got the impression he was getting ready to lump me, so I made sure I kept at least ten feet and my revolver between us at all times. Ten feet, as it turned out, was easily enough because Bob couldn't walk more than a few feet without stumbling into something and I figured I must've knocked his balance off when I popped his eardrum. Parky was very much in the 'Let's find some way of getting the fuck out of here' camp, whereas Jimbo was cautiously non-committal.

As for Patsy, Patsy was long gone. He hadn't answered any of the calls I'd placed, so he was either on his way to the airport or already in police custody. I kept on trying, nevertheless, as he was our one glimmer of hope, but I wasn't optimistic.

'Look, Milo, you heard yourself what he said: the longer we stay in here the worse it'll be on us in the long run,' Goody pointed out. 'Let's just get it over with and give up now. I mean, we're not going anywhere but nick, so why fight it?'

'And it'll definitely be less than ten years?' Norris asked.

'Yeah, less than a third, but not less than a quarter, so that's, say, six years.' Goody added up on his fingers.

'Yeah, but you don't do six years, do you? You only have to do half that these days to be eligible for parole, so perhaps we'd only end up doing three and a half years. Maybe only even three,' Norris said hopefully.

'Three fucking years, Jesus!' Bob moaned.

'That ain't that bad ah spose,' Jimbo said, less than sincerely.

'Yeah, it could've been worse,' Goody said.

'What d'you reckon, Milo?' Norris asked.

'You know what I reckon? I reckon we'll all get twenty years. Even if we get a good lawyer, a good judge and a jury made up of bank robbers and our mums, we'll still get twenty years, twenty at the very minimum, and we'll definitely end up doing at least twelve. That's what I reckon, and that's what I know, so pick the bones out of that lot if you want to, because that's the reality of what we're facing.'

The lads didn't like hearing the naked truth any more than I liked telling them it, but at least I wasn't bullshitting myself.

'But he said . . .'

'Goody, I know what he said, but none of that will matter when me, you and his honourableshipness get together. Even if he was telling the truth, which I very much doubt, he's got nothing to do with the sentence. The judge will make up his own mind about how long we'll do, and there's nothing those cunts love better than sending a load of working-class blokes like us down for half their lives for trying to pinch little more than what he'd think of as his lunch money,' I said, though I think the term 'working' confused most of them.

'But what if we was to get it in writing first . . .' Norris started, but I just shook my head and told him to wise up.

'Well, what are we going to do, then? I mean, we can't stay here for ever, can we?' Parky observed.

'Maybe not, but I'm in no rush to get banged up. See, once I'm inside, I know I won't get to see another Wagon

Wheel for twenty years. Out here, I've got a whole box of them to myself,' I said, slapping the box I was sat on.

'Give us one of those, you cunt!' Parky said, making me notice how, as the years had gone by, almost all of my mates had substituted the term 'you cunt' for 'please'. I passed the Wagon Wheels out, and we all ended up having three each (either I've doubled in size since I was a kid or Burtons are a load of fucking crooks). The sugar boost was much needed, as I was starting to get a bad case of the Shakin' Stevens. I'd been awake for almost twenty-four hours, and I'd used up a lot of energy in the last eight. I wasn't sure just how much longer I could keep on going and decided, whatever we did, I'd have to have a couple of hours' kip beforehand to ensure I didn't end up getting grilled in some interview room when I was so bleary-eyed I could hardly see what I was signing.

'Yeah, we could have a party, man. Some booze, some smoke, some nice grub. Go out in style,' Jacko suggested.

'Yeah, I mean, we've got some nice-looking birds next door,' Bob mused, stroking his chin at the possibilities.

'Not a chance. Stay away from them,' I warned them all. Only Jimbo offered me any sort of support on this decision, mumbling something about how he was so shit scared he didn't think he could do anything about it even if he wanted to, but the rest thought it had the makings of a blinding idea.

'We're not talking about . . . you know, forcing ourselves on them . . . just having a few drinks and a bit of a knees-up and seeing if any of them fancy joining us, you know what I mean?' Goody said, flapping his eyebrows.

'You don't get it, do you? If the birds in there wanted to have sex with masked men, they'd go walking on the common at midnight. I'm telling you, any one of you messes with any of them in there – and I don't care whether they rip their clothes off and drag you into the sweets cupboard

– the lot of us'll go down as sex cases and have to get used to eating shepherd's pie with broken glass in it for the next twenty years. Just leave them alone, will ya?'

As much sense as I was talking, the lads seemed far more preoccupied with the fact that I seemed to be always telling them what to do.

'You know, I'm getting pretty fucking sick of this,' Bob said, standing up. 'I mean, what's going on here? Who the fuck do you think you are, ordering us about all the time? Do this, do that, can't have a drink, don't shoot no one, leave the girls alone, stay out of there, stick that up your arse. Who the fuck put you in charge?'

'Who put me in charge? I'll tell you who put me in charge: you lot did when you dragged me into this fucking mess. I didn't want to know. I tried walking away, but none of you wankers would have it, would you? So I agreed to come along, show you how to do it, help you get the money, but on one condition: that you did exactly what I said, when I said it and how I said it. And you lot agreed. So shut the fuck up and sit the fuck down.'

There was a bit of a standoff between me and Bob for a few nervous moments before Jimbo and Goody got him sat back down and Parky struck up.

'Look, this ain't getting us nowhere. I'm with Milo, all right? And I don't want no party and then go to no nick. I do, however, want to get the fuck out of here, so why don't we have a think about that before the fucking Babylon come busting in and taking us all down?'

Good old Parky. This got us all back on a common footing again, and we scratched our heads for a while before Goody suggested giving Patsy another try. I went upstairs to get a signal and phoned the phone I'd given him, but it went straight over to voicemail again. Either it was off or he'd slung it. I was about to try the shop when Patsy's own mobile, which I still had in my pocket, burst into life. I looked at the caller and saw it was my brother, Terry.

'Hello, Terry.'

'Patsy? No, who's this? Is that you, Darren?' I told him it was. Terry asked me where I was. I asked him why he wanted to know. Terry reckoned he was watching an interesting item on the news and wondered if I was starring in it. 'Are you in MegaSavers?'

'Who's with you?' I asked. He swore he was on his own, so I chose to believe him. 'Yes, I'm here.'

'You fucking arsehole. What are you doing, man?'

'Living up to everyone's expectations once again, I guess. Believe it or not, it wasn't meant to work out like this.' I took a minute or two to explain what had happened and how it had all gone wrong (leaving out the fact that we'd shot someone) and told him what we were facing. 'Is there any way you can help me?'

'What do you want? I'll do what I can,' he promised.

'Can you get a fast motor?'

Terry was flabbergasted; he'd meant he'd do anything legal he could for me, like getting me a lawyer, or bringing me my toothbrush or something. He hadn't expected me to ask him to *Dukes of Hazzard* me out of here.

'Oh don't worry about it, then,' I told him. 'Here, can you see the place on the telly at the moment?'

'No, not at the moment. Why?'

I told him to keep watching and give us a bell back when he saw my message. I looked out of the windows and clocked the TV vans on the hill up by the main road, then found a big white sheet from the linen section and some shoe polish. I'd seen old lags in prison riots do this a lot on the telly and always wanted to do something like this for myself (unfortunately, I'd never been anywhere nearby when one had kicked off). After ten minutes of writing, I opened one of the front upstairs windows and unfurled my banner. Unfortunately, it was too windy, so I had to pull it back in and thread the bottom corners through a couple of tin can ring-pulls to weigh it down, then I unfurled it again. Terry phoned ten minutes later.

'That's you, is it? FREE MEGA STORE 7? It sounds like they've got a sale on: you know, buy one, get seven free?'

'Does it?' I asked, knowing I should've included the word THE in there somewhere. Still, fascinating to think that I had just done something that had been seen by millions of people across the country, probably (or maybe just in the TVS area). It made me wonder if we could use this to our advantage somehow. Rather than hanging stupid slogans out of the windows for laughs just to get on the telly, perhaps there was some way of manipulating this to our advantage. I racked my brains but couldn't think of anything except, WANTED: HELICOPTER. WILL PAY CASH but that was just stupid. Then it struck me. I cut the sheet loose and got another one, then wrote a second message, one aimed not at millions and millions of people this time, but just the one. Goody and Parky came up to see what I was doing and chipped in to lend a hand when I told them.

Terry phoned again as soon as he saw my message on the telly, but I told him I'd have to put the phone down because I was expecting another call.

'Darren, stop fucking about. Just get out of there, otherwise they'll shoot you.'

I told him I was working on it, but I really, really had to go because I needed to take this call.

'All right, then. Just be careful and don't do anything stupid,' he said, though it was a bit late for that. He was just about to let me go when he decided to ask about the banner. 'One last thing, Darren. Who's Mr D?'

Bringing in a patsy

20

It took another hour for Mr D to ring, but when he did there was much relief among the lads. I'm not sure why. There was very little he could actually do. I just thought it might be handy to have someone on the ground behind the Old Bill who could look for possible chinks in the armour. Patsy was over at his newsagent's, trying to act as if nothing had happened, when I rang and told him to shut up shop and get his arse back over here. Patsy reckoned he didn't really fancy it, but I told him if he didn't we'd squeal him up for being in on the whole thing from the start. However, if he came back and helped us out as best he could now, all the lads would agree to tell the Old Bill, in the event of his capture, that he was only party to this whole cock-up after the event, a mate we belled to come and help us out. And that wouldn't get him more than a couple of years, if that.

'A lot better than twenty, wouldn't you agree, Pats'?'

Patsy whimpered and whined like a trapped animal, but what could he do? He finally agreed to close up for the day and make his way over with some little binoculars. I could tell he was almost wetting himself with fear and put money on it that he started crying as soon as he put the phone down. Of course, there was always the chance he'd just clear the newsagent's safe out, grab his passport and jump on the first plane out of town while we were all sitting around waiting for him to come charging over the hill on his white steed (after all, that's what I'd do), but knowing Patsy as I did I was confident he'd come. See, no matter what sort of fantasy life Patsy pined after, all he really wanted was his wife and his nice little life back again. He didn't want to go travelling around Thailand or India or anything like that; he just thought he did because he didn't want to be the sad little divorcé who worked in the newsagent's, no matter how big his new bird's tits were. If you gave him the option of getting his old life back again or seeing the world, Patsy would always take his old life. He was born in this two-horse town and he'd die in this two-horse town. Mind you, if this all went stupid, so would I, and a lot sooner than Patsy.

While I waited for him to get his arse over here I finally leaned out of the window and answered Weasel's repeated calls for me to show myself. He'd been on the foghorn ever since I'd started hanging messages out of the window, but up until now I'd chosen to ignore him. However, the longer my silence went on, the more suspicious he grew, so I waved a little white flag out of the window, poked my head out and asked him what he wanted.

'What's all these banners for? Who are you signalling?' he demanded.

'My brief, if that's all right with you. We want a little legal advice before we go giving ourselves up, so just be patient and we'll be out soon.'

'Your brief's Charlie Taylor. Who the fu—' (suddenly notices cameras trained on us) '—who's Mr D?'

'That's Charlie,' I lied. Weasel dropped the foghorn and talked to some copper close by, but I couldn't hear what they said. He lifted the foghorn to his gob again and asked me why I hadn't just used the phone like normal people. I had a think about this and told him I couldn't remember the number. I don't think he believed me.

Goody and Parky looked down at Weasel from windows on either side of me but neither said anything. Parky, however, did catch Weasel's attention with a wanker gesture, but that was about it.

'Your time's running out fast,' he warned us. 'You can't hide in there for ever, so give yourselves up and let's sit down and sort this whole silly mess out together.'

Oh very carey sharey of you, I thought. Goody suddenly found his voice and shouted down that we would be coming out just as soon as we'd used up all the food, and me and Parky half laughed at that.

Well, you have to keep the old spirit up, don't you? Norris suddenly appeared and asked us who was out there.

'Weasel,' we told him.

'What's that cunt want?' he asked, rather pointlessly in my opinion.

'Milo? Milo, are you there?' Weasel called up again.

'What's up?'

'Give us some of your hostages,' Weasel demanded, without even saying please. How had they let this arsehole anywhere near the loudhailer?

'For what? You haven't done anything for us yet. That's how it works: you give us something we want and we'll give you some hostages in return for whatever it is you give us.'

'Besides, we can't,' Goody whispered to me quietly. 'We haven't finished killing them yet.'

'You want to stop fucking about, Goody?'

'Well, what do you want, then?' Weasel asked and we all knocked our heads together. Parky and Goody both thought a couple of helicopters and a jumbo jet would just about do it, but I told them to be sensible. That sort of thing never worked. Hadn't they seen *Dog Day Afternoon*?

'We don't really want anything at the moment, thanks, just a bit more time to consult with our briefs,' I shouted back down. Weasel looked disappointed.

'OK, you've got it, but give us some of your hostages first.'

'The fucking cheek on this bloke,' Parky mused.

'Why don't we let some of them go?' Norris asked. 'They're only sitting down there moaning about how hungry they are or how thirsty they are or how much they need to go for a shit, so let's just get rid of them. Why not?'

'No, we may need them yet. The Old Bill won't dare move in while we've got that many people in here with us, and if we do decide to make a break for it a hundred bodies might make an excellent shield to hide behind.' The lads looked at me with concern until I explained that I meant live bodies, not dead bodies. 'Look, we better rustle them up some more grub and step up the bog visits. Can you lot go down and see to that? I'll stay here and talk to this idiot.'

The lads made to depart when Goody stopped and turned.

'Here, Milo. I've just had a thought. What about the day manager and his family? We can give Weasel him if he hasn't got 'em already.'

That was a thought. We'd be giving him some bodies (again, hopefully alive) and building the old trust bridges without weakening our own position any. I shouted down all the details to Weasel and he seemed very interested. He got straight on the radio, dispatched a squad car to go over and investigate, then asked me if we'd tied anyone else up around town.

'Only all the fucking cops,' I told him and shut the window. That would get him thinking.

I found the electrical appliances aisle and took a trolley-load of kettles, toasters and microwaves down to the canteen, then got Goody to break out the Pot Noodles and instant curries and stuff like that and handed out some wine. I restricted them to the boxed wines rather than bottles, because I didn't fancy anyone cracking me over the head when I wasn't looking, then I got two of the shelf stackers to go and find some bin bags to tidy up some of this mess. Several people asked me when I was going to let them go, but I just told them they'd have to be patient. 'We're working on getting everyone out alive,' I explained, putting the willies up everyone no end, which was the general idea.

Patsy finally rang back and told me he was about half a mile away, almost as far back as the little parade of shops we'd parked behind and that was about as close as he could get.

'The Old Bill have the dual carriageway all roped off, and they're turning everyone back. I had to park up by the parade and walk it to see what was going on but they keep telling us to fuck off.'

'Us?'

'Yeah, you're attracting quite a crowd. Half the town's turned out to see what's going on. The other half are stuck in their motors wondering why they can't get to the shops.'

'Exactly how close can you get the motor?' I asked him, looking out of the window towards where he was calling from. Not that I could see much. Past the car park, which surrounded the megastore like a moat, there were steep embankments with wasteland beyond them: trees, bushes, shrubs, a few strips of concrete that used to be some factory's floors and a few thousand used condoms and roach butts. I couldn't see the parade from the supermarket's front windows – well, not unless I stuck my head out all the way, and I wasn't about to do that when there were so many people down there who wanted to blow it off for me – so I just had to estimate where he was.

'Well, I can get the car about a hundred yards past the

parade – you know, where that mini roundabout and those big billboards are? That's where they've got the road cordoned off, but I can't stop there because there are a load of coppers there who are waving everyone on. I'm just opposite them on the other side of the road with a big crowd of people,' he explained.

'Well, where's the closest you can get to without being moved on?' I asked.

'Probably the parade. The Orion's still out front. So's the Saab.'

'Are they? Good. OK, that's something, at least,' I said, racking my brains as to how we could reach them with all those size nines outside. 'OK, look, park up at the parade and wait for us there.'

'Wait for you? What are you talking about? How are you going to get out of there?'

'I don't know, do I? I'm hoping to think of something, though,' I told him, less than convinced myself. 'And make sure all your doors are unlocked and that you're not blocked in.'

'Milo, you're going to get yourself killed. You can't get out of there. Just give yourself up.'

'No,' I told him, no way. 'There's plenty of time for that later.' At the moment there was still a chance, just a tiny, minuscule, almost invisible little chance. Until you were in the cells, there was always a chance. I didn't know where it was or how I could use it best, but I did know I still had a chance, and I wasn't going anywhere while that remained.

I told him to get to where I'd told him to get and check out the waste ground for cops. If I could just get past the ones in the car park outside I might just be able to make it to Patsy. And if I could make it to Patsy, then I might just be able to put a bit of distance between us and them in the motors, then hide somewhere, or switch cars or something. All I needed was that little bit of breathing space and I was confident I could disappear. I didn't know why I was so confident; I'd never been able to do it before. Perhaps it was the fact that I had been caught so many times before that it was that that gave me hope. I knew the score now. I knew which way they'd come from, how they'd chased me, how they'd communicated with each other, what sort of terrain they hated and what not to do. I almost felt like I'd been vaccinated against the possibility of being nicked – if only I could get a head start.

I phoned Patsy back again and told him to knock some holes in the fence behind the parade so that, if we did make it that far, we wouldn't have to clamber over the bastard. Not that we'd be able to clamber over anything after doing the half-mile sprint. But it was good that I'd thought of this; the little details were occurring to me every now and again to keep my spirit up, and they gave me hope that the big idea would hit me sooner rather than later. I hadn't thought of one yet, but there was still hope. After all, the fence hadn't occurred to me until I'd visualised myself running across the waste ground and getting in the car. I even had the best route picked out once I was behind the wheel (I'd insist on doing the driving; Patsy was like an old lady) to shake off the cops. All I needed was to rewind my visualisation back a bit so that I could see how the fuck we were going to get out of here. I hadn't got it yet. Every time I'd imagined myself slipping through the skylight or crawling through a drain, there'd been Weasel waiting to slap the cuffs on me.

Allow me to walk you through my plans.

PLAN 1
We'd all get eight shelf stackers each to surround us like human shields, then we slowly walk out together. The police wouldn't dare shoot us (hopefully) for fear of hitting our guests, and they wouldn't be able to nab us

because we'd keep a gun to the heads of one of the old ladies (or maybe one of the young birds actually: less likely to shoot and I could have a sneaky feel while I was at it). They'd have to back off and give us room, and we could slowly make our way up the embankment and across the waste ground towards where the cars were parked. Hopefully, Patsy would've knocked holes in the fence big enough for nine people to slip through at a time (see where the cracks in this plan were starting to appear) and then we'd quickly duck into the motors and put our foot down. Unfortunately, moving so slowly, the cops would be able to keep pace with us every step of the way. They might give us a wide berth, but the whole shooting match would walk across the waste ground with us so that we were no better off than we were at the moment. The only difference really would be that we wouldn't have a supermarket around us any more. No, that was a shit idea. OK, what else?

PLAN 2

We'd demand a helicopter to take us to the airport. We'd give them some hostages, then we'd get a plane to take us to . . . I don't know, I'd figure that out later. Somewhere where they couldn't extradite you from (I'd have to ask Charlie). We'd give them some more hostages, then the rest when we got to wherever we were going. How was that? That was exactly the same plan Al Pacino had in *Dog Day Afternoon* and look what happened to him. More to the point, look what happened to his mate. I did actually lean out of the window and sound out Weasel about the possibility of getting a helicopter for some hostages but he just shouted back at me through the loudhailer to 'grow up'. No, Plan 2 was even worse than Plan 1. So on to Plan 3.

PLAN 3

Plan 3 was like Plan 2, only we'd get a coach instead of a helicopter. Hmm, what was Plan 4?

PLAN 4

Plan 4 was we hid. They didn't know how many of us were in here, so a couple of us could squirrel ourselves away among the rafters and wait for everyone to fuck off once the rest of us were caught. It might take a few days before everything got back to normal, but we could stock up on choc and pasties and lemonade to keep us going, then slip away without anyone noticing. Of course, only a maximum of two of us could hide, as the rest would have to sacrifice themselves in order for the plan to work, and who was going to agree to that? We could draw straws for who got to hide and who got to do twenty years, I suppose, but I wouldn't trust those bastards not to sell me out the moment they got in the interview room. Plus, the Old Bill might not believe there were only five of us in here; all the staff knew there were more and they'd soon squeal on anyone hiding in here. They might even bring the dogs in to sniff us out, though I was half thinking about hiding a load of raw chickens and steaks around the place to throw them off the scent, but it still wasn't much of a plan. It might work – as an absolute outside chance – for just one of us, but that wouldn't be me, because Weasel knew I was in here already. And it wouldn't be Norris either; everyone had his number, so that was some small comfort at least. No, hiding wasn't much of an option.

PLAN 5

Plan 5 was we ran for it. We let all the hostages out the front and caught the police on the hop. Hopefully, most of the coppers' attention would be drawn away by the sudden appearance of a hundred people, so we'd dart out the back and run like fuck. If we got past the few coppers left, we'd get our heads down and run as fast as we could until we got through the fence, then it would just be a case of piling in the motors and shooting off. They couldn't shoot us in the back if we were unarmed – again hopefully – so it would all come down to who could move their legs faster.

Again, there were great holes in this plan, not least of all the fact that most of us were totally unfit. In Jacko's case, he'd smoked so much he could hardly stand at the moment, let alone outpace the Old Bill, and there were swarms of them out there. We'd be seven people; they'd be a hundred. We wouldn't stand a chance.

PLAN 6
The same plan, but we'd dress some of our guests up in our masks and combats just before we shoved them out of the door. It might divert the Old Bill's attention long enough for us to slip out the other way dressed as shelf stackers and leg it for the cars. It was a thought, but then how many of our guests were likely to agree to dress up like us and walk outside when there was that lot out there waiting for them? Not many, and even those who were would be grabbed the moment they filed outside and they'd still leave enough coppers out back to nab anyone trying to slip through that way. They weren't idiots, you know, which was a bit of a shame really.

PLAN 7
We all dressed as shelf stackers and filed out the front with them. Maybe in the confusion of so many people all dressed the same, we could slip into the bushes and make a break for it. Again, this was a nice idea, but again the Old Bill weren't stupid; they'd hardly leave us all to mill

around unguarded out there. No, they'd herd everyone up into a tight little group the moment we stepped out into the sunshine and go through us one by one at their leisure. Not that they'd need to. Duncan and Mike and whoever else would point us out to the Old Bill in a heartbeat. No, this was the dumbest plan yet, but there had to be a way. There had to be.

And there was. But it wasn't me or Goody or Patsy or any of the others who suggested it. It wasn't even Duncan. It was the Old Bill themselves. They provided us with the missing piece of the jigsaw I'd spent so long scratching my brain for. They showed me a possible way out. It wasn't a perfect plan, by a long way, but it was a chance. And that was all I needed.

Plan 8 definitely gave us a chance.

Getting the money

21

'So, how close can you get?'

'I told you, Milo, they've got it cordoned off at the roundabout,' Patsy told me.

'No, I mean the other end. The motorway end. Have you tried it from that end?'

'Yeah, I got on at junction four, got off at junction five, but the Old Bill have that roundabout roped off too. All you can do is either drive straight round it and get back on the motorway or cross over the bridge, but the supermarket's even further away over that end than it is over this.'

This was deeply frustrating. Why had they roped off the road so far back? It was probably a half a mile or more in both directions. It was a long way to make a break for it. The main road was a good hundred yards away from the supermarket entrance as it was. Didn't they think that would've done? But half a mile? They were probably trying to prevent some kid getting the sticky end of his lollipop blown off while it was sticking out of his gob or more likely trying to stop a great convoy of rubberneckers backing up the traffic to London. Or, even more likely than that, they didn't want any witnesses when they gave us all that fucking good hiding they were planning. Yeah, I'll take box number three, please. Still, half a mile back in both directions? That gave the whole crime scene a wide circumference. They couldn't possibly guard it all.

'Is there a lot of people hanging around?' I asked.

'Yep, hundreds. Fucking ghouls.'

'So what? You must have hundreds of coppers back there keeping them back?'

'No, not really. Just a small handful really,' Patsy told me, and I was much surprised.

'Really?' I asked, incredulous. Was this the chink in the Old Bill's armour I'd been looking for? If it was, I couldn't quite see the significance of it at that moment, but I knew I'd stumbled on something. 'Well then, how are they keeping all those people at bay?'

'They're just telling them to stay put,' Patsy told me, but this didn't make sense. There was a big designer robbery going on at their local supermarket with SWAT teams and SAS and all the rest of them silly fucks. Didn't anyone want to get a better look? Surely they couldn't see nothing from the back at the parade. I would've snuck through if I'd been out there and no handful of coppers would've been able to stop me. What was stopping them? Respect for authority? In this town? Surely not.

'They're frightened,' Patsy told me.

'Of what, a stray bullet?'

'No, they don't know it's a robbery. The Old Bill are telling everyone there's a bomb down there. A massive one, like 9/11, so everyone's staying back. But not too far enough back that they'll miss the fireworks when you all go up.'

'What, that's what they're telling them?'

'Yeah, sneaky lying bastards, aren't they?'

'They are,' I mumbled, lost in thought.

'You what?' Patsy asked.

'Look, I'll call you back. I've got some thinking to do.'

'Milo, wait. I don't . . .' but I didn't want to hear it. This was it, this was definitely it. But what? I felt a few missing pieces and my brain grabbed hold of them and twisted and turned them in all directions, trying to get them to fit into position, but I couldn't quite see it. And that was more frustrating than anything.

I went downstairs to see if the lads could make anything of it and found most of them congregated around the canteen entrance. Only Bob and Norris were missing, watching over the loading bay and the shop floor doors respectively, but I wasn't fussed about their opinions, to be honest.

Goody asked me if I had any good news so I told him we were all going to get knighted by the Queen at Disneyland. He didn't appreciate that. I was about to tell them what Patsy had told me when something caught my eye: Jimbo was leaning against the trolley of Calor gas bottles. This caught my eye because I remembered they were the same Calor gas bottles he'd so reluctantly taken shelter behind during the Battle of the Loading Bay, so it seemed odd that he'd be happily leaning against them again.

Then it hit me. My God, it was like a blinding flash of inspiration, like when that bloke invented the light bulb and jumped out of the bath shouting at Ulrika. Everything suddenly fitted – the hostages, the supermarket uniforms, the bomb, the Calor gas bottles. Suddenly, I saw a way out. Like I said, it wasn't as good as a Get Out of Jail Free card, but it was definitely an idea. And not a bad one at that.

I'll come back to it in time, but there was something else I had to take care of first.

'What's up, Milo?' Parky asked.

'Does anyone know what time it is?'

'It's . . . look at that, it's almost midnight,' Jacko said, speaking for the first time in ages.

'No, Jack', it's almost midday,' Goody corrected him. 'We haven't been here that long yet.'

Everyone shrugged their shoulders and asked 'so what?'

'It's past eight o'clock, isn't it? In all our excitement we didn't notice: the safe's open now.'

Again, everyone just shrugged and asked 'so what?'

'What difference does that make any more?' Goody asked.

'Well, we came for the money, didn't we? Let's at least go and have a look at it.'

'Wassa point?' Jimbo asked, but the others were made up with the idea.

'Come on, Jimbo . . . er, I mean Mr fucking whatever. Let's just go and have a look,' Parky told him, giving him a dig.

'Why bovver?'

'You doing anything else at the moment?' Goody asked.

I poked my head in the canteen and told Duncan to report for duty front and centre.

'Look, when are you going to let us go?' Duncan demanded impatiently when he stepped out. 'We've been in here for twelve hours now and frankly there's only so much of this we can take.'

'Well, I've got good news and bad news for you on that score. The good news is we're going to be leaving pretty soon.'

'What's the bad news?' he asked warily.

'That'll have to be a surprise. I've got things to do for the moment. Right, first of all, me and Mr B here would like to go to the safe and get the money.'

'You want the money?' Duncan asked in confusion.

'Yeah, that's the whole fucking reason we came here in the first place, and had you not dicked us around with the timelock we could've all been in bed by now.'

'But the police, surely . . .'

'That's who it's for. We're bunging them a few quid to let

us go,' I told him. 'They're all bent as coat hangers out there. Didn't you know that?'

Duncan didn't know what to make of that, to be honest, but it got him thinking. I told Goody to grab us a few more hostages so that we could crab-walk to the office sheltering behind them like in Plan 1 and told him to make sure they were young birds. I told him this because I figured young birds would be the least likely to try and *Under Siege* us like some blokes would or collapse in a big annoying hysterical heap and refuse to go on while a dozen gun-wielding cops were aiming their guns at us, like the old ladies probably would. Besides, if you had the choice to be sandwiched behind four or five warm bodies, wouldn't you rather go for attractive young women? If you're honest?

Goody wheeled them out and I explained what I wanted of them, then led them up to the shop floor entrance and got them all to gather around me. Goody did the same, and I had to congratulate him on his selection. I had nubile young totty buffeting me in all directions, and it wasn't something I hated. Another time and another place and I would've loved this for all the wrong reasons (or all the right reasons, depending on how you look at these things). Perhaps if, one day, I won the lottery or, I don't know, even more fantastically actually got away with this fucking job, I'd indulge myself in some of the same at some later date. At the moment all they were to me were bulletproof jackets. Sexy young bulletproof jackets, I'll admit, but bulletproof jackets all the same.

I looped an arm around the girl in front to stop her from straying too far away from me and checked to see if Goody was ready. He was OK to go, and that was just about what we were about to do when I noticed Duncan almost sexually assaulting four young human shields of his own.

'Duncan, what the fuck are you doing?'

'I just thought . . .'

'No one's gonna be shooting at you. You girls, get around me and him,' I told them, indicating myself and Goody. Jesus! 'OK, let's go.'

Norris stepped aside as we pigeon-stepped past him towards the doors, and I called out to the Old Bill that we were coming out.

'Don't shoot. We're coming out. Don't shoot.'

My little huddle passed through the rubber swing doors and stepped out into the aisle to see two dozen tactical firearms officers crouching behind freezers and shelves of cat food and stuff.

'Lower your weapons,' I told them as me and six other pairs of feet moved aside to let Goody's group out. None of them lowered their weapons or indeed looked like they were likely to do so in the near future.

'Stop where you are,' a voice commanded us, but we ignored it and kept on edging slowly down the aisle. Goody now emerged into the firing line with a protective posse of his own, then Duncan stepped out nervously with his hands raised.

'I said stop where you are. Don't move,' the voice repeated.

The twelve of us carried on shuffling along, down the aisle towards the office door, and we managed to pick up half a dozen policemen and take them with us for the ride.

'Stop there right now!'

'We're armed and not afraid to use them,' Goody shouted back. 'Don't give us any fucking grief.'

The lead officer spoke quickly into his walkie-talkie and told whoever was listening that something new was going on in the shop, and within thirty seconds Weasel and Inspector Blakey appeared and came motoring towards us past all the checkouts to ask us where we thought we were going.

'Just stay back,' I told them, even though they'd stopped a dozen yards short of us.

'Milo, Milo. Fucking stop,' Weasel told me, holding his hand up like a school crossing policeman, probably frightened if he fucked this up that would be where he ended up. 'Just stop there.'

'We're going over to the office, so just make room and keep back,' I told Weasel, peeking out at him over my sexy young intimate's shoulder.

'What are you going to the office for, Milo?'

'I want to see what the view's like from in there.'

'The view's exactly the same from there as it is from anywhere – obscured by coppers,' he told me.

'The money. They're going after the money,' some bright spark aiming his Heckler & Koch at us finally pointed out. Weasel and Blakey looked at matey and then back at us, as we continued our slow migration towards the office.

'You're not serious, are you, Milo? You're not really being this fucking stupid, are you?'

'Fucking stupid is as fucking stupid does,' Goody replied, stumping even me for words.

'You can't get away!' Weasel screamed at us, making several of the girls around me cry. 'You touch that money and you'll double your sentence.'

'Bullshit,' Goody shouted back.

'At the moment we can do you for attempted armed robbery and false imprisonment. You touch so much as 5p of that money and we'll have you on the full charge.'

'Fucking bullshit!' Goody shouted again.

The girl to my front gave a little worried whimper as our exchanges grew more heated, and I clutched her to me tighter still.

'Just back off, just back the fuck off. We don't want anyone hurt, but we're going to that office.'

'You're sunk, Milo. You just sunk yourself.'

We reached the end of the aisle and had to manoeuvre our way through the last narrow checkout slip to reach the office on the other side. I had to let several of the girls go ahead of me but kept a close hold on the one immediately shielding me as I quick-stepped through past the till. Once on the other side I clustered all the girls around me again and waited for Goody to catch up. Weasel, Blakey and half a dozen cops crossed over a few tills up and took up positions ten yards off.

'Duncan, get the door.'

Duncan looked at Weasel for divine inspiration, but Weasel just told him to do as I said.

'Go ahead, then. You get the money if you want, but you're not going anywhere with it,' he told us, then whispered something to one of the firearms boys and they rushed off to check out whatever it was he'd just told them to check out.

Duncan opened the door and we all backed inside the office.

'Well done, everybody,' I said, shutting the door behind us and patting my little mate on the arse by way of a thank you. I stationed half a dozen of the girls up by the door and half a dozen up by the window, then invited Duncan to do the honours. Duncan put his key in the lock and twisted the handle and a sudden deafening alarm went off the moment he yanked it open.

'I thought we got that switched off,' Goody pondered.

'There are several alarms that have to be deactivated before you can open the safe. You only deactivated one,' Duncan told us.

'That little rat. So even if it hadn't been on a timelock, we would've still set off the alarm?' I asked and Duncan told me that was right. Norris? What a twat!

'So why didn't you tell us about it, you fucking arsehole?' Goody demanded to know.

'Yeah, what do you think that ten grand was for?' I put to him, grabbing the girls' attention. Duncan grimaced and flinched and tried to wriggle out of it, but I pressed him into (quietly) admitting that he would've deactivated the other alarm this morning if the police hadn't shown up.

'I tell you honestly – people, they're such unreliable cunts,' I told Goody. 'OK, let's get this turned off now, please. It's doing my head in.'

Duncan said he couldn't, so I poked my head out the door and told Weasel to get it killed. Weasel took his fingers out of his ears long enough to hear me, and three minutes later we had blissful silence again. By this time we'd dragged all the money out on to the floor in front of us and we were handling it with wonder.

'Look at it all,' Goody gasped. 'There must be millions.' Silly cunt.

'We should count it,' I suggested, but Duncan said there was no need and went through a few printouts for us and told us exactly how much was there.

'Three hundred and forty-six thousand, four hundred and fifty-six pounds. About ten thousand of that is made up of coins.'

'Fucking hell, Milo, we would've been rich,' Goody said, pawing through bundles of notes. 'Look at that. Look, it's as thick as a book, only a book made of money,' he said, holding up a wedge for me to see. 'Three hundred and forty grand – what's that come to each?'

We all stood around in silence trying to work it out before one of the girls by the window told us it was about forty-three grand each ('Forty-two thousand, minus Mr Bramble's cut,' she added, looking Duncan square in the eye and endearing herself to me no end).

'Forty thousand quid,' Goody muttered to himself, sounding almost heartbroken. 'What a bastard! What a real bastard!'

I picked out what would've been my forty-three grand and stacked it up a dozen different ways to see which way made it look the most, then I stood back and admired it. It was beautiful. So beautiful, in fact, that I'd almost be loath to spend any of it had I got away with it for fear of detracting from its beauty. I admired it some more, then added an extra two-grand bundle of twenties to it when Goody wasn't looking. Then slipped another into my pocket.

Well, where was the harm in it?

If Weasel was right and we didn't manage to get away, it wouldn't make any difference how many extra bundles I gave myself, so in that respect who was I ripping off? With this in mind I slipped another one into my pocket, then gave one to Goody and told him to keep it to himself, then pocketed two more while he was stuffing his one down his trousers.

'Cheers, Milo,' Goody winked. 'You're a star.'

'No problem,' I replied, then suggested we took a couple more, just for the road. 'Well, they don't know how much is here, do they? They only think it's a hundred and twenty.'

Goody thought on this long and hard for almost a quarter of a second before we both started stuffing bundle upon bundle down our trousers.

'There really is no honour among thieves, is there?' Duncan tutted, so I gave him two grand and told him to shut up.

'I thought you said ten grand,' he complained quietly.

'You ungrateful old crook. You want it or not?' I replied. Duncan took the money and stuffed it in his pocket when he thought no one was looking. I was suddenly in a pretty generous mood, so I then gave each of the girls £250 and told them to hide it down their knickers. All but two of them took it.

'No one will ever find out,' the others badgered the abstainers. 'Not if we all take it,' and this proved enough to convert one of the doubters. I handed her a bundle of notes and told the last of them that she was spoiling it for the rest of them.

'If you don't take the money, the others can't, and how do you think that'll go down with your friends?' I asked her

'I don't care. It's wrong,' she insisted, looking around an office jam packed with people stuffing money down their pants.

'No one will ever know,' one of her mates told her.

'I'll know,' she replied, then begged the others not to take any of the money. 'Please, think about what you're doing.'

'Julie, have you even seen what we're charging for Head & Shoulders these days?' my friend with the little arse pointed out as she padded out her bra with twenties.

'Take the money,' I absolutely insisted, handing Julie her £250. 'Chuck it away or give it to charity when you get out of here if you like, just fucking take it and stop messing it up for everyone else.'

Julie reluctantly took the cash and put it into her pocket, though I could tell it wouldn't stay in there for long. Jesus, what was it with some people?

Goody had pocketed an extra ten grand while I had God knows how much tucked away in my shirt. We were just slipping the rest into shopping baskets to take back when Duncan asked us what we were doing.

'We're taking the money back for the lads,' I told him, wondering what he was getting at.

'But what good will it do you? What good will any of that money in your shirt do you? You're caught.'

'Hey, I ain't caught yet,' I told him, tucking one last extra bundle into my sock.

The lads were well impressed with the haul of three hundred-plus grand in used notes we'd found in the safe. We'd left behind the coins simply because they were too bulky and heavy to take. If there'd been no police about we would've had them away, but our break for freedom was going to be hard enough as it was without handicapping ourselves heavier than thoroughbreds entered in a donkey derby.

'Fucking hell, Milo, three hundred grand,' Bob said, smelling the notes and giggling like a little schoolgirl. 'I mean, fucking hell!'

'Fat lotta fukkin' good that duzzus, tho',' Jimbo pointed out.

We were all sat around a table at the front of the canteen, counting through the money while the staff watched with salivating mouths.

'There you go, not so stupid now, are we?' Norris declared triumphantly, waving a big bundle of notes at his former work colleagues as the sound of police helicopters motoring around overhead rattled through the building.

'How much do we get each, Milo?' Parky asked, but Jimbo disturbed my concentration as I tried to work it out.

'Wassa point?'

'Don't you want yours, then, Jimbo?' Parky asked, sensing a greater share of the pot.

'Ah just carn't see the point in takin' it, that's all. We ain't goin' nowhere.'

'Hey, don't go counting your chickens before they're nicked,' Goody advised him sagely.

'No, no, it's his decision, and if he don't want to take none then I respect him for that,' Parky said, licking his lips and piling up a big load of bundles in front of him.

'Not so fast, Mr P. Let's give him a chance to make up his mind properly,' I told him.

'But he already said he didn't want any,' Parky argued, so I double-checked with Jimbo to see if this was his final decision.

'Is it? Jimbo, you don't want your share?'

Jimbo thought about it, then conceded it didn't make a difference one way or another.

'Oh you bastard!' Parky spat in disgust.

'If only to stop this greedy cun' geddin' his hands on it, then,' Jimbo shouted, making everyone except Parky laugh.

'So it's seven ways,' Bob said, starting to go through it.

'Eight,' I reminded them all.

'Eight!' everyone exclaimed.

'What about Mr D?'

'You can't be serious,' Parky objected.

'Mr D is still a part of this gang and as such he gets a cut.'

'Mr D isn't here any more, and he'd probably be the first to say how glad he was about that. I say fuck him, we divide up the money on the basis of who's still here.'

'Just because Mr D is outside, it doesn't mean he's not working for us. He's exposing himself to all sorts of risks trying to find us a way out of here, so I say he gets his share. Anyone object?'

No one said nothing, so I started bundling up Patsy's share.

'You know, I can't believe you blokes. We went into this thing on the understanding that we split everything equally, yet at the first sign of cash you're already stabbing each other in the back,' I lectured them, shaking my head but doing it slowly so as not to shake any of the extra bundles out from under my shirt. Goody just stared at the wall.

'Here, do I still get my expenses back?' Bob suddenly remembered.

'Jesus, Bob, you've got thirty-seven grand there already. Don't you think you're being a bit greedy?' But Bob wasn't being shook off this easily.

'Fuck that, Milo. You said I'd get it back, me and Jimbo,' he demanded.

'Fine, fine. Well, the split's been made now. I'll have to give it to you out of my own cut,' I moaned, then gave him a bundle off the top of Norris's pile when neither of them was looking. 'Happy now?'

'That's odd,' Norris started, staring at his pile, but I told him whatever it was he could keep it to himself. I had enough on my plate already, 'thank you very much'.

'Nice,' Jimbo muttered, stroking his dough. 'But it don' make no difference, we're still fucked.'

'Yeah, but at least we'll go to prison rich men,' Parky smiled, as if this meant anything. 'I've never been a rich man before, and I don't think I'm going to get too many opportunities in the future, so it'll be nice to look back on this when I'm old and grey and say I had forty grand on the hip once.'

'When you're old and still wearing grey, you mean?' someone rather unsportingly pointed out, pouring cold water on Parky's little fantasy.

'Well, I don't know,' I mused. 'At the risk of sounding a little corny, I've got a plan.'

'A plan?' everyone said.

'I wish you had a fucking tunnel,' Norris muttered.

'What is it, Milo? How are we getting out of here?' they all clambered to know, so I told them to belt up and listen.

'First of all, we ain't going to need these fucking things any more,' I said and peeled off my ski mask.

The lads looked at me a little unsure and Goody asked if I knew what I was doing. 'Yes, I do. They're slightly redundant when the Old Bill already knows your name and address, so we might as well get rid of them.'

'But they know who you are. They don't know who we are,' Goody told me.

'Look, you think they won't know all of you within an hour of us getting out, if we get out? Man, we're clocked. All we can do now is run. Besides, for my plan to work, we've got to ditch the masks anyway.'

Still the other six stared at me warily before Goody

followed suit and pulled his woollen hood off over his head, gasping with relief as he rubbed his red sweaty face. One by one the rest of the lads unmasked until the only one left was Bob.

'Come on, Bob. Get it off.'

Bob wobbled and wavered, conscious of the fact that the whole of the canteen had been fixated at the sight of us finally revealing our faces, and he turned around to them and told them all to close their eyes. We laughed at this and told him he wasn't getting his cock out, for fuck's sake; just pull it off.

'Come on, Bob. Don' be shy,' Jimbo urged him, and Bob finally threw his mask on the table.

'This better be one shitter of a plan,' Bob warned me.

'It is, don't worry,' I reassured him, then suddenly went white. 'Oh fuck! Oh shit, I got it wrong. Quick, put your masks back on!'

Bob snatched his cold, wet woollen hood back up and pulled it on in a total panic while me and the boys all stood around and laughed at him some more.

'Fucking idiot.'

Plan 8

22

I outlined the plan to everyone and made sure I collected the last of the ammunition. We'd got away without killing anybody so far only by the skin of our *schnutts* and I planned to keep it that way – whatever happened to us. There were a few objections, and I had to have a stand-up blazing row with Parky before he agreed to hand over the last of his shells, but finally we were an unarmed gang once again.

Well, almost. One of us was still armed.

I found some packing tape and we started taping our money to our bodies. I did this away from the rest of them for fear they might clock just how little of me they could see after I'd taped my share on to my body. Arms, legs and back all had to be used, and after I'd taped on Patsy's share too I looked like some kid on work experience at the Royal Mint.

'Milo, do we not want to wait until night to do this? You know, these plans are traditionally better in the dark,' Goody pointed out.

'Fuck me, Goody, that's another nine or ten hours away. I can't sit in here with this lot another nine or ten hours,' I replied.

'Would you rather sit in a cell for another twenty years?'

'Goody, mate, the numbers out there are only going to grow. We can't sit around for nine or ten hours while they fill in every chink of light and the SAS fill their sights with our brains. We have to get out of here, and we have to do it now. I ain't fucking waiting around for another half a day with this lot in here, that lot out there and Patsy pissing himself halfway up the road. How long do you think he's going to hang around for us?'

'Yeah, you're right, I guess.'

'No, I'm not. That's just the fucking problem. I don't know if I'm right. And I don't know if I'm wrong. I'm just keeping my fingers crossed and hoping for the best.'

Goody accepted this with a philosophical smile and got on with his preparations, though one bloke who was absolutely determined not to be philosophical about this whatsoever was Norris.

'Are you absolutely sure this plan is going to work?' he asked once I was all dressed again.

'No,' I told him.

'But you think there's a good chance of it working?'

'No,' I told him again.

'Yeah, but there's a chance, a fair chance?'

'No.'

'Fifty–fifty, then?'

'I can't see you getting those odds anywhere.'

'Sixty–forty?'

'I doubt it.'

'Seventy–twenty then?' Stephen Hawkings then asked.

'I don't know what you want from me, Norris, but I haven't got it.'

'But we have got a chance, though, haven't we?'

'No. We've got a possibility at the absolute outside. A very, very slim possibility, next to zero.'

'Then why are we doing this?'

'Because a possibility's better than a certainty. And that's all we've got at the moment.'

Norris pulled his hair out some more and tried to shake me down for reassurances until he got on my tits so much that I decided, what the fuck, he could have them.

'All right, all right, you're right, Norris. There's a very good chance of us getting away. A very, very good chance. This is the last thing they'll be expecting, so they won't know we're gone until we're gone.'

'Really?' he pleaded.

'If you like.'

I left Norris to his fingernails and tried my new shelf stacker's overalls on for size. They felt tight around my chest and sides where I had the bulk of my cash taped to and I tried jogging on the spot to see if any of it came loose. The cash stayed where it was, helped by the tightness of the overalls, but the sticky tape played merry fucking havoc with my body hair. I wasn't looking forward to unsticking that lot.

The only part of the plan I'd dropped was the idea of making some shelf stackers dress in our combats. It was too much of a cuntish thing to do. Sure, they might act as a decoy to grab the Old Bill's eyes while we made a break for it, but in doing so there was also a danger they might get shot, and that wasn't something I thought I could live with, so I booted that particular idea into touch.

'How do I look?' Parky asked, modelling this season's megastore overalls.

'Like you were born to work here?' I told him.

Jimbo and Bob came and told me they'd finished the bomb and asked if I wanted to have a look at it. I told them I'd be delighted to, and we all went down the short corridor to the rear of the loading bay to examine what they'd put together.

The 'bomb' was a trolley loaded with Calor gas bottles.

They'd wrapped them up with a few miles of tape, connected all the valves with a dozen different wires and had them feeding into a lunch box which contained something that looked, and rather suspiciously smelled, like a big dollop of marzipan.

'It's meant to be plastique,' Bob told me. 'Looks all right, though, doesn't it?'

'Yeah, not bad. It'll do the job, I suppose.'

Of course, our 'bomb' had about as much chance of exploding as my socks did. But then, it wasn't meant to. It was just a bluff, same as every other part of this stupid robbery; just a big dumb empty bluff; something to get our guests' minds and legs moving and create enough panic and confusion once we were all outside so that a few of us could slip through the lines in the mêlée. And that was the Plan, the much-hyped Plan No. 8; shit everyone up and get them to charge about outside like headless chickens in the hope that this mass stampede might create a window of a few seconds for me – I mean, for us – to get beyond the first line of the police and make for the motors.

Didn't sound too promising, did it? No, but then it was the best of a bad bunch of not-very-good ideas and we were all out of options.

'Hey, it'd be good if this place was built on an old castle and there was like a secret passageway out of here or something, wouldn't it?' Jacko said helpfully.

'Man, I hope they don't put us in the same cell together,' Parky replied for all of us.

I went upstairs one last time and phoned Patsy to make sure he and, most important, the motors were still where he claimed them to be. It would be typical of my luck right now to bust out and get all the way clear only to find Patsy had lost his bottle and put his foot down before we were halfway across the waste ground.

'I'm here, Milo,' he told me all jittery.

'OK, then. We're coming, and we're going to be coming fast, so engines running and doors open as soon as you see us make our move.'

'How will I know when you make your move?' he asked.

'Believe me, you'll know.'

I rang off, slipped the phone into my back pocket and took a moment to say a little prayer. I didn't know why I did this. I wasn't a staunch believer in God, I didn't go to church or play with the rector's organ on Sundays or nothing, but by that same token I didn't disbelieve. I mean, who knows how these things work? Cleverer men than me hadn't figured it out, so who was I to vote one way or the other for sure? Agnostic, I believe they call it. Hedging my bets would probably be a more accurate way of describing myself. Either way, I needed all the favours I could call in if I was ever going to get out of this.

'Help me out of this one, God, and I swear I'll never steal again. Never, not even a shirt button. Nothing. Not even a tenner off an old lady, like that one I could've when I got out of Brixton, you remember? I could've had it as well, you know that. But I didn't. That was like a test or something you set up, and I passed it with flying colours. Well, test me again, test me all you like, just give me a chance to prove myself to you again. Please, let me get away with this seventy grand and I'll never nick again. I'll even give a couple of quid to charity or the church or something, I don't know. I'll have to have a think about it. So, go on, please, let me get away.'

I looked out across the sea of flashing lights one last time and crossed my thumping heart with my fingers, the same as they did on *The Godfather*, then went and talked to our guests.

'OK, as most of you are aware, the Old Bill are outside and at the moment we are all nicked.' The staff eyed the seven of us at the front of the canteen with trepidation. I could see the mounting worry in each of their eyes as they began to realise what a truly desperate pickle we were in. 'Each of us is facing a minimum of twenty years, and that's not something any of us fancy, so we've decided to make a break for it . . . or at least, die trying.'

A wave of panic rippled over the canteen when I said this, and I had to tell them to shut up five or six times before I could finally speak again.

'OK, now listen up. Quiet and listen: this is something you need to hear. Just listen to what I'm saying and you'll probably be OK. Now, outside in the loading bay we've rigged up a bomb . . .'

Mass pandemonium broke out as girls screamed, blokes jumped up and down, old ladies faded away like flies . . .

'Everyone sit back down and shut the fuck up, I'm try-ing to save your lives.'

Off to my left, I heard Goody mutter in Bob's ear, 'What a hero!'

'He's going to blow us up. He's going to blow us up,' one of the girls was screaming uncontrollably, and I knew I had to do something to get them to hear me out, so I fired a shot into the ceiling, whipping everyone up into an even bigger frenzy.

'Shut up!' I shouted at them. 'Shut up or I really will just blow you all up.' This got their attention and half of them shushed the other half quiet so that I could finally spell it out to them. 'Right, now fucking listen this time. Don't worry. You'll all get a chance to panic, but not until I tell you to, OK? Right, now, we've made a bomb using Calor gas bottles and a little bit of plastique we brought with us to blow the safe.' Duncan put his hand up, but I ignored him and carried on. 'Now, our plan is to let you all go, then blow up the supermarket behind you and hopefully escape in the confusion. Now – and listen closely because this is where you all come in – we're going to detonate the bomb as we're letting you go. None of you will be directly near it when it goes off, but it's a big fucking bomb so you'll need to get clear of the place as fast as you can. Dawdlers will get wounded, maybe even killed, so as soon as you're clear of the loading bay, you run like greased lightning and you'll be OK.'

More panic, more wobbles, particularly from the old ladies who didn't look too nimble on their plates.

'The police will try and hold you back and prevent you from getting clear. This is because they don't know about the bomb, but you can't let them hold you back, otherwise you're in big trouble. Just scream your guts out and warn them about what's going to happen and try and get as far away from the supermarket as possible.'

'This is madness,' Mike declared. 'You can't do this.'

'Hey, you don't like it, why don't you go and live in Russia?' Goody told him.

'Listen to us, just listen to us. You'll all be OK. Just run fast as soon as you get outside and you'll probably be fine.'

Lots and lots of panic; people jumping to their feet, blokes shouting at us, girls howling, old ladies praying, Duncan eyeing me very suspiciously; it was going off in all directions.

'I'd better go and talk to Weasel one last time, prime him that we're coming out. You keep this lot simmering,' I told Goody, slipping out of my supermarket overalls and getting into my hood and combats again.

I walked through the loading bay, waving my little white flag, and poked my head out into the car park. The Old Bill were still there. How disappointing.

'Is that you, Milo?' Weasel shouted at me through his foghorn. I located him in the mill and gave him a wave to show that it was. I stepped off the loading bay step and out into the car park, and I could feel a dozen gun sights trained all over my body. I gave my flag another little wave to make sure everyone had seen it, then pulled up sharply. Oh my God, there with Weasel . . . what the fuck? That low-down dirty bastard!

Weasel handed the foghorn to Alice and showed her how to use it, then stepped back and let her say what they'd brought her here to say.

'Darren? Darren, is that really you?'

I said nothing. I just stared back in disbelief, then slowly nodded.

'Take the mask off, Darren, please. I need to see that it's you.'

'No,' I told her. 'I can't.'

'Why not? If we know who you are, why can't you take the mask off?'

'I can't let you see me like this, not like this, Alice. I'm not Darren any more, he's long gone. I'm just Milo now,' I told her deeply. This was actually a load of bullshit. The real reason I didn't want to take off the mask was because I didn't want every copper in the car park knowing what I looked like when I tried to make a break for it. Weasel and a couple of others knew, but to the majority I was still rel- atively faceless, so I shielded my face and my intentions behind a load of profound gobbledygook.

'Why have you done this, Darren?'

'I don't know,' I replied, and at that precise moment in time I really didn't. 'Why not?' I shrugged. The coppers around me didn't like this answer, and I could sense I was losing the audience.

'Why not? Darren, when are you going to fucking learn?'

'Oh don't start all that again.'

'What's the matter with you, Darren? Are you an idiot or something? Why can't you just grow up, you pathetic little boy?' Weasel tried wrestling the foghorn off Alice, but she held him at arm's length long enough to tell me I was a loser as well.

'Hey, why did you even come down here, Alice? What's my life got to do with you, anyway? Shouldn't you be at home with McCann? He'll be wanting his tea about now,' I shouted back bitterly. Alice yelled some reply, but I couldn't hear her, so I told Weasel to give her back the foghorn. Inspector Blakey gave him a few prods as well, and reluctantly he let go of his favourite toy.

'Is that what this is all about, me marrying Brian?'

'No. It's got nothing to do with you. The world don't revolve around you, you know?' – though to be honest, mine did.

'Just let it go, Darren. Move on and sort yourself out, for fuck's sake, before you waste your entire life.'

'I did. Last time I went away I swore to you that it would be the last time, that I'd go straight from now on and I meant it,' I told her, then realised how daft this sounded. 'Admittedly, things haven't worked out so well for me recently . . .'

'Look, I haven't come down here to argue with you or wash our dirty linen in public.'

'Then why did you come? We never got to that.'

'Terry brought me down here. He thought I might be able to talk some sense into you, get you to let those people go.'

'I will,' I reassured her.

'No, I don't mean in three days' time or whenever you finally decide you've had enough playing the big man. I mean now. Let them go now before something happens that you can't undo.' Alice let this hang in the wind for a moment, and the fifty of us stood in complete silence while we waited for her next words. 'Let them go, Darren, and give yourself up.'

'OK, I will. I'll let them all go in a minute,' I conceded.

'Will you come and visit me after we're all done in here?' I asked hopefully.

There was a suspiciously long pause before Alice told me that she would. Proof positive, if ever I needed it, that people will say anything to get you to throw in your advantage. What a bitch!

'I'm going to go and let them all go now, OK, so hold your fire everyone,' I told them and made to go back inside. I took one last long look at Alice and realised that, no matter what happened, this was more than likely the last time I'd ever see her. It made me so sad to know this. Up until yesterday there was still a chance, the briefest tiniest little chance, even smaller than the chance I had of getting out of here, that she might've broken up with McCann somewhere down the road and taken me back. I would've welcomed her with open arms, her and her son, and we could've lived as a normal family for the rest of our lives. This was the fantasy I'd clung to despite all I'd said and done over the last few months. This was that tiny private little dream I comforted myself with in the middle of my sleepless nights. This was my hope – and now even this was gone. I looked at her for the longest possible moment. Her face was stern, her arms crossed in that oh–so–familiar way they always were when she was disappointed with me and her hair was flapping in the breeze. She looked absolutely beautiful. My God, how had I let something that special get away from me? What the fuck was wrong with me? I was almost afraid to turn my eyes from her, because I knew they'd never fall on her again, but eventually I did. I turned away, climbed up the steps to the loading bay and headed inside, all the time with Weasel's voice at my back.

'Nice and slowly, do you hear me? Bring them out nice and slowly.'

Milo's run 23

I dumped my mask and combat jacket once and for all and slipped back into my supermarket togs. I pulled up the collar like Humphrey Bogart then pulled it back down when I saw that I resembled a supermarket worker trying to look like Humphrey Bogart (or Eric Cantona) and that, I figured, was more likely to draw attention to me than just trying to wear my overalls like everyone else.

I went into the canteen, told Goody to turn his collar down, then addressed our guests for one last time.

'OK, we're going to go now. No pushing, shoving or running until you get outside, otherwise we might end up blowing it early. We're going to file you out into the loading bay, then when I say "go", you go and go as fast as you can. Everyone clear?'

Most people said they were, but there was one tear-streaked lad who just kept saying over and over again, 'Don't do it,' making Bob chuckle.

'OK, on your feet and let's make our way to the loading bay.'

I turned to the lads and made sure we were all singing from the same song sheet. 'Don't let them run out in dribs and drabs. They all have to leg-it together, otherwise this won't work.' The lads nodded their heads like they understood, so I wished them all the best of luck and pulled Norris aside. 'You know where we're going once we get out of the supermarket?'

'Thailand?' he speculated.

'One step at a time, Norris. No, I mean do you know which direction we're running to when we get outside?'

'Yeah, over the waste ground, back towards the parade of shops,' he confirmed.

'No, we're not. That's just what I told them to send them off as decoys. We're actually going the other way, left, down to the motorway. That's where Patsy has the motors,' I lied.

'Oh right. Cheers, mate,' Norris said, giving me a grateful dig in the ribs, then he smiled sadistically. 'None of them know you're stitching them up?'

'No, they're wankers,' I told him, then felt an enormous glow all over. How very satisfying.

We herded the staff down the short corridor to the loading bay, keeping them bunched up together as densely as possible. Bob was at the head of the line (well, a couple of bodies back, keeping a firm grip on the shirts of the guys in front), waiting for the signal, while I'd squirrelled myself in among the throng about two-thirds of the way back. I figured this was the best place to be when the stampede started, not at the front or back, where I might get grabbed, but somewhere in the middle so that I'd emerge at that optimum moment when the thin blue line was stretched to overwhelmed by the surge of bodies. At least, this was my thinking on the matter. Having never done anything like this before, I was no expert; I just had to hope luck was on my side.

Luck, surprise and a mountain of determination, and I might just get through.

'Everyone ready?' I shouted when we were all in position. It was hard to make myself heard among so many gibbering and jabbering bodies, but the lads finally answered me the third time round.

'Ready!' Parky shouted from behind us somewhere.

'Ready!' Goody shouted from up front.

'Ready!' Bob called back.

'Ready!' Norris squawked from up ahead.

'Yeah, yeah, yeah, ready!' Jacko told us close by, not sounding very ready at all.

'Weddee!' Jimbo confirmed.

'Best of luck, then, fellers. OK, Jacko, trigger the bomb the moment we're all outside,' I told him.

'What? Oh right, yeah,' he suddenly remembered.

Lots of luck, Jacko.

'OK, then. let's GO, GO, GO!'

The corridor immediately condensed and I was crushed front and back as a hundred individuals started fighting to pass through the tiny tight bottleneck. I tried to move my feet, but the feet of the blokes in front were still there. I tried to push back to give myself some room to manoeuvre, but the force behind the swell was too great and after only a few seconds I found it difficult to breath. 'Back off, back off,' I croaked, but the panic had set in and people were almost climbing over each other to get a few feet closer to the outside world.

'Back off . . .'

Crushing, screaming, panicking, trampling, punching, clawing, crawling, but none of us making it any nearer to daylight. I tried to calm everyone's fears and restore some order, but I had neither the space nor the strength. I tried to look around, but all I could see were shapes in the darkness. It was pandemonium at its worst.

'Stop . . .'

A hundred people were crushing each other to death in here, and there was nothing I could do about it. More to the point, a hundred people were crushing each other to death in here, and it was all my fault. Why hadn't I seen this? 'Stop! Stop! There ain't no bomb,' I tried to yell, but I had the breath squashed out of me. I'd spent so much time pre-occupied with my own flight that I hadn't seen the dangers of panicking this many people in this small a space, and now it was too late. We were all going to die; crushed, suffocated, trampled. After all I'd done to ensure the safety of our guests, I'd gone and done it myself in one foul swoop on a scale all the lads put together couldn't have managed.

Forget twenty years, I'd be answering for this one for all eternity.

If I was lucky, if I was really, really fortunate, I'd be one of the ones to die. There was no way I could look anyone in the eye again after this.

Just when I was starting to give up all hope, the pressure suddenly eased in front of us and we all surged forward. This movement came as such a surprise that several of us almost went over on to our faces. In fact, the girl next to me did go down, and I had to grab her and drag her back up to her feet to stop her from being walked over.

More forward movement and more room to step; we were really starting to move now and daylight was rapidly approaching. Guys were hanging on my shoulders and step-ping on my heels behind me, but I was able to keep pace with the crowd. The nearer I got to the outside, the louder the cries were from out there.

'There's a bomb! There's a bomb!'

'Stop where you are!'

'Grab him!'

'Stop them!'

'There's a bomb!'

'Everyone back!'

The guys in front of me suddenly disappeared off the edge of the loading bay and, for the briefest of seconds, I was able to view the chaos I'd created. The quiet, ordered

lines of uniformed and CID officers had vanished under a
tidal wave of shelf stackers. People were fleeing in all directions, rat-running, climbing over cars, grappling with the
Old Bill, screaming in their ears. It was absolute bedlam.
Quite a few had made it past the lines too, and I spotted at
least a dozen supermarket uniforms clambering up the grass
banks towards the main road. This restored my battered
confidence, and I hit the ground running and went full tilt
off to the right.

'There's a bomb. It's going to blow,' I screamed as I ran,
frantically waving the Old Bill away. 'Get clear, run for your
lives.'

I dodged a couple of coppers who tried to stop me in
my tracks and sidestepped another who settled for rugby-
tackling the bloke next to me. I quickened my feet and
looked towards where I wanted to go. There was a large
concentration of Old Bill off to the left but a relatively clear
run hard against the supermarket wall, so I darted down this
route and nipped and tucked between cars and vans as I
closed in on the embankment. Suddenly, I ran straight into
some painfully young copper hiding behind an ambulance.
He looked as startled as I did by my unexpected appearance, but not half as startled as he looked when I smashed
him in the face and yelled at him, 'There's a bomb,' though
he was suddenly too preoccupied holding his nose in place
to hear me.

I scrambled over the bonnet of a police car to avoid a
ruckus at the boot end and stayed at arm's length of several
uniforms by leaping from roof to roof of two more motors
before hitting the car park again. There were coppers everywhere, some running, others waving guns, but most were
standing their ground and trying to grab as many people as
they could as we all flew past. It was like one almighty game
of British Bulldog, only much more fraught and not half as
much fun. Off to my right, someone suddenly exploded

with notes and I just turned to see Jacko rolling around on the floor with two coppers on top of him. His top had come open when he'd been grappled to the ground, and scores upon scores were fluttering across the car park tarmac.

This got everyone's attention.

'He's one of them,' one of the Old Bill shouted.

'No, let me go, there's a bomb . . .' Jacko was yelling until he disappeared under an avalanche of coppers. I turned away and used the commotion as best I could to slip past a few more plod before they woke up to what was actually happening.

Go on, go on, keeping running, I pushed myself. Don't stop for anything. Just keep on moving.

I tried to run and keep my head low at the same time, though it was difficult to slump the shoulders with all my money taped up all over me.

'Stop! Just stop there, sir,' someone was shouting close by, while the foghorn was appealing for calm and ordering everyone to stop right where they were.

Out of the corner of my eye I saw some determined young flatfoot closing in on me like a guided missile. He seemed to have only eyes for me and trailed me around and over the labyrinth of motors until he was nearly on my arse.

'Stop right there, you bastard,' he was shouting at me, and I wondered what it was he knew. I stared over my shoulder at him in horror as he closed to within a couple of arms' lengths of me and even reached for my gun when, miracle upon miracle, some panic-stricken shelf stacker charged blindly out of left field and smacked right into him. There was a sickening christening of heads and both went down on to their knees. Neither looked like they'd be getting up again any time soon, and I was happy and relieved to show them both a clean pair of heels.

'Don't let any of them get away. Stop them all!' the

foghorn was yelling, though I was through the worst of it by this time. I reached the corner of the supermarket and made the short sprint the last twenty feet to the bottom of the steep grass embankment. To my left, Parky was already halfway up, while Goody and Jimbo were just emerging from the mayhem behind us. There was no sign of Bob or Norris, though I hadn't expected to see the latter.

I raced on to the short slope and scrambled up on my hands and knees. It was dry and dusty and I slipped down two feet for every five I climbed. Parky seemed to be having the same problem, despite almost being at the top, though Goody and his all–fucking–terrain army boots made short work of his climb.

'Come on, get up there!' I screamed at myself, as great clumps of grass came away in my hands. Before I was even halfway up I was super–fucked and ready to slide back down on my face and look for another way up, but the sounds of a dozen size tens closing in fast gave me the extra impetus I needed to claw my way to the top.

Goody grabbed my hand and hauled me up the last few feet, and I looked back down the slope and saw at least half a dozen coppers scrambling up as we had. There were also a couple of genuine shelf stackers who'd taken it on themselves to follow us, so I kicked out at one of them and sent him tumbling back down, taking out some copper in the process.

I was just about to leg it when I clocked someone else emerging from the scrum, shouting and pleading with me to wait. It was Norris. The suspicious bastard must've been watching which way I ran and followed me.

'Fuck him,' I told Goody. 'Let's go.' I forced my exhausted body onwards, and the four of us started across the waste ground. There was no fence separating the car park from the waste ground – I guess they thought the embankment would tell shoppers all they needed to know – but there was an old wooden job right over the other side of it. If Patsy hadn't done as I'd asked him to and knocked a few holes in it, we'd be in all sorts of schtuck when we reached it.

There were maybe nine of us running across the waste ground in total. Four of us were trying to get to Patsy and the motors, three of us were trying to stop four of us from reaching Patsy and the motors, and two of us thought the supermarket was going blow up. Off to my left, maybe a hundred yards away, was the main road. There were police cars, ambulances and even a couple of fire engines cluttering up the whole drag.

I wondered what things would look like once we'd got to the parade.

Patsy had promised there weren't that many Old Bill up there, and I hoped he was right. Of those that were there, if my luck held out, they might only be specials (part-time coppers), drafted in to redirect the traffic and keep the nosy locals at bay. All the CID and armed boys should be concentrated back at the supermarket, where they were expecting the action to be, in which case I might be able to safely wave the hobby bobbies aside with my shooter without too much fear of getting plugged. The theory was sound, but then so was the idea behind robbing this fucking supermarket, and look where that had got me: running for my life across some abandoned pikeys' encampment with half the county's constabulary after me. Man, if I could just get out of this one, that really would be it for me. I know I've said this before and no one believed me then, but I'll say it again: sprinting across this broken, rutted and overgrown field with seventy grand in cash taped to me body, an illegal handgun in my waistband and three coppers hot on my heels, I'd finally learned my lesson.

'Stop right there!' the police were taking turns to shout. 'Stop, police.'

Well, duh.

One of them even tried, 'Stop or we'll shoot,' but I paid this no attention. They didn't look like firearms officers to me, though even if they were I knew enough to know that they weren't allowed to shoot people in the back, not even suspects. The genuine shelf stackers didn't know this, though, and they pulled up sharply and slung their hands in the air. The first cop to reach them chained them together like the Defiant Ones, then leaned on them to get his breath back. This left just two after me, Goody, Parky and Jimbo. I thought about turning around and firing over their heads, just to make them stop chasing us, but then it occurred to me that this would tip our hand. At the moment, the Old Bill behind us didn't know us from every other shelf stacker they'd been ordered to stop. If they did, we would've had more than just the three up our arses . . . I mean, eight. Fuck, where had they come from? Five more uniforms popped up from nowhere to help with the chase, and I couldn't help wondering if something – or someone – had tipped them off.

My chest was burning and I had a stitch in my side so painful that I wondered if maybe I'd been shot in the back after all. I clutched at my side and soldiered on as best I could, but all too soon I had next to no strength left in my legs. I wobbled and stumbled across the hard ground, only too conscious of the fact that one trip or ankle twist now would cost me twenty years.

Keep on going. Keep on running. You're fucked now, but it will be worth it if you get to those motors, so find the strength. These were the things I repeated in my mind over and over again as I mopped the sweat from my brow and scoured the approaching fence for holes.

Run, run, run. Come on, Milo, run.

I was oblivious to everyone else except myself, the field and the coppers behind us. To me, this was all the world that mattered for the moment, though my blinkers were ripped from my head a moment later with what happened next.

'Grab him! Grab him!' someone was shouting behind me. A sudden anguished shriek followed by a cry for ''elwp!' made my heart miss a thud. Oh Jesus, they'd bagged Jimbo. He'd been the furthest back of the four of us and trailing quite badly. I turned around just in time to see four of the chasing pack pin him to the ground and slap the cuffs on him.

'Milo, 'elwp me!'

It pained me to hear him cry after me like this. I hadn't known him very long, only since we'd come together to do this job, but I'd definitely taken to him. Of the eight of us (myself and Patsy excluded, I guess) he'd shown more brains and common-sense than the rest of the gang put together. Mouth full of marbles or no mouth full of marbles, I'd been glad to have him on the team, but now he was gone, and there was nothing any of us could do about it. At least he took four coppers with him, so that was something.

This left just three Plod in the chase. One for me, Goody and Parky.

We reached a broken concrete floor (all that was left of the old factory) and made better time across it than we had done across the uneven field. Unfortunately, our pursuers then reached it too and gave themselves the same break so that we were all square again.

'Come back here you little bastards,' one of them kept shouting after us. 'You'll be in big fucking trouble if you don't stop,' he promised.

'There's a bomb,' Goody yelled back, but we were so far from the supermarket now that the place could've had a hundred bombs in it and we would've probably all been all right.

The fence was close, probably only another hundred yards or so, so I ran my eyes along the length and saw there, just in the corner, a few boards had been kicked out. I pointed my feet at the gap and milked myself for every last ounce of strength I had as I went all out for freedom. I left the concrete floor and leaped and scrambled with everything I had over the tinder-dry scrub, stubbing my feet and catching my trousers as I ran.

Unfortunately, it didn't look like I had enough. Plod was closing in fast. Goody and Parky were way out in front and all three Old Bill seemed to have made up their minds to home in on me. The bastards. I was so close to escaping, and so close to collapse. It wasn't fair. It wasn't fucking fair. Why couldn't they give up and just let us go?

Fifty yards from the hole and I could hear their legs thrashing through the long grass behind me. Forty yards . . . thirty . . . Parky had made it to the hole. He smashed into the fence and almost fell through the gap as he hurled himself through to the other side. I spurred myself on but I was running on empty. I could almost feel their hands on my back.

Twenty yards . . . ten . . . and Goody was there. He dived through the hole and glanced back at me, and when he did, I could see from his expression just how close I was to being bundled over.

Nine yards . . . eight . . . I could now see someone out of the corner of my eye.

Seven yards . . . six . . . I felt someone lunge.

Five yards . . . four . . . 'Come on, Milo!' Goody screamed, though I knew I wasn't going to make it. That half a second I needed to check my stride and jump through the hole was all they'd need to bag me. I was caught. After everything I'd gone through, I was fucking caught.

Three yards . . . two . . . I reached into my overalls and pulled out my gun. The time for fucking around was over. These guys wanted to take my life away from me, and it didn't get any more serious than that. I had enough strength to click off the safety and cock the trigger before I reached the hole.

One yard . . . none . . . I spun, slammed into the fence, aimed and fired off three quick shots all around their feet, kicking up dust and forcing them to dive for cover. The nearest actually crashed into me and sent me tumbling over. When I righted myself I found him clinging on to me and screaming for help, leaving me no choice but to brain him with the pistol until he let go. His mates sprang to their feet and looked like they fancied their chances at overpowering me, so I pointed my gun at the closest and told him I'd kill them both if they didn't back off.

And I meant every word of it.

Dozen of reinforcements were now pouring across the field towards us, including several firearms officers. I wanted to push matey off my legs and take the plunge through the hole, but I was so fucked I couldn't do this and keep my gun trained on the cops.

'Fuck off, fuck off,' I pleaded with them, but they wouldn't back away.

'Give yourself up. You're caught,' they told me. 'Just drop the gun. Drop it now.'

Drop the gun?

I was caught?

I was going to get twenty years?

No, this couldn't be possible.

This wasn't supposed to happen.

I was supposed to get away.

I was supposed to make a new start.

I wasn't supposed to go to prison again.

I looked at my Get Out of Jail Free card and wondered if I had the balls.

I cocked back the trigger and decided not to think about it. Just quickly do it and know it was the best of a bunch of not-very-good options. I took a deep breath, then another.

Then I took one more, then one for the road, psyching myself up to turn the gun around, but no matter how much I psyched myself up, my arm simply refused to play ball.

I couldn't do it. No matter how hard I tried, I just couldn't do what I had to do.

Mercifully, the big guy upstairs finally came through and rescheduled our appointment by getting Goody to turn back and point his gun through the hole. He told both coppers they had exactly one second to hang on to their balls if they didn't get going.

'Go for it, Milo!' he yelled at me, waving his empty gun in their faces.

This finally did the trick and I had enough time and space to pull myself up and throw myself through the hole. Goody half covered, half dragged me to safety, tearing my trousers and slicing open my knees as I went, but it didn't matter – suddenly I was on the other side of the fence.

Half a chance (at best)

24

Fuck, this was where it had all begun.

Had it really only been twelve hours since the eight of us had set off from here? Me, Goody, Norris, Patsy, Parky, Jacko, Bob and Jimbo, all laughing and joking about DNA on fag butts and Patsy's stupid fucking mask. Twelve hours ago? Was that all?

It felt like a lot longer.

For Jacko, Norris, Bob and Jimbo it was only going to feel longer still.

A shudder ran down my spine.

Best not to think about it. Best just to move on. Do what I had to. Get doing. After all, I wasn't exactly in Copacabana myself just yet.

'Come on, come on, let's fucking go,' Goody shouted, pushing me towards the front of the shops.

One of the coppers tried climbing through the hole after us, so I turned and blasted a slightly smaller one just to the left of him as a warning, making him screech and fall back out of sight.

'Quit firing that fucking gun, Milo, or you'll get every cop in the neighbourhood after us,' Goody honestly said.

'Bit late for that, mate.'

We ran/staggered around the front of the parade and

found Patsy in his motor, engine revving and doors open. Goody dived in the passenger seat. I dived in the back.

'Where the fuck is Parky?' we asked, when we saw we were a robber light.

'He ran off down that way. I don't think he saw me,' Patsy replied, white with terror. 'What shall we do?'

'Well, we can't sit here waiting for him, so put your fucking foot down,' I shouted back at him, and we spun into the road just as half a dozen policemen sprinted around the corner of the shops.

I rubber-necked them over the back parcel shelf as they shouted and screamed and wafted our smoke from their faces, but a roundabout, right turn and thrashed engine gave us a minuscule head start and rid my line of sight of cops for the first time all morning.

'Where are we going?' Patsy asked, breaking a dozen new laws to add to all the shit we'd already done today.

'As far away from here as possible,' I fervently hoped.

'Thailand?' Patsy suggested optimistically.

'Possibly,' I said, patting our shares through my shirt and trousers. Goody looked over his shoulder at me at that moment, and I managed to catch his eye and give him a wink. 'Though I'll be fucked if I know how we're meant to get there with no money, Patsy.'

The look on his face.

Of course, I was only joking with him. I couldn't really hold out on a friend. Especially one who'd come back for us. Once we were clear of the Old Bill and safely away, I'd divvy the cash up and give Patsy his rightful share, as promised.

You know, all £15,000 of it.

As agreed.

Hey, don't look at me like that!